Ageless Winona

Merle Hanson

WAGONBRIDGE PUBLISHING

2021

First edition, paperback

ISBN: 978-1-953444-03-5

This book is a work of fiction. While care has been taken to provide accurate historical background for the work, the characters, events, and locations presented within are the products of the author's imagination or have been used to create a fictitious story.

Wagonbridge Publishing
661 East Howard St.
Winona, MN 55987

In Honor of Joseph Ives
1949 - 2021

"I tell yah Hanson, he ain't right in the head. Poor boy has a different way of thinking in him. Upside down. Inside out, nuts. He can't think, talk, write like any of us. He don't make no sense till he does."
-- James Edwards, 1872

"He needs a haircut. Looks like a burn out from the 60's. Give him the nicest cut in the world and 10 minutes later it looks like it's been a year since he had it cut. He sits in the barber chair and starts talking to people not there."
--Ben Lee, Barber, Hurry Back. 1954

"We tried all the drugs. Dead folks just keep pouring out of his thinking. Something's not right."
--Doc Wilson, 3rd floor,
Ted Maier Drugstore. 1962

"I love this town."
Merle Hanson 2021

Table of Contents

Introduction

This is my hometown. I grew up here, learned here, left here, and eventually came back. That journey is part of my identity and the myth of Winona is at the core of my being. I feel it in my bones, my joints, my kneecaps, my thinking. Now, I never met any of the folks who lived in the First Ward, Windom Park but they were part of my growing, thinking, and learning.

Parts of my family came to these parts in the 1850's. My great, great grandfather was part of the 4th Vermont and was just outside Gettysburg when the fighting began. He ended up taking a bullet at The Spotsylvania Court House. He and his wife are buried out there in the Wood-lawn Cemetery. He told stories and I listened.

I didn't think much of it until I started school up there on the hill. St. Mary's. I was seeing people and shad-ows that weren't there. The whispers and the cries talking through time kept coming, and my mind crumbled. Time turned a different way. I ran and the faster I ran the more they showed, the louder they became and the more they challenged my thought. That's when I really met Grandpa. Woodlawn Cemetery. 1977.

I'm a pretty lucky guy. I could be dead or living un-der a bridge, locked up or losing my mind. One lost mind is enough for any mind and I figure I've lost at least two.

The dead people started talking to me just as I was entering adulthood. I tried ignoring them, running, denying. I went to see doctors who worked behind closed doors and locked units.

I put them, the voices, on the back burner, when raising the kids. It doesn't mean they stopped talking. They lay dormant and waged their war in my conscience. I'm fortunate I slept well.

Eventually, I started walking rather than running and the houses, the streets and the storefronts started telling their story. I find wisdom in trees, woodwork and alleys of living. I walk and hear yesterday's people down by the river or the tracks.

I walk behind the Holzinger Lodge and Woodlawn Cemetery and I feel death, a calm content death lying in the bluffs of this town. You can feel spirits who'll talk to you about life lived. They whisper all times of the day. And they like the quiet cold nights of crunching snow and a clear night sky. The spirits dance filling the streets and skies of Winona town.

I hear the sounds of old drunks, the sounds and the cries of the preacher and the souls of our forgotten. Death, it stretches to every corner of this fine town, and after over 150 years of living we all got some crazy in us. Welcome to Winona.

Part 1 The Journey

Chapter 1

I have always liked watching people, and in all these years of watching Lucille made me realize how much she meant to my living. She sat over there just the other side of the bend in the bar.

She had this big schnoz like Jimmy Durante and she could talk like the grand man himself. She was twenty years and then some past her prime. Her jokes had stopped being funny, but the old guys would laugh, ask about Tommy, and get back to the talking.

I was young when I started hanging at the Hei 'N Lo. I liked listening and the old stories made me laugh. I never said much, being they were older, wiser. On top of that, being a writer I'm not a real good talker.

I never met Lucille's Tom. He used to sit right next to Lucy, the old boys told me. Sad, just sad, they would say as they shook their heads. One day she caught me looking and beckoned me over. The boys stopped talking and watched as I slowly made my way.

She was wearing red lipstick, a polka-dotted dress and a kind of white button hat. It was winter and past 8 in Minnesota and she wore sunglasses. White rimmed.

"Tommy is taking offense at your staring," she said. "Tommy?" I asked.

"Yes, Tommy," she snapped. "Best man Winona ever had. This is our night out and he wants to know why you are staring at me. Hitting on me? Let me tell you something, young man. I have no emotional or sexual interest in you at all! Nothing, you hear, nothing. There is only one man, and Mr. Tommy James is his name." She pointed to the chair beside her.

There was nobody in that chair. Most everyone in the bar was looking at me and not talking. I started apologizing when she started again

"Can't you feel the pain running through me? You see everything in black and white. Live, die, right, wrong, heaven, hell. Need I go on? Tommy is not dead. He got put in the ground, but that don't mean I stop feeling. He feels good next to me as I have my beer. So quit staring and get back to your corner of the bar."

Evan had one poured for me and the boys still talk about what happened now and then. They told me Tommy had a motorcycle accident, and Lucille never recovered from her loss. The boys took care of Lucille, and I helped out. We made sure a neighbor kid mowed her lawn, and that her roof didn't leak, her snow got shoveled. We paid for the cab to pick her up and take her home. Evan gave her a free beer and nobody sat in the chair next to her.

We all grew to love Lucille. She gave us a sense of place and a feeling of relief that we had escaped the burden she was living. On Valentine's Day me and the boys pooled our money and got a dozen roses delivered, signed "Love, Tommy."

Chapter 2

Winona is a town like no other. A big, little town built on a crooked bend along America's greatest river. The stories of the people and town go beyond seeing. I was living a lost soul life, stumbling down Main Street one Saturday evening. The sun was setting in the western sky filled with evening colors. I'd been drinking since before noon a lifetime ago.

Science Girl Cheryl had told me I was done on that morning. Cheryl knew how to get under my skin. Mostly good things. She had helped me overcome some of the roadblocks I put in front of myself. Can't do this, can't do that.

She got me to Zipline and walking in the nighttime woods with the stars as my guide. Got me in touch with that spirit world. The dead folks deepened her own understanding as they worked their way between us.

I had heard things, sensed things for a good long while. Covered them up, thinking when you died, life stopped. It took a long time for that river that runs through me to make any sense. But sometimes it got to be too much for Cheryl.

"Honey, these dead people are more than I can handle. You need to talk with a psychologist or somebody."

"Living or dead?"

"You see? You can't even have a normal conversation without dead people being a part of it. We got no intimacy. Never just the two of us. A relationship cannot stand when there is always at least three people in the discussion!"

It never dawned on me this was her way of saying goodbye. I hadn't seen it brewing, so wrapped up in me like

I was.

"Take your sleeping bag," she'd said.

I slept under a tree that night on the Levee. Not too far from the Hobo Jungle where some of us had our beginnings. Never going home again, some of them said as they hopped a train. Life had hit these boys and the rails were how they saw this country and their stories still echo in the hearts of old townies.

I called a cab, figuring the need to forget precluded driving. My cousin, Robin, picked me up and we started talking about the dead'uns. Family trait. It was Sunday morning, just after my night on the Levee.

Robin dropped me off at the Hei n Lo. Robin wondered if Bobby Rut was holding up, and I worried my old friend, Darrel Holzer, an H and L regular, dead now, was going to give me hell. Robin said to call when I needed a ride.

Gina was working the bar. It was quiet and the sun was lightly filtering through the big corner window. Dale was sitting at one end of the bar and Lucille was talking with Joe on the other. I was bleary-eyed and still carrying the broken relationship.

"Messed up with your girl again, I hear," Darrel said, talking at me before I even sat down. "How long is it going to take you to learn? We all got something a bit off in us. It's the river. The East end is actually south. It's like our orientation is off. That Science Girl balances your sanity. Keeps you upright. You best get it back together and really you ain't nothing without her. You can almost talk. She's a saint putting up with you."

"Gina, I'll have a Hamms." I tried to ignore Darrel as I took a look around.

Big D hadn't changed much. Gone, going on a decade now, but here he was helping me over a rough spot. They were all staring at me. A bit unnerving. Gina and I were the only live folks in the Hei 'N Lo, and she didn't seem to be noticing any dead.

"You can't be so hard-headed. You have to let go," Darrel said

I wanted to respond, but I noticed Gina was staring, looking worried, puzzled.

"You all right?" she asked.

Darrell started snickering. "Tell her you are fine. I'll keep the secret. Don't need to get locked up for what you got inside your head."

"I'm fine, Gina. A beer can settle my soul. Bring a bit of clarity to a foggy mind."

Gina said, "I hear you and Cheryl split last night. Your ego, keep you from listening?"

"I'm sure. It isn't easy having the dead rattling in my head, and sometimes I can't keep them bottled up."

"Let me tell you something, young man. You best appreciate what you got," said the raspy voice sucking down cigarettes at the end of the bar. Eleven in the morning on a Sunday and Lucille was all decked out in her polka dot dress. She was wearing a hat that had a bird in it. She wore this red-orange lipstick, laid it on heavy. Hanging over her eye flaps she had painted a hot pink. I called her ravishing. She proceeded to tell me I was no match for Tommy James. I heard the crowd rumbling that Hanson is at it again. Egging on the people. He should have gotten whacked in the head, some said. Knock some sense into him. He can't hardly talk.

I heard Darrell respectfully say, "Lucille was one fine

lady. Never recovered. Sad. Brought me to my senses. She could do that. Pam too."

I was feeling the walls pounding. Too much tension. Too many voices. I dialed Yellow Cab. 3331 "Have Robin pick me up. What's the special down at Ruth's over on Third Street? Ribs, you say? Thanks."

Robin was there in 5 minutes. She had a funny look on her face as she said, "Dead folks?"

"Left and right, see-able and not so much. I hear them, you know."

"You got it bad."

Robin drove me over to Ruth's and dropped me off. The boys were all there at Ruth's. Billy K. and Chief. Lenny having his graveyard stew. Chinky and Charlie Stock. Literski.

"Aw, Johnnie Lavell, so nice to see you." I nodded to one of the old boys at the other end of the bar. Johnny carried an orange soda, a hamburger, and a smile in his being. I felt my grief breaking, feeling his goodness spreading.

The place filled up with businessmen wearing suits and ties. Napkins covered their shirts. Good food, good service, good people.

"Put him in the back booth," I heard someone shout from the kitchen. Before I could hardly sit down, Ann had a cup of hot black coffee in front of me.

"Ann," Darlene yelled. "Tell him to get his head screwed on straight."

I ordered the ribs. Now, I've had ribs from all over. St. Louis, Kansas City, Memphis, but I never tasted a finer rib than those I got at Ruth's. The flavor oozed through those ribs as my mouth tasted paradise.

"Otis, Otis how many servings we got left?" Darlene

17

asked. "One, did you say?"

"Railroad and Lumber boys like their ribs, Darlene. Those boys like to eat. They took a hundred of them," Otis, the cook, said.

I wasn't the only one listening to the chatter. Chinky and Charlie both pounded the table. "Mine," they said at the same time.

Their arms started swinging and the snuff was flying! They were tearing each other up.

"It's mine!"

"No, mine," the other one said. And the boys cheered them on knowing the story would be retold for years to come. Come on, Charley. Grab him, Chinky.

"Otis, call the cops!" Darlene said.

Chapter 3

Night was closing in when I left Ruth's and started walking. It wasn't long before a voice broke into my thoughts.

"The cemeteries and the churches aren't the only place in this town where spirits roam." He had long, black hair, dark eyes, and a long nose. He softly whispered in that rumbling way of wisdom talking. "The earth spirits woke when the white man came. No finer resting spot than along the big river. It gets in your bones, this way of life, and you carry it to the grave. The stars of this world are bright, so bright but down there, down there."

He looked down. "That is where the bones rest. Man, White Men came and knocked down our mounds as they lusted for power and money. That pursuit of the American dream had a price for those that stood in the way. But the nice thing about dying is you get to see. You living folk are blind to what awaits you. You trampled our freedom. It all ended when the white man came. You built your homes on the lands of my people, on the graves of my forefathers. Our dead woke and our spirits rose, our heritage trampled. The place of our eternal rest."

I was missing Cheryl. My nose was cold and though I thought the Indian dead, I wasn't quite sure what was real anymore. I took a deep breath of the night air and saw the beautiful stars of downtown.

I heard the quiet voice of an old friend I could barely remember. "That hole you dug with Cheryl just got a bit deeper. How are you going to fix this?"

Sounds and voices circled my head. I turned to see an old Peterbilt jacket with Wayne embroidered on it. When he'd been living, he had been part of my conscience. All that was decent about a man seemed to be him, to my way of thinking.

"Stars are nice," I said. Small talk is something I'm not good at.

Wayne's voice kept at me. "If it helps you soften that thinking, those dead set ways, you have to let go. Not enough people I know bring drinks to a graveyard. Us dead folk like that. We get to see, hear, and listen like yesterday. You feel not like a stranger but family."

Another voice took up the advice. "Strangers visiting a neighborhood cemetery where most everybody was related in one way or another. Made their day and then you played gin. Cracked the dead up and they still talk about the day you showed up to shoot the breeze. We want to hear about the grandkids. Wisdom is supposed to outlast living and you young folks have stopped listening."

The dead Indian chimed in again. "He is right. The white man stopped listening to spirits long ago. People don't hear the sounds of the dead because they don't care to stop and listen. You ignore what you can't see. When death swallows you, your eyes see for the first time." The dead Indian's head began bouncing as if hearing some far away voice. "The savage ways of the white man opened the mounds, disrupted the lives of our ancient warriors and you spat them out. The ancient ways that all who die, live forever in this beautiful river valley. Time flows on the other side of living. The journey starts when the dying begins. Here on the land called Keoxia, great warriors whisper truths to the blind. If you walk the lands, you find quiet spots where great warriors rest. The line is long with people who want to share their story. Spirits still play in the land between the river and the bluffs for those that hear."

Daunted by the idea of so many dead, so many voices, I left the levee behind for now.

Chapter 4

I found myself in a car with another old friend, just trying to clear my head. I gripped the door handle. "Specs, drive faster! Drive faster! Drive like tomorrow might not get here. Let's get the fog cleared from my head. Find me somewhere stories are set in the walls. I don't care where, anywhere in this town. Monument makers, cemeteries, and bars. Part of the history, our past, our roots. Hurry!"

Specs was looking through his rear view mirror. He wore bottle glasses and had stopped shaving moons ago.

Tired of cutting himself, I think, but how a guy who can't see becomes a cab driver escapes my thinking. Crazy thing is I never felt safer than when he took me where I needed to go. He could drive fast enough to keep the dead ones from talking.

That's why he was staring at me for so long. Specs could feel things because his eyes didn't work too well. He knew how to listen to the sounds of a man and his voice, the feel of his heart.

"Women problems?" he asked.

"More my problem."

"Honest?"

"I think it was my creating. Dug my own hole."

"Caught up in your way of thinking?"

"Don't we all, Specs? What do I owe you?"

"I can't charge you until I leave the curb. You need to go see Dr. Herb."

"I'd like to try EB's first."

EB's corner is pronounced as if it were a set of initials. Neighborhood place, alongside a brick road in the west part of town. A throwback to earlier days. I walked in the front door, wearing my Packer hoodie. The inside was dimly lit, with nice windows. I felt myself relaxing, breathing. Then I saw I was being stared at. I was in a land of purple delusion, and green and gold wasn't seen often here.

When they greet you as you come in the door you know you are drinking with some townies. Edgar has been gone awhile, but his spirit still echoed in the stools of EB's. His hair was long and greasy, and his eyes sparkled, all lit up. He started shaking when he saw me. "I'm Edgar. We aren't much for Packer fans in this bar. I've a right mind to throw you out."

His hands started moving and his head was spinning all round. Something was twitching, waking to life. "Vikings," he yelled. "A, la la, luche le lah," he started mumbling. "Maga, booga, eder," he roared, so loud he was nearly shaking the ceiling. His movements sped up. His words became pointed, his eyes lit up like the fourth of July, and his words were elsewhere.

Butch was on my right, sitting in his monogrammed chair. His nose was crunched up, and he started talking out the side of his mouth. "It's your attitude that rubs us. Rubs us the wrong way. Bad enough I don't like nothing about Wisconsin. No sir, no way. Pecker fans." He waved me away. "You feel proud, getting a man like Edgar all wound up? You all right in the head?"

I let that settle and noticed a woman on the other side of the bar staring at me. Her black hair was piled high and she wore her black dress with pearls that said yesterday. I could feel her talking.

"Big boy, come share a drink," she said. "Sidle up close."

I smelled the hamburger and onions on the grill and made my way to her side of the bar. The wrinkles of hard living showed as Patsy Cline sang "Crazy" out of that corner music box. All eyes were turned on me and yesterday's dame.

"Blanche DuPage." She extended her hand and pushed her breasts up close to my face. I smelled the scent of lavender and heat. "I'm into real estate. You?"

"A writer, just a lousy writer."

"I've always liked writers. The good ones are able to get inside me. My head I mean," she stuttered sweetly.

Butch chuckled. "Hey Hanson, ask Blanche how

she made her money."

She ignored him. "Do you like my car?" Her words were smooth as honey. "The red Cadillac right out front. Nice day for a ride. Top down."

Butch plowed on. "Two dead husbands. Took the life Insurance money and bought real estate. Worth a fortune but she'll rent you a room by the hour. Still turning a nickel. Are you her new toy?" Butch asked.

"Miss Blanche?" I said.

"Yes, dear?"

"You seem to have a bit of melancholy running through you."

"Yes, I need a young man to lighten my burden, jolt my bones, and make me relax."

I started shaking my head.

"Oh yes! Would you like another drink?" Her red smudged cigarette filters filled the ashtray. She smoked funny, her cheeks squeezing together as she inhaled, almost swallowing the cigarette. She moved her cheeks and smacked her lips after inhaling and before exhaling. "Jameson, for the young man."

"Miss DuPage, ah, ah, ah. I don't think that's..." I shook my head.

"Oh, you'll do just fine. You aren't one of those funny boys are you? Never had one of them."

"No, no." I kept shaking my head. "Riding the gut in a bright red Cadillac, top down? Third street in Winona? Driving in line behind Chico, Stueve, Remlinger and the boys? Now what do you think my girl would think?"

"Honey, I have a nice apartment. Chocolate, wine and the finest liquor. A nice steak. Oh, Mr. Lawyer, you think like a lawyer. Dirty and scandalous." She waved her hand, "But your way of talking stirs my insides, deep, deep down. You must write lovely stories." She tried snatching my arm. Her long fire engine red fingernails spoke nasty.

"Miss DuPage, I don't want to mislead you. You are an exquisite gem of another time. I have always been more interested in a girl's thinking than I was in those other things. You stood tall as you faced life. Now you are a beautiful girl, Miss DuPage and it is an honor that you thought maybe but Cheryl is my only girl."

She wouldn't give up. "I wouldn't say a thing, Darling. Just a little secret between you and me."

Butch saved me. "You see Wild Bill, yet?" Butch had a way of bringing people to their senses.

I shook my head no, downed my drink, put on my Packer hat and headed out the door, chirping "Maybe next year boys. Packers by 10."

Chapter 5

I needed to walk, get away from the clamor, space to think it out. I always liked walking down Broadway and biking down Seventh. Traffic moved slower there. Past St. Theresa, past the great homes and people of Seventh, the old hospital, the train tracks and a thousand more memories. Comfort routes in my growing up days, working my way from one side of town to the other.

I always thought Fifth Street had more shadows. Felt it closing in on me. I was always fearful. I avoided it except when I went to a movie. I got the feeling it has something to do with the fear of not being able to breathe, suffocation. Crazy.

24

But my feet took me there without my head consenting, so the voices of the dead caught up to me.

The first was a lady I didn't know. "You have a strange way of thinking, Hanson." Her voice interrupted my thoughts as I walked near the old hospital. All apartments now. "My name is Quinn. Also, a walker. Been dead a long time."

"Nice to meet you," I mumbled.

"The spirit runs through you."

I looked at her, puzzled. Her hair was long, white and wispy, flyaway. Her eyes were ablaze as if hearing a different drummer. She walked with a purpose guiding me through the land of the dead.

"Being able to see the other side of living. My Indian friends say you have a spirit. They say it happens when the earth rumbles and loud voices rule. They buried them on Wapasha's Cap, the great spirits of our past."

"You buried the dead on the Sugar Loaf?" I asked.

"Our greatest spirits, holy men ground up. Dynamited and crushed. Like ashes to ashes. Your freedom trampling our way of life. They were forgiving people, the great ones. My Indian brothers had their spirits raised, interrupted. They walk amongst us, in the trees and in the laughter of the children. Their spirits have never left this valley. They are here. Can you hear them?"

Walking wasn't helping. I felt a need for a smoke and a place to sit down. The church steps were always available for sitting and the 500 Club was just up Fifth. Queenie was probably down in the basement. A place now called Fast Eddies and he always brought good talk. My phone rang. Someone named Holzinger. I figured it was a sign and dialed 3331. Time for a cab.

Chapter 6

The sounds of traffic echoed between the bluffs. Seems like it is everywhere, white noise, that living noise, intruding upon our living. It is getting harder to find quiet. Our forefathers knew the value of parks. Even the pillars of commerce realized man needed a place to get away, to think, apart from the hustle and bustle of now.

I walked the trail of my past through the falling leaves and the comfortable path behind the Lodge and Stone Circle. I walked to Bluff View park. A nice walk just up from town.

I saw him up ahead. Long white beard and a walking stick.

He started talking as I came closer. "It was a political battle. Some folks didn't think much of parks. Work, work, work. The woods let us look at the world through fresh eyes. The founding men valued trees and parks. Now, there is a bit of hypocrisy in what I'm saying, being we raped those old forests. We've learned as time passed to rebuild, reseed, recreate. Don't be messing with Mother Nature. Parks make for thinking, happy people."

"Hello sir."

"Name's Horton. I lived in the Laird Bell house. Fifth street on Windom Park. Even the founders who cut trees knew parks and the wisdom that comes from sitting in them, walking in them. Bluffs, River bottoms, Coulees, Ridges, all part of our makeup. We built the town and homes and we made sure there were parks every way you turned. Understood value in dollars and cents, but knew a day in a park sure beat one in the office or the plant. Some nights, I remember sitting in that Windom Park hearing the cries of Mrs. Huff from the tower that Henry had atop his house. There were spirits in the walls of that Huff house. They find you if you listen. He sold the city and didn't much care for the Indians whose land we trampled. Henry Huff sold the land upon which we built this fair city. He had the meanest set of eyes I've seen. And a heart that matched. A scoundrel. Being dead I can tell you I always thought Henry would wash ashore one morning along the river. The old boys used to say, even the big catfish wouldn't touch the son of a bitch. That house is carrying some hauntings, some stories that need telling. The whole neighborhood was nothing but wealth at a time when a man raised a family on a buck a day and still found a way to give to his believing, his churching. You want to feel spirits, step inside the prayer houses. Deep feelings there, just beyond the seeing."

I nodded, realizing he made good sense. Winona's dead live on in this old town.

Encouraged, he continued. "Take the Secretary of the Treasury of the United States of America, William Windom, lived on the corner of Broadway and Harriet, across from Windom Park. In 1891 his face was put on the two-dollar bill. Or think of Harriet of Harriet Street was Henry Huff's dead wife. Wilson, his dead son. Henry always claimed it was the Indians that killed his children. Windom, Garvin, Bell, Choate, Hodgkins. Lumbermen, Bankers and Sash Makers, Merchants and Railroads. Boom town. Secretary Windom was Quaker stock, with Pennsylvania roots." He shook his head. "Windom had a deep thinking in his bearing. He was Secretary of the United States Treasury and took care of himself like politicians have long been known to do. I chuckle thinking how us men of the old ward took to Windom like fly to shit. Almost made him President."

"Hmmm?" I hadn't known that.

"Yes sir. Secretary Windom would have stayed here but Mrs. Windom caught the winter gloom and so they lived out East. Winter cast a deep shadow on Mrs. Windom. She spent a lot of time staring into her fireplace. The deep thoughts burdened her thinking. Winters can be hard, big house like they had and Bill out cutting deals in Washington. You ever really listen to a crackling of fire till the embers die, Hanson? Spirits, you see, know how to talk. Come along." He began moving further down the path. "A way of thinking has always circled this town but in the gloomiest of times a light would shine. Maybe, it was the Indians. Maybe it was a blessing. The spirits still walk beside us. The dead never die. They loved this land, thinking it far grander than their life and themselves. Maybe it's the river or the bluffs or all the animals that used to walk when there were no streets. Or it could just be that the character of the people drawn to the river, that make up who we are. Always thought it a tragedy his roots weren't here, glory days, somber tones. Not easy living, everything by hand."

I turned as I heard another voice join in. He was a small man, thin with white hair and wire rim glasses. "Oh, yes Windom he belongs in Woodlawn. We see a lot, this side of the curtain, greed getting in the way." His voice creaked. "Never enough. You think heaven awaits those with piles of gold? Now the good lord isn't looking to revenge your evil doing, but he does look at your footprints, those people you crushed as you get to judgment day get to say their piece. Money doesn't go far in the world of the soul. They'll be finding it sets them back."

It was cloudy as I kept walking past Bluff View Park and then to the cemetery. The leaves were yellow, damp and moist. The air felt good, filling my lungs and letting me breathe. Drifting, drifting from the worries of living.

The memories of summer past followed my walking. I thought of the smells and the sounds of the time passing. Old friends where we said goodbye, never really thinking it would be the last time. Thanking the spirit of the falling leaf and all that it brings brought me to the edge of where spirits live.

A voice filled my head. "Welcome. I am your guide through the path of death. No name. No name. The stones are of people. Good people who see life in a different light. Hear, hear their voices. Their words, their calls, their visions."

I heard the sounds of ducks, birds and geese and started my journey.

Chapter 7

I walked until I found myself at Woodlawn, wandering the farthest reaches. I stopped by a hand chiseled stone out on the hill called Potter's Field. Baby Boy Smith. 1931. As soon as I saw it, the voices started talking. It was a quiet whisper.

"That's me. Baby Boy Smith. Never thought I'd get to say a word. Ma you see had a hard time forgetting my dying and Dad reminded her every day that she was at fault. I never made it out of the womb you see. My life not meant to be." The wind sighed through the trees and I sat down to listen.

"You keep thinking on this side," the baby voice went on. "No stress, no stress. It's life in a different light. Patterns in thinking, acting, cropping up time and again. They called me Blue baby. Came out dead, never saw the light. Dead."

I was shaking like the leaves overhead, but the voice went on, soothing." Hanson, Hanson don't be scared. We know who you are! What took so long? It's hard watching life from this side. Dad, Dad he would rage. I could see it. He'd start pounding the table, Slow anger, you could see it building. Blaming would follow, then the rage. He couldn't let go, couldn't let go of my dying.

"Mama caught his anger. Food was overcooked, undercooked, never good. Dad was home less and less as the demons rose. House was never clean enough for him, beer wasn't waiting. They used to have a beer every Friday. Dad started down that path of drinking alone. I screamed and he didn't listen.

"Ma ended up living hard and died at 42. Twenty years of black eyes and bruises. I couldn't do anything, just watch. You see a lot of hurt on this side of living. Her life as she knew it ended, when I came out dead. Dad beat her and showed man at his worst.

"For a while, I thought I was responsible for their actions. It was their own sense of self and their views on things that got in the way of living for them. Everything changed after me, their body language, their talk.

"I think I would have liked baseball. You ought to hear the graveyard during baseball season. People are just happier. Night ball in the old stone yard is a nice, nice place. The stars can be so pretty when the lights of the city dim down. I just want to fly."

Chapter 8

The dead folk were lined up on the paths of the cemetery. Folks clamoring to be heard, blocks upon end waiting for a chance to be remembered for something other than social standing, their job, or the amount of money they had.

"I want to talk about my mistakes, my missed steps. Keep my children and grandchildren from making the same mistakes. I see life differently. Can you reach my children and grandchildren?" The voices of the dead cried out.

"You don't tire on this side. Your mind feels nimble, light and young. Your burden has been lifted. Your own doing. Worries gone. No need for food or money. The burden has lifted."

I said, "I'm not quite where you are at and I get tired, living in two places like I do."

Someone unnamed whispered. "Thousands of people waiting, just waiting for you to open up the door."

Chapter 9

The sweet songs of a violin echoed through the quiet reaches of the Woodlawn Cemetery. Hauntingly, quietly refreshing as it played the songs of tomorrow.

"I am the angel of death. I lift them, raise them up. I walk the narrow paths, playing the songs of the heart as the sun sets upon another time. I plant seeds of goodness, calmness, and those seeds settle into the minds of the hereafter. Rest, sweet friends. Let the ancient battles duel. Lucifer and Michael and the great ones play their game. There are no swords or stones in the deep sleep. A different light upon which to look at life. It is there where life begins."

And the teachers and musicians clapped as she played the songs they taught. Carlson, Guenther and Lehmeier stood weeping in the brilliant light that fills the valley.

Chapter 10

I left the cemetery to walk back to town, toward the East End. The green stands of Gabrych Park used to fill up for games. Ladies and men filled the stands and kids scrambled for baseballs at the park named for a dead soldier. It was a chance to meet girls from the other side of town and feel part of something bigger. It was as close to the big leagues as most Winona boys would get, although a few of the local boys made it to the big time.

An old soul, a fan from days gone by, approached me. He was a tall, thin man who talked slowly, weighing his words. "I always liked sitting near Sticks Ditzinger," he began. "Something was bound to happen when Sticks was near. Never met a man who got so wound up for a ball game. Never even drank, not a sip. I sometimes wonder if that wasn't his problem. He just needed to breathe. Bench jockeying the boys on the field was his release. He left us more than a few years back. Right after that LeJetz nearly won the National Championship.

"I remember it was a sticky July evening in a long month of sticky days, must have been the early 50's. The wind stopped moving and the heat had set in the valley. Everybody was tired of everybody in those days before air conditioning. Hecklers were lining the fence to get inside

32

the players heads. The cops were out amongst the crowd. When the Polish National Alliance boys were playing the boys from the West end, the town felt different.

"Dime admission and kids could get a nickel a foul ball they brought back. Nickel a baseball and corner grocery stores selling baseball cards. Always betting going on and the bars in town had a steady stream of customers in the weeks leading up to the game."

"We bet on everything and there were five or six of us who put money in the pot betting on which inning it would be when Sticks got kicked out of the ballpark. I had put my money on Sticks getting booted out by the fifth. He sat behind that 1st base dugout. In a big game like this, Spike Kaehler was behind the plate calling balls and strikes.

"By the third I wasn't sure if he would make it to fifth. The PNA catcher Max Molock was jawing with Spike. I think Sticks was getting mad that Spike wasn't hearing Sticks. Sticks wanted the attention. By the fourth Sticks ran onto the field swinging at Max. Even wearing the catcher's gear, Molock was light on his feet. Cops led Sticks off the Field and wallets, mostly shut their whole life, opened up. Old man Anderson was all smiles as he won our pool."

The old man faded away, replaced by the voices from the radio playing on inside my head.

"Top of the seventh. LeJetz down by one, top of the seventh. Men on 1st and third. Two out. Bauer to the set. He did it! He did it! The big lefty picked him off! Ronnenberg with the tag! Headed to the bottom of the seventh. Austin 2, LeJetz 1."

"This is Yvonne Lindquist of KAGE radio and Merchants Bank, proud sponsor of Winona Athletics from Hannibal Choate to Greg Evans and Rod Nelson. Putting

33

kids and customers first."

"This is the always entertaining Mike from Owl Motors with a bit of lost history. Some of the boys stored moonshine just off the basement parking garage during the prohibition. The feds walked into front rooms of the town, hauling men off and closed the bars. Sent men to jail, families having to fend for themselves. Stills all over Buffalo County, bars with back room operations and a police force that didn't like federal men."

I remember Winona drank a lot of Coke covering up that bad moonshine. Heh, heh. I chuckled and nodded at someone else from the past. "Hi Archie, Archie Gilbertson, you got Fords marked down to everyday low prices? Galaxies priced to go at Owl Motors in downtown Winona." Then it was back to you Chuck from Owl Motors."

"Come on LeJetz," could be heard coming from the big green stands."

"Good as the bones will carry me. Not as fast as yesterday. We are open Sundays. Stop on down and share your story. This is Charley Beck from Charlie's Bar on Main Street in downtown Winona."

"Thanks Charley. Chuck Williams and I'm reporting from Gabrych Park with the Kuhlman Brothers post Game Report. LeJetz win tonight, 3-2, in a dramatic fashion with a suicide squeeze in the bottom of the seventh. Jim Scovil laid down a perfect bunt and Mike Semling beat the throw. I'm here with Mo Godsey. Mo, what do you think?"

"So proud of the boys," Mr. Godsey said. "Thinking, executing, under pressure. I was sitting next to Julie Wera. He told me before the squeeze he thought it was coming. Said he thought that Austin's first baseman had hard hands and would struggle getting the ball out of his glove."

34

"This is Chuck Williams signing off from Gabrych Park where the Winona LeJetz beat the Austin Red Hawks 3-2. Back to you Bill."

Chapter 11

Leaving the East End, I walked back toward downtown, until I stood on the corner of East Second and Lafayette and looked around. This building at 79 East Second has stood for a long time. It was a chocolate company, a bar, a brothel, and a gift shop. If you need a gift head down to Cheri's Pieces of the Past. Open Sundays for all your gifting needs. That brick building behind us was five stories of chocolate. Sweet tooth, all points west of the Mississippi. Latsch Sr. had those Swiss chocolate connections. Got the supplies and the finest chocolate west of the Mississippi was found here, made here.

Past Cheri's on Second Street I saw Tick Tock. Tick Tock was a real Winona Legend. A good, fine man with a great name. Sold watches to make ends meet. He was wearing a long London Fog jacket. When he opened up the jacket, there must have been 30-40 watches. All still running in perfect time. Tick, tock, tick, tock.

"How did you get all these watches? Steal them?" I asked him.

"No, no. The cops would have been all over me. I was a handyman, mostly raking, shoveling, lawn mowing. Widows sometimes paid me with their dead husbands' watches. Here is a nice Longines. 5 bucks. Where else can you get a Cartier watch for 10 bucks? The boys wore nice watches while living and Morgan's Jewelry sold the best."

He showed me his arms, each adorned with six watches, then went on. "I loved this town and the people in it. I wasn't quite right. I got by. I liked eating at the Steak Shop. Day old Sunbeam bread at their store down on third street. It always smelled so nice downtown with the smells of the bakery and fried onions and grizzled meat.

"I used to clean the Hurry Back, late evenings. Only place to find stories in town was in that pool hall, corner bar and greasy spoon. The newspapers brought the world to our doorstep. My heart beats for the Hurry Back.

"You see things in a different light here. We were the characters in this town. I had this watch obsession. I got hundreds of them in the house on Second. They get right inside you. Doc Tweedy calls them obsessions. I can hear Doctor Bob saying they take over your mind. It is all that matters to the obsessed.

"Hey, kids used to get into mischief, the thinking being it was a normal part of growing up. Explore, think, learn. People, young, old, would be out and about. The Hurry Back was one of those places. Grifters and pool sharks and to some lawyers it was a gold mine. It wasn't too far from the courthouse and the stories have gotten better.

"Pool hall, barber shop, bowling alley, shoeshine. Everybody smoked. Old toughs and younger toughs, learning what tough was. They weren't fighting for turf. It was a sanctuary for stories of life turning. Guys would relax. Youngsters would come in tough, hear the stories, get the feel. Pinball machines tucked away so as not to bother the pool players. Quiet was understood, revered, there was money on the table and distractions weren't tolerated. Teddy Bath ran a tight ship. I tell yah, air conditioning messed up our lives as much as anything. Hot and cold.

We started staying inside. Moved from our front porches to the living room. People used to spend summers on their porch watching the day pass by. They kept an eye out for kids running across their lawn and the widow on the street corner. When air conditioning came in, they retreated and life became about themselves. They forgot about the widow and those kids running through yards once TV entered their thinking. Doc Tweedy and I used to talk of things like that. Right down the street, upstairs in Ted Maier drugstore where the boys learned to do a bit of reading on the shelves where magazines were displayed. Art Gallery there now.

"I mean everybody knew I wasn't right in the head. Kids would stare, and Mamas would shake their heads. My sleeping was never normal, mind was never rested, unless I was gardening. There I felt a stillness. Right down on Second, had a front yard garden. I liked tomatoes. Nothing like a tomato off a vine. Fresh with Sunbeam Bread. Some of that Watkins pepper. Heaven on Earth right here in this river valley.

"At night I cleaned the bathrooms and felt the stories of the day settle my bones, I would start talking, I'd be looking at myself in the mirror, sizing myself up. I had high aspirations once. That was a long time ago, before my mind started going and my window, my view on the world was through shattered glass. Lotta talking to myself in that mirror. I didn't care people were looking, watching. Some nights I would think about being a gangster and work myself all up, yelling and screaming as I cleaned the bathrooms. Even thought about carrying a few guns under the jacket, turning fast and seeing the look on the faces of the boys watching me from outside. Those boys got Walt,

Walt Neumann to thank.

"I remember Walt saying to me, No gun for you Tock. No gun for you. Some men aren't meant to carry. Walt had a way of speaking. Some things were more important than money to Walt. If you see him, tell him Tick-Tock says hello."

Tick, tick, tick. Tick…tick..tick tick. I listened as the sound faded away and I kept walking.

Chapter 12

I continued down Second Street where Merchants Bank Drive-thru and parking lot is now. Walt Neuman was sitting outside his store on Second Street. I joined him on the rickety bench under an old Canada Dry sign. He had a short-pointed nose and was scrawny. Glasses, big glasses and today he was wearing a beret. He seemed to be happy, a life well lived. He started right in, talking about John Latch and his son.

"The two of them were different; fathers and sons are like that sometimes. Those two were complete opposites. Always been that way, a town of strong wills."

"So I wasn't alone in not getting along with my Dad," I said.

"No, no. Now, I never met Latsch Sr. and only met John Jr as a boy, but the stories you heard in this town all carried a sliver of truth." He put out a hand for me to shake.

"It is an honor," I said. "There are some living and half dead boys who would do anything to see you. Tick Tock says hello."

"I haven't thought about him in a long time. He'd come in every day and have himself a week-old Bloedows. Fleck the black spots off them and give me a couple tomatoes for the stew I had brewing for the poor folk. I didn't always like to be distracted, you know. I'd act ornery but I liked the young people. Kept me breathing." Walt chuckled.

"To a man the others all said you were one of the kindest men they ever met. Feeding the bums like you did."

"They were the best of men, the railroad riders. They'd sleep all night out there where the Art Museum now sits. Not too far from the tracks. Life was no fairytale, living that life. Life doesn't fall evenly. The kids seemed to like talking to this grumpy old man and it kept me from getting lonely."

"But you fed them, Mr. Neuman."

He laughed. "Things more important than money, son. I had it and I wasn't going to take it with me."

"No, I suppose not. Old Man Latsch was tough?"

"Boys used to call him Iron Fist. Heck of a businessman, not so friendly. But to a man they had a deep affection for the first Mrs. Latsch. Now she was a beautiful person. Kind and generous. The boys thought she was different, wearing a flower in her hair like she did, right out of her garden during the summer. That was where John Jr. got his decency from. That gift of land John Jr. gave to the City of Winona made our town what it is.

"Yes sir, she started the tradition of bringing food to the store to give to the neediest. I carried on that tradition. Latsch Sr. did a great deal of the building down near and around the Levee. He built them right, his buildings he did. Location, location, location and down there by the tracks and where the steamboats used to land was the place to be for a grocery wholesaler in a boom town. You know, you would have liked Second."

"Oh?"

"You wouldn't have had to leave the front of my store to find characters. Not much left on Second except dead people walking around and not enough of you living folk pay attention or got the skill to see the shadows. They are just searching for old haunts. Even a name. You should have heard old man Latsch when they tore down his building."

"Not happy?"

"Emotions are different on this side, so let us just say he was sad. As close to sad as you living folk get. You wait. There is some sadness you go through upon dying. It hits you. Feelings last a good long while. Now Latsch Jr. used to sleep upstairs in that red building especially during the summer. The Mississippi ran slow from bluff to bluff and floods happened often until the dikes and dams controlled the river flow. He used to talk about how canoeing under a full moon was as good as it got. Not quite like today where everything is channeled, controlled. Got up way before the sun to go river paddling. Building still stands looking better than it ever did to my recollecting.

"He was a nice man. Brother Eddie, everybody liked to say, was even smarter than John Jr., but he couldn't hardly talk. He was a different kind of bright. None of the Latsch kids married. I can't remember the sister's name. Things get foggy when you age. She died young as did the first Mrs. Latsch."

"Family just ended?"

"John Jr. never married. He donated so much land

to the city. He liked his nature. I tell you, if you couldn't find what you needed in Winona you weren't looking too hard. The Park Brewing Company just down by the river made a fine beer. Five brewers in town before the moralists waged their war. The Volstead Act. It was a going business, gangbusters and people got all high and mighty thinking societal ills were because God was mad. We were dealing with the grieving. Kids died in that first war. It was a dirty, ugly war of ancient hates, and it takes time to recover from hating. Then what the war didn't kill, the flu did. We need-ed an escape from the decade that ended with a war and a bad case of the flu. We escaped all right, right into the Depression, but first we tried to forget by partying.

"They tried taking away our drink, the moralists and the government. That's what they did. Our sons came back from Europe and they couldn't even share a legal beer with their grandpa.

"Still We partied through that decade. Townies and barkeeps filled their cups with moonshine and covered it with Coke. It only took a few years before Congress rescind-ed that law. Still, the Kuhlmans did quite well for them-selves during Prohibition and the years following.

"I never much listened to their thinking and I dealt in second-hand goods, first-hand goods, dented goods and a person's heart. I got my moonshine from my cousin across the river. Covered it mostly with Coke made right down the street by the Kuhlman Family.

"We were in different times. A lot of bad things and our churches carried the gloom that God was punishing us. Our boys had died across the waters during the First World War and more citizens died from the flu than the war. Lotta people thinking God was punishing us for the lives we were living. Alcohol was evil to some people's way of thinking. Morally uptight is what we became."

"What has that to do, Walt, with our Levee Park?

"The Volstead Act, prohibition son. Shut down the brewery business. Moral compass is what people thought. We do get fearful as a people."

"Oh."

"I was fortunate. Grew up in the Grocery Business. Building still standing. Even rather sturdy. Computer place in there now, 3rd and Franklin was where my Dad had his grocery business. That's where I first met John Jr." He looked at me. "Have you ever been to my store before?"

"No sir, but I feel like we've met. Everybody who knows anything about Winona has a Walt Neuman story. Part of our myth. A legend, a real live legend. It's a shame your building, your history is now Merchants Bank's parking lot."

"You sure enough got that right." He shook his head and continued his train of thought about the Latsch family. "The thing about Latsch Jr was when everybody was done, talking, yelling, John Jr would have his say. Men with hard heads just nodded. All forgotten, forgiven. Jr became mayor in the lumber milling dying years. The town leaders were worried about lumber leaving, being the mills and harvesting were now being done out Washington way. The end of an era.

"My pops got me started running a store like mine. Third and Franklin. I think the Hauser family still owns the building. Winona was bustling, and he sold the best of the best right next to the dented cans. He would buy damaged goods. Right from the railcar. Old bread from the bakers who used to fill this town. Watches from down and out gamblers and poor widows. Pa had a soft heart for the not so lucky. His gift to me and when we see each other nowadays I let him know. He calls me soft hearted and I carry that with pride.

"I carried everything in this store down here on Second. Most things had a story attached. It was how I figured out where things came from. Carried a lot of broken dreams in this store on Second."

"Did you carry guns?" I asked.

He nodded. "Guns, paint, week-old Bloedows. I even had a shooting range downstairs. Right into the sewer. Best prices in town. My store represented Winona. Everybody in this town had some hurt running through them and yesterday's goods showed where a person had been. I was a lucky man, I got to hear stories through that broken glass window.

"Everybody sees things different. Learning gets filtered through belief structures you got inside you. Learning peels away the blindness that fills us all.

"Old Man Meyer, down at Lang's Bar tells me he heard his best stories through a cloud of alcohol and smoke. But he also said that alcohol can wreck a man and his thinking on the world. Too much alcohol darkens the soul."

I'd heard that before. "Tell me about it," I said.

Walt went on as if he hadn't heard. "Old Father O'Boykin would come stumbling down here about two every Saturday afternoon. Told me that preaching wasn't for everyone and he had a liking to the church wine, cigarettes and dancing. People said he was the best priest they ever met. Of course, Bishop Cotter wasn't the fondest of him. Didn't think much of alcohol or socializing with the customers. Old timers used to tell me nobody could bring in the cash on Sunday like Father Tom O'Boykin.

"He told me he liked the confessional booth. Said it made him smarter, more insightful. Never, never did he speak of those deeper, quieter thoughts but he attached meaning to all he heard. In silence came wisdom, he used to say. Him and the bishop would get to disagreeing and arguing over that sense of right and wrong. Sometimes right out in the open. Two different ways of looking at things. The good father saw life with a twinkle in his eye and the Bishop was more of a black and white thinker. I consider him, Father O'Boykin, one of my best friends.

"Second Street was the best place for people watching. I'd sit out here and hear the stories of the past. Everybody stopped in and talked, hard to get anything done. I was young enough to hear the stories of the boom years by those that were there. I heard laughter and hardship all sitting on this bench watching time go by.

"You ought to see this town during Christmas season. Nothing quite like it, dead people from all over. Everybody has forgiven everybody, grudges all let go and people get carrying on, just like they used to. It is a bit of a mess for a few days considering all the buildings that have burned or been torn down, and the names in the windows of the buildings are all different. All the old haunts gone. Get inside, get a feeling for the old lumber and bricks and you'll feel a lifting, a smiling of your heart.

"Mrs. Pitelenko, she lived upstairs. A kinder renter was not to be had. She scored baseball games and swept my steps. I had the best renters, roomers."

"Could a fella find a deck of cards in your place?."

"Got some in the back. There were some big poker

games in this town. Those riverboat captains used to run games as they moored their boats. Surprised there wasn't more shooting, considering the number of games going on. Dad got me started collecting cards, even some signed ones on the shelves.

"Fortunes won and lost. Johnny Latsch, it was said, could count cards. Gave his dad a bigger stake. A kid gambling with the big boys. Lotta fortunes won and lost on that Poker table. All around town. Always a game going on."

I was feeling a bit overwhelmed by Walt's words. All the forgotten history. In spite of his warning, I needed a belt. A good hard drink. I stood and waved goodbye to Walt.

"You run into some of the bums, the boys, you tell them a bowl of soup will be waiting."

Chapter 13

I wandered into Stovall's cafe on 2nd Street downtown Winona. The cafe was in a brick building that had seen better days. Winona gathered here for cheap coffee and eggs. A lifetime of memories where the walls could talk. First person I met was Mrs. Latsch. "Mrs. Latsch, how are you?" I asked.

She smiled and said, "I've been waiting for you. I just loved talking and I thought death took that away. 1877. We've been watching and waiting, you know. We weren't sure you were going to make it. Welcome."

Mrs. Latsch, mother of John Jr had died early and the town grieved her passing. Her spirit could be felt from blocks away. She wore flowers in her hair and danced as she walked. In the darkness of a post-civil war society, she was a most welcome sight.

She used to skip through town. The town folk couldn't quite agree. Some thought she was plain nuts as she talked of the dead spirits out and about.

Others said, "You see what happens when money comes to you? Makes you a bit nuts in the head, eccentric." And others said she was just happy being away from Latsch Sr.

I asked her of Mr. Latsch and she told me he came back from war a changed man. "He signed up leaving John Jr. and me to fend for ourselves, right across the river. President Abe Lincoln paid a good wage and money was scarce in our early years, so that money helped us get started. But John Sr. came home possessed and the love we once had was gone.

"He would fly off the handle at the least little thing. Little Eddie, our third child, didn't much talk. Fear of his father gripped his tongue. John snarled as he walked, talked, yelled his way through life. The man had disagreeing in his bones. I was married to a man who didn't take kindly to war. They don't always come back the same. Seeing blood and death gets to some men. He had that mangled hand from the farming accident. It was nice not having to be in the same room as him. But I refused to allow him to brow beat me."

I miss talking to the old folks who talk in the way their grandparents did. We've lost the art of telling a story as radio and TV drive our thinking, learning and anger. Sad, the old people say.

Lulu filled our coffee cups saying, "Hanson, you tell

those living people how special Mrs. Latsch was. She'd load up a wagon and deliver food to the boys living in the hobo jungle. Never met a better lady."

Mrs. Latsch waved away the compliment. "Different thinking, always been part of Winona. Characters walking and talking the streets. I like walking the alley Hanson, meeting people in their relaxing times. I knew everybody and they knew me. John, he didn't like me talking to people he didn't know. 'Stay in the garden or in the house,' he used to roar. I told him you see people at their relaxed best in the alleys. All gathered around, telling stories. I'd go for my morning walk as soon as he left for work. Let the spirits rise," Mrs. Latsch said.

Mrs. Lastch was changing. Her eyes were in a different time as she started talking about how the eyes revealed their soul. "A lifetime of reflections and sadness" she said. "After the war these lands were covered in the shroud of death. I come from a time where spirits roamed and hauntings were haunted. Dark forces beyond the seeing. We'd get the tent revivalists coming through town. I never missed a one. They could shake the worries right out of me."

I took a slow sip of the dark, hot coffee, letting its heat wake my insides. Nothing better than talking, and I had a whole town of incredible people like Mrs. Latsch to meet up with. I kept listening.

"After the war, we needed something to hold onto," she said. "So much death, just hanging in the air. Families torn. Hard times. How to escape the pain we asked? Some of us found the dead, others the bottle and others work. We all had something hanging, something we couldn't see that we needed to lean on."

I nodded my agreement.

"War made John unhappy. He took it out on who-ever got in his way. He ran a wholesale grocery business. Look at those buildings he built, but he was never able to escape those sounds of the Civil War. He came back a different man. The love, innocent love was gone. He carried the darkness of war."

I looked around. Of all the buildings that were built by the Latsch, not many were left standing.

Mrs. Latsch looked tired, dark circles rimming her eyes. "The entire town heard the echoes of war. Long, long after the shooting stopped. Every bar stool in every neighborhood carried the war. Didn't have to even shoot a gun to hear it talking. I mean we were all products of the European wars and we left that way of living. I tell you a lot of immigrants hoped the civil war would end all wars because we were tired of fighting."

She shook her head as if to shake off the gloom. "Now John Jr. was a different story," she said.

That's when my computer went kerplunk.

She said something about machines taking over the world and that I should learn how to write with my hands.

I hoped my friends at The Computer Dock located in Walt's old grocery store would be able to help me with my problems. Always been music at the corner of 3rd and Franklin but without my computer I would soon forget.

Chapter 14

"Being dead isn't so bad," the old soldier said "You don't have that unease you do when living. Being dead is about being in the present, the now. It is a different feeling over here."

I was back at Woodlawn. My phone had rung while sitting on the steps of the Heise Clinic. Private Bell, the display said. I ignored the call, but Private Bell was waiting for me at the cemetery.

"Your mind just won't rest." Private Bell's voice was as clear as could be. "It starts going when you first wake in the morning. One thought after another, thousands of thoughts upon thoughts as time passes. It starts when you are young, just a baby. The white throats pound you with their sense of right and wrong, then parents and grandparents fill you with the myths."

He seemed happy being dead and all, so I asked him, "You mean those myths ain't real?"

"Hell no. I ain't found hell, not even hot water. Talked with a lot of people. Outlaws and crooks. None of them ever felt the burning hell. Main thing is, you get to do a lot of thinking, and for some that ain't easy. In living, they start pounding you even before you can remember about right and wrong. Traditions, myths. This is the way it is. You be a good little boy and you get to go to the glorious place called heaven.

"I know outlaws and Bible thumpers and it's the Bible thumpers that take a bit longer here. You start coming to the minute you step on over. It is a nice place, son. Being dead that is. Earthly living is hellish. You got men caught up in their sense of self- importance. Anything for power, money. Punish the weak. Tell them what and how to obey this white haired, bearded angry old man! Pompous bastards they are!"

He was gathering steam and I'm guessing when living, he spent some time sitting at the bar. I was learning

49

that you carry on some traits. I was beginning to like these dead people. They seemed comfortable with their place.

"I was no saint," Private Bell admitted. "Hell no. I drank and stole cars from early on. Rules-- they were meant to be broken, was my thinking. I was surprised, yes, Joshua Bell was surprised when the casket closed."

"You sound a bit insane, there's life after death?"

"Of course, nothing like you living make it out to be."

"Huh?"

"There is a tender spirit running through these parts. Light, a bit ego-less, you see. You got none of that ego here, that sense of self-importance running through you. No burdens here. It's a delightful place. Your mind is rested, relaxed. After a bit you get back to feeling things, but your heart no longer carries the hate and anger in it. Damn frustrating."

"Frustrating? Sounds like a pretty nice place."

"It is, but it took dying for me to realize that. That sense of "I" gets in the way of the spirit. Yep. That sense of "I" really does more harm than good. Runs against the quiet spirit. You find over here there's a different way of thinking. Of responding. You start to realize you could have thought differently every step of the way and life would have been a whole lot easier. You'll find as you walk through the home of the spirits a quiet stillness. I'm telling you, you don't have to die to find peace."

I smiled. I was missing Cheryl. My heart lifted thinking about her. Maybe there was hope after all, and maybe I was not alone. Poor girl, putting up with me.

Chapter 15

I had to think about what I would say before I called. I had to get it just right. I wasn't looking forward to another night under the stars. As I walked my way out of the cemetery, a couple of the dead folks said I could spend the night there. Saw Jerome Pickett, his wife Margaret. I smiled at Mrs. Urness telling her Coach says Hi. Their goodness filled me.

My phone rang. I saw it was Science Girl Cheryl, and I answered right away.

"Some guy named One Shot has been calling every hour on the hour. Wants you to meet him at 2 p.m. Manhattan Club. 4th and Center. Across the street from the Lumber Exchange," she said.

"One Shot Kelly?"

"That's his name. Do I know him?"

I grew quiet. Merrit Kelly had been gone twenty years. Everybody knew One Shot.

"Are you there?" She wouldn't give up.

"Yeah, I'm here. One Shot, Mr. Kelly has been gone twenty years."

She has always had a way of talking with her quiet, her silence. No sound from the other end.

"Can I call you later?" I asked.

Silence, and then a quiet bye. The phone went dark. I took a breath. It put us back in the game. Black and white movies, dial tones and slammed phones. Tough guys, slow moving cars. Now she was hearing the dead, just not so loud. Those early ones are the toughest so if you see her tell her I love her.

Chapter 16

I looked at my watch. 11:30. Time to stop by to see my friend, Shorty Jung, at his restaurant, just across from the railroad depot. I went even though Shorty's Restaurant is burnt now down.

"Mr. Hanson, how are you?" Shorty greeted me when I walked in.

I took up a seat at the counter.

"Down on your luck, I hear." Shorty could always tell when I needed someone.

I nodded my head.

"Listen, you got some powerful people in your corner. I don't know a person out here who doesn't want to tell you a story."

He still spoke with a soft German accent. Shorty has a welcoming smile and a nice place to eat across from the Amtrak Station. First place anybody stopped when they got off the train. Lotta people never went back to where they came from. Made Winona home. Once they met Mr. Jung, they felt this was the place to be.

It had been a classy joint, but then like all buildings age started creeping into its bones. It began to feel different. Shorty passed. The building grew gray, and the sad stories started filling the booths. The classy joint became a thing of the past.

"Story? What do you mean, Shorty?" Was he right? All those folks just itching to tell their stories?

"Life over here. I would have never thought it. Not while living. I was hoping when I died that there was something other than darkness, but never thought it would be anything like this."

52

"Feeling thirsty? Hard to relax the mind. Do this, do that. This was due yesterday, tomorrow's worse. A million miles an hour." He turned and called out to the cook. "Keep the fish coming." With an apologetic smile, he set down the rag and rushed back into the kitchen. The batter on the fish was really quite good and the coffee, hot, black and fresh.

I look back now and wonder about Shorty's secret ingredient.

Chapter 17

After leaving Shorty's, I sat outside the Manhattan Club. Fourth and Center. It's a bike shop today. We bought clothes at Nash's growing up and in the early days it was a Jewish gathering spot. Even had another floor to it.

It was a classy joint with the Lumber Exchange, Winona National and the First National all just a few steps away. It was owned by Harry Czaplewski and the bartenders wore ties. I waited for One Shot inside. One Shot was the photographer of the Winona Republican Herald. He was seen most everywhere there was news to be had.

The bartenders dressed with class and you stood at the bar waiting for a table. Musicians played in the way back part. I was thirsty wondering where One Shot was. I saw old man Hodgkins, who lived in the Windom-Christiansen House, headed into the Arlington Club across the street. Deep pockets.

Winona has a nice collection of park benches, scattered haphazardly in different directions throughout the town. In the old days before TV and air-conditioning, men would sit on these benches, talk with strangers and neighbors alike.

Money rolled through this town like few others. Yet, figuring out who had the deep pockets based on the car they drove, clothes they wore or way they talked was an endless pursuit nowhere.

"Don't blow it. You only get One Shot."

"Mr. Kelly, you've been part of my life a long time. I can feel it in my bones. Straighten up, One Shot was on the scene and he only takes one shot. Get it right."

"It was a lot of things that caused me to take only one picture." One shot steadied his camera. "I can still taste the depression. Waste was not something we did. Hunger was close to our upbringing." He always wore a black suit. Never knew much about him "One shot," he whispered mostly to himself. "Don't, don't think. Find the zone, let it happen."

Just like that a bright light flashed and I heard the quiet call.

"One Shot."

Chapter 18

Some of the ladies wore pearls and the men had polished suits. Prosperity echoed in the walls of the club. Cigar smoke lingered and young wives cozied close. Smelled like young power and the sounds of a grand life were heard in the whispers.

"You need a coat and a tie to come in, Hanson." The head waiter was ready for me. "You look like you slept outside last night. You stink, what the hell? Here put on this coat, and this tie. Sprinkle some of this on your face. I'll have to send this coat to Haddad's after you leave. I'll send you a bill. What'll you have?"

"A double. Irish, need something to get me thinking. I'm in a rut. Here to meet some old teachers. Got a call from One Shot Kelly."

"Been a long time since I seen him. You remember all those little league teams? Wingold Flour and Sunbeam Bread. Auto Electric, NSP, Standard Lumber. One shot used to take pictures for the Winona Republican Herald didn't he?"

I nodded. "The age of our innocence."

"Good times. We played those Saturday morning basketball games in all the grade schools and then summer it was baseball."

"They were all different. I remember watching those old Winhawk games in that auditorium. The old high school. Seemed like the whole town was there. Sitting far up. So far up. You could feel that energy, overwhelming. My brain was never in the present. Don't remember a thing except for the fans."

"You been thinking too much?" The waiter straightened my borrowed tie.

"I sometimes wonder, but what is a guy to do? It starts working in the morning and it just don't rest."

"You can have those demons. Not me. Here, have a shot of this fine Spring Grove whisky, Giants of the earth. It'll make you let go."

"Let go of what?"

"That stupid stuff you carry in your thinking."

Damned, if I can remember his name. Like I didn't have enough on my plate and Alzheimers was starting.

The four women I wanted to see were seated in the back. They looked up as I came near. All my old teachers itching to keep on correcting me. "Come here, young man. Stand up straight. Shoes, tied right? Not polished. What has happened to you?"

I looked at Cleo Reiter and told her I would like to thank her. I turned to the rest. "All of you, all of my teachers. You told me, instilled in me that if you wanted to be good at something, that there was a price to be paid. My world expanded as I heard the stories of your life and what you liked and didn't. My home away from home when I was in your classes."

To her right, Miss Dunley wore pearls, had dancing eyes, but her demeanor was strict. She smiled with clenched teeth. Her eyes sparkled, and she spoke in tune with the piano that filtered through the room. "It was my life, teaching. I lived across from the Christiansen-Hodgkins-Windom home on Broadway. I lived in a beautiful home, beautiful neighborhood. A Winona Banker. George Mahle owned the house that became mine, Sixth and Harriet. August Riesling had first owned it. I can hear the sound of old bankers in its walls. I played the piano nightly and watched Walter Cronkite."

"You helped me read. Not just the words, but the meaning and you made the world come alive. A place to explore," I said.

"I have a hard time with all these tests nowadays." She frowned. "I remember those Iowa basics. The thing is parents wanted their children to do well. Still do, but life has gotten so busy. Both parents working. Children raising themselves. No money and so off to work we go. The written word wakes up a different part of the brain. Losing our

56

patience. We always have to be somewhere else."

I sat at the table with my old teachers and accepted the Irish whiskey the waiter brought.

Cleo nodded to the waiter. "I'll have a martini, extra dry, neat." She turned back to me and continued. "But the biggest change in academics from all my years of watching is the one parent family. Not enough time in the day. I laugh when I hear divorce is wrong. Kids see right through it, when their parents aren't making it. It is man's ego I tell you. Time changes people. Their interests, their world expands. If you don't embrace it, you begin dying. You get set in your ways. Your mind shuts down."

Kay Dunlay. Miss Kay Dunlay, my 2nd grade teacher sat next to Cleo. I never remember her talking loudly but I listened when she spoke. Now she was just nodding in agreement.

Miss Doris Pennel spoke next. "Did you ever walk through a Nursing Home?" She was tall and gangly. She taught us Run Spot Run. Dick and Jane. At least for me she made reading a good thing. "You ever take a look at those that reach 90 years of age? We stay active. Even when our bones stop working. We do crossword puzzles and read and knit. Listen to music. Keeps our minds going. Children nowadays have a short attention span. The world is moving faster. It's louder. It is just noise, white noise. Everywhere. The kids don't even realize it, because it's what they know. Every time you hear something the brain responds, reacts. It gets conditioned to a short attention span. A teacher who gets set in their ways gets old quick. Hard to grow up in today's world."

"Oh Doris, that is why I so liked teaching at Phelps. The energy of a College keeps a person young." That was

Opal Foster, 3rd grade teacher.

Cleo Rieter was staring at me. Unhappy. I'm guessing she was looking right through the borrowed jacket and fresh splash of cologne. She expected everything to be in order, shoes, notebooks, pencils.

Miss Dunlay spoke up. "Do you remember Liberace in Winona?"

"Yes, yes, Armistice day. So talented. The College of St. Theresa. Those nuns were some serious educators. They knew talent and music. He was here before he became famous. There was such a storm that day. People dying, freezing, up by Weaver. The storm came up so fast."

"Did we go to that together, Cleo?"

"No, no. We've forgotten, Kay. He never made it. He got stranded in LaCrosse because of the bad weather. He was a bit strange. His mannerisms were different. It wasn't until a few years later that he started wearing the bright colors and wild suits. How many died the night Liberace was supposed to play?"

"Never mind that. So young man, how are you going to get back in good grace with Cheryl?"

Chapter 19

"It is a scourge of growing old." Another dead man stopped me to talk.

"What is that, Sir?"

"Getting set in your ways. Thinking you have all the answers."

"Generational thing?"

"The dying gasp of a generation, trying to impose

their beliefs upon those that follow their footsteps."

"You mean like old people trying to impose that sense of right and wrong they got running through them?"

"You see it over here, from this side. The second you get set in your ways time begins passing you. Life moves faster and you never catch up."

"How did you make your living?"

"I counted money for Laird Norton. Down on Liberty where the Polish Museum stands."

"Family member?"

"No, no. Just good with numbers. Never came across a smarter lot of people." He chuckled. "They had an understanding about how things are connected. Almost made Windom President is what they did. Built the western United States right here. Running lumber down river, milling it and shipping the lumber west. Right here. Winona, Minnesota.

"I come back now and then just to sit, just to listen. Kids and birds. I like these benches. There is an energy here, in this neighborhood. Richardsons, Murcks, Caldwells, Fosters. Kids everywhere running through yards, playing kick the can and ditch. But laughing, always laughter, even in the saddest of times. I'd rather be nowhere else than right where I am sitting.

"I'm one of the faceless faces of history. I had a circle of friends, family. Time, the recording of that time will forget us. Only thing left will be that stone in the yard. Never had children, Alice and I.

"She died first and I've yet to find her. I can feel her, sense her. Always almost there. Maybe it means I've not yet found the peace which is the other side. That comfort I always felt next to Alice is out here, I can feel it."

Love it weaves a tangled web. This Alice, I hoped to meet. A shame to forget the lives of regular people. Cheryl has made me appreciate it all the more. I had forgotten what real living was. Walked around with my head wrapped inside itself. She taught me how to see beyond the bond of my own thinking. She reminded me time's short.

I dialed the phone. "Road trip?" I said as soon as she came on the line.

I could feel the pause.

Then a hesitant, "Just the two of us?"

"I'll turn them off." I hoped I could do that.

"Well, I don't want you boring either. Just don't want you looking behind every word and action for some dead relic of mine or somebody else's past. Where are you?

"Sanborn and Franklin. Walking towards Broadway."

"See you in 15."

Cheryl was back and he had left. Never knew his name. Yellowed newspapers and dusty bins, good people forgotten. A stone in the yard now covered with moss that had a final say.

Chapter 20

I started walking along Broadway, watching for Cheryl. The dead surrounded me.

The judge's voice was harsh. "Army or jail? Up to you Ray. You go serve this country or I'll lock you up for five years. And I'm not talking about Winona, where your cousins are more often than not sitting in another cell. Ten seconds to take my offer or you are headed to Stillwater."

Ray walked along with me. "Judge Libera, changed my life. There was a man who didn't mess around. Third generation Polish Immigrant who believed in toeing the line and doing things right. It would have been at least five years behind bars had I chosen that route. Hut two, three seemed like a no-brainer. It used to be common thought. Military straightened a young man up."

I was needing a smoke.

Ray kept pace with me. "The judges knew jail would never be the answer for me and my cousins. We ran and drove the streets and alleys of Winona. We grew up by the time we hit thirty. And then as long as we avoided the disease of drinking we became upstanding citizens. We started early, thieving, drinking and having fun. But stealing the car of Lawyer Lamberton was the best time I ever had I must tell you. All my years of living. That car engine purred, money can buy nice things. Best ride I ever had."

"Judge Libera must not have thought so."

Ray just grinned, thinking of the old times. "I remember my crazy Uncle Billy told me once not to steal anything from the hand of the law if it wasn't worth the money except if you really didn't like the guy. I kept his wise words with me, long after he left us. Lamberton, he had it all. Never could like a guy with so much to spare."

My head was spinning. The dead were occupying my every moment. Story after story. "Hurry up, Cheryl. I need a break," I whispered.

Ray wasn't giving up. "It was late. We must have been twenty. Lamberton kept his wines locked up under that tree in his yard. Fifth and Huff, still there, little storage under a tree. That little bitty lock was putty in the sweet hands of my buddy, Mike. But you know, the Huff place, it was haunted. Huff had built his house on top of the souls of Indians. Built his fortunes on lands where the Lakota lived. Those Indian spirits had a way of remembering what people said. We noticed the house was dark and after the first bottle we started thinking about breaking in. I always felt a bit of the rush before I broke into a place. I could feel the chase. We headed to the garage and saw the Packard.

"Now I was just a poor kid. We got parts for our cars when we needed them from Sam Weisman. Did you know this town had 30 junk dealers at the turn of the century? Nine of them or so from one family. Millers are still at it today. They fought tooth and nail with each other. A grandson of one of them turned out to be mayor of this town a good many years later.

"In the early days this garage had been a barn for the horses. Back in the forties when we stole it you could still smell the animals. Reminded me of my great uncle's place up there on Vinegar Hill. This Packard was like nothing I'd ever seen, much less driven. Shame to be sitting in an old garage. I asked Mike, 'What do you think?' That buddy Mike of mine. Brothers with no blood between us. Did everything together and he still makes me laugh.'"Look, Ray, the keys,' Mike would say. 'Right there in the ignition, like an open invitation.' I smiled, turned the key and the engine started purring. I started feeling the pull of the road as I backed the car out of the garage looking every which way for lights.

"We were cruising down West 5th. 'Ray,' he says to me, 'you ever been to Texas?'

"I shook my head. No. Mike, never had to tell me anything twice. I hung a U turn and got to Old Stone Road, now Mankato Avenue. We hit the highway and headed downriver. It wasn't until St Louis that I felt myself relaxing. We drove hard. We had found 200 dollars in the glove box. We didn't stop until the flashing red lights of a Texas Ranger showed up in the rear view mirror. Best time I ever had, outrunning the law. Judge Libera didn't think so and so I served in the Second War. Straightened out."

I heard the sirens of Praxel Ambulance, thought of an old friend, and saw Cheryl pulling over. Ray and Mike disappeared.

"Hop in," she said.

Chapter 21

The ride was quiet. I felt my heartbeat. Breathe, breathe I said to myself. "Let's get a drink," I finally said.

"I can see they still got hold of you. Another night under the stars is what you need."

"Okay, but how about a drink to warm me up first?"

Her eyes sparkled. She cackled and drove. We pulled into Sportsmen Tap, now called the No-Name bar that was once Beauj and Anns. Corner of Third and Franklin.

Cheryl ordered a Stella and I got a Coke.

Beauj, former owner, bartender, bottle washer turned to me, "Bill Laird used to sit in that stool. He was a fine newsman, running the Winona Republican Herald like he did. He used to walk, then drove a carriage and finally got a car. Always found the time for people. He had it in his blood, the ideas and a better way. Town was full of Masons and that pursuit of theirs. Mr. Laird was high up in that world of Masonites but he never forgot his friends."

"What does a newsman, lumberman got to do with

Coke?" I asked.

"Bill told me that you scare people to cause change. Change only comes about through thinking. Why they used to have Cocaine in our Coke and that stuff will do something to your thinking."

The Judge took up the story. "This bar was once owned by the Kuhlman Family. Right down the street they owned the Coke plant and across the street, if I remember, they owned the Schmidt distributorship. You are in the Sportsmen's Tap. My place, we bought it. He used to say that fear sold newspapers. Put it in headlines. Bill was right. Think of the fear driving us in time. In the 50's it was bomb shelters, blacklists and the Russians coming.

"Now the place wasn't always the No Name. The Gaertner family owned it and before that it was the Burmeister Hotel. But the bar back has been there for a long time. Used to have a grocery store and then Thorne's refrigeration on the Franklin side.

"It was fun in here. Diedroski, the Polish Newsman would come down here and him and Bill would talk for hours about the affairs of the world, argue might be a better word. Those two tried throwing darts into the others' thinking. Newspapering in their blood I would guess and if you were a stranger, you might think they had little in common, but they were of the same inquisitive spirit. Newsmen at heart."

Others joined in to tell the story. "Why there was a cigar maker just down by the Coke plant. Him and his son n law used to argue. Sometimes it would start right in this bar. One afternoon the son in law shot the old man. Week later, they were back in here drinking, like nothing ever happened."

"Goltz, the medicine maker, just down the street. His medicines could make you forget what ailed you."

"The Pharmacist on third?"

"Grandson or great grandson."

"See that little guy in the corner. That is Mr. Hub. Finest violin maker West of the Mississippi. Yep, right down the street."

I closed my eyes to shut out the cacophony of voices.

Cheryl turned to me. "They just won't leave you alone."

I shook my head, drank my Coke, and hoped she would find understanding.

Chapter 22

All around me they kept talking, the dead, the ones with stories left to tell. Too many to keep track of. I sipped my coke and listened.

"The devil is the smartest of all. So many ways. You have to look at the seeds planted. The devil's seeds, they sprout. The seeds turn to flowers, bright beautiful flowers and then luscious fruit and we just suck it up. The devil's fruit right inside you. Sets down roots. Mess up a person and his thinking. That devil is a master at turning a person and his thinking upside down."

"God and the Devil been fighting inside the head of man since the days of walking upright. Just the idea of good and evil battling. Matters of conscience. All our forefathers had these thoughts. Often around a campfire or with the drink of the times. They loved, they laughed. Something beyond instinct. That feel. The follies of man."

"You sit on enough bar stools in this town you'll hear about everything. Some good, some not so good. There are some mighty smart folks in this town. All skilled in many different ways. Wise men who work through life's problems with the help of drink or a friend. A lot of mistakes and old friends, laughing in the times of sadness that all that the great bars carry. Life upside down."

The fists of life had pounded their heads. The machines running our lives have exacted a toll on our living. I could see it in their eyes, tired eyes and eager faces, needing to talk. Their language is an odd mix of yesterday and tomorrow.

"I spent a few nights in the county jail. They were nice but I have no interest in going back. I grew up not far from William Mitchell. He ended up being Hoover's Attorney General. Sr. Mitchell if I remember founded the William Mitchell Law School. Money and power run deep in Winona town."

"Hoover, the President?"

"Yep, Winona has always had some heavy hitters. Settled in NY is what Bill Mitchell did after working for Hoover. Well respected man. Presided over the Pearl Harbor Commission. Winona raised them smart."

"And Bill Windom he lived about a mile away. William Windom. Lived over in one of those big houses. Dollar Bill we called him. Tawney, the House speaker just lived up Broadway a bit."

"Here in Winona?"

"Sure thing. A genius in making deals. His people talked long and hard about William. They, his immediate family, couldn't understand why he would want to do anything but carpentry and raise a family surrounded by

66

his elders. He was of Quaker stock, Pennsylvania if my remembering's right."

"I drink to remember, the good times, the soft times, the slower times. The world moves too fast, too damn fast. Sometimes you have to escape the machine. We didn't have all these machines in my time. A man can't keep up."

I closed my eyes for just a minute, overwhelmed by all the stories. Lives tilted towards the absurd were the folks of Winona's bar stools. Song and dance. A character on every bar stool and a mean bone hard to find.

Cheryl shook her head as the dead roared, but she didn't leave.

Part 2 Remedies?

Chapter 23

The Heise Clinic, built in the 1940's, is on the corner of Sarnia and Franklin. William Heise was a German immigrant, a country doctor. His five sons all became doctors. I met him when I went to the clinic a few days later.

"Listening and understanding your patients is the key to good doctoring," he told me when I sat in the office. "Dr. Herb got called out to an emergency surgery. He left me some notes. The dead talk to you?"

"You are?" I needed to know that much before trusting him with my stories.

"Dr. William. Founded this clinic along with my five boys. Educated at Rush in Chicago. My office used to be down on Third."

"They show up, the dead people," I said.

"What medications are you taking? Blood Pressure seems normal. Lab results are all in line."

"A cocktail of blood pressure medications. Took Drs. Nolan, Turner and Ferris to fix me. Winona guys. They hear a bit different."

"Sign of good doctors. Tell me, is there a visual or auditory onset?"

"You mean does something happen before they show? No, no, except my bones ache."

"Have you tried anything? Haldol, Stelazine, Thorazine, Lithium?"

"Yes, they gave me time. Gave me a chance to process information, stimulus."

"Are you saying they were always there? The voices, the dead?"

"Yes, your friends at Mayo called them voices. A little paranoid schizophrenic they thought. Good men."

"I knew Charles and William, the brothers. They had asked me to join their clinic when we were first getting started. The best of friends. I wouldn't leave Winona. The town and its people gave me a sense of place."

"They were before my time."

"The real question is these thoughts, that you say you've had for a long time, how did they become the faces of death alive?"

"That's why my friends said I needed to see Dr. Herb."

"I must say this is an interesting case. I'd like to set up another appointment in a week. I'll consult with my sons, but I think I might have to go through some old medical books and my German isn't quite what it used to be. Never quite heard of a case like yours. One week? 11am?"

I sat down on the steps for a while, wondering how much help a dead doctor might be. Couldn't hurt, I decided, and started walking. Saw the beautiful lake and the red building that was supposed to be a swimming pool. Land donated by the Watkins after a drowning in the lake. I saw the Sugar Loaf and remembered how it used to look when it was Wapasha's Cap and thought of my spirit friends.

Chapter 24

I was still sitting on the steps of the Heise Clinic when he showed up. He was a vet. The grandfather of a friend.

"I've been watching," he said as soon as he saw I'd noticed him.

"Do I know you?"

He shook his head. "I served in the Second War."

I nodded my head. He lightly sang Texas as he spoke. He sat down and I could feel his warmth, his caring.

"I spent my life never talking much about war. It seemed there were so many better things to talk about. I buried the stories inside me. We all did, us vets that is. War was hell on earth, a nightmare lived." He seemed to disappear for a bit, then started up again, "I blocked most of what I saw, felt. Those were not fun times as we made our way across Europe. I chose to forget. Should have told more stories about the dying.

"I was at Pearl Harbor and my heart hurt for a good long while. My friends died, never knowing what hit them or getting a chance to say goodbye. It was such a quiet morning when those bombs fell.

"What followed was a war of all wars. Hate and revenge was on every street corner, every town, every village. Everywhere.

"I had enlisted when I graduated in 37. I was not prepared for that day and what would happen. Every day, the rest of my life I tried to forgive and forget.

"All these years later, the most powerful moments were surrounded by quiet. That awful Sunday morning in Hawaii and again when I entered the concentration camp in Europe. I'm sure noises were there but I mostly remember the quiet. The crunch of my boots, the sounds of death, spirits. You can hear them. The air swirls differently when death is present. The dead bodies of a world gone bad were strewn across Europe, Asia and in the harbor of quiet Hawaii.

"Amidst the ashes and bones of the death camps, I felt things I never felt before. Life after death and from where I'm sitting it seems true. The spirits were all around as we tried to give the lost ones all the respect we could muster.

"It ended, finally and I'm not certain, if it had not been for Winogene and the farm how I would have kept myself together. Dairy cows brought a bit of calmness to my being. And laughter from children, grandchildren and just plain kids, family, kept the dark demons away."

"And your name?" I asked.

"Not important, but it is Laird. There are guys lined up shoulder to shoulder wanting to talk with you. They'd like to say goodbye to their loved ones. I'm just a soldier, who got to live."

Chapter 25

That Laird fellow was right. Lines of people waiting to talk, just to say their piece. I didn't have to seek them out. They found me. The next one introduced himself.

"George Tenorbell. How do you talk to the dead?"

I shrugged my shoulders. "A gift," I said, maybe believing it. "How long have you been dead?"

"Since 1928. Gettysburg man. 1st Minnesota. Made

me who I am."

"George, you were nuts," Sergeant Stanley Stankowski from the 1st World War interrupted him. "After war, men change. Not always well. We take care of those who lose something more than life on the battlefield. That is honor, the ways of a Warrior. George, how long have you been seeing Dr. Heise?"

George was staring straight ahead watching the cars cruising down Sarnia as he talked. "I started seeing him three times a week after the war. I died that first week of December in 1928. That is a lot of sessions. I could tell you how many, if you give me a minute. Do you want to count the one I'm headed to?"

Stanley quietly whispered, "Best guy was George. We loved him. But he could never think normal. Like now he is calculating how many days, hours, minutes and seconds. Always thinking.

"He walked from one end of town to the other nearly every day. He liked wearing the uniform and there were days when his thinking got the best of him. He would start drinking at Johnny's in the East Side and end up over in Goodview. Go till his legs stopped working. It's my job as a soldier, once a soldier, always a soldier, to take care of George. Hasn't changed on this side. You want something done right, you hire Stanley Stankowski."

George looked up from his reveries. "With emergency visits, 200 hours a year. 87 years. Shortage of men you know. Met a lot of girls. Winona had the prettiest girls but ten minutes of talking with me is all it took. They'd go off talking to another man. I never did find a girl. They always kissed me before they called it a night. Deuce would pour me another beer and Stanley would make sure I had a place to rest."

Stanley picked up the story from there. "George was in St. Elizabeth's Hospital after the war. Big Hospital in DC. It's still a hospital. It's where they sent John Hinckley after he tried assassinating President Reagan. Anyway, George headed west. On foot. Walked all the way to Winona. There were hundreds of men walking across this country. The tragedy of war. Lost minds. Living casualties. We understood the price of war by then. We knew our neighbors and heard mamas cry clear across this country. The cry of a thousand deaths fell across this town and all across this country for decades after the shooting was done."

Private George Tenorbell stood and said, "War is hell. Got to go see Doc. Poots at four."

Stanley left too.

I always felt a quietness come over me when they left. A deep stillness. I heard the songs of my youth, smiled and thought of pretty girls, friends, and long summer nights.

Chapter 26

I grew up next to Republicans. Staunch Republicans. Good men who at their core were good people. Mr. U. Mr. P. My Uncle Cletus. Dad. Mr. M. Like a whole bunch of other people in this town,these were some of the men who shaped my living.

The old boys, gone now, still talk to me. I visit them and they like to tell me how their outlook on things has changed. It hurts them deeply to be called a RINO and in such a disrespectful way. They fought for this country, its ideals, compassion, its sense of right and wrong.

I'm a liberal so many people think I'm not quite right in the head. I like it that way. Following an order, hut two-three has never been how I rolled. I got a hard head. Without it, I might very well be writing stories drab and boring.

Those Republicans I grew up with worked endlessly and had a curiosity in how things worked. Their minds were with ideas, the pursuit of a new idea, an improvement drove their life. These are the guys who started and ran the companies.

Many didn't do their best learning in the classroom. Keen observers of life, often moving when doing their best thinking. Learning, searching for insight. Doesn't matter the field, nor the obstacle, they liked the challenge of understanding. Peaking curiosity seems like a worthy endeavor for our young people.

These boys have become persistent, at least the dead ones, in lamenting the decline of the Republican Party as they knew it. They were thinking men and tell me they are nothing like today's Republican. Dad reminds me that dying has changed his thinking.

They liked a bit of Baileys in their coffee. They tell me even on the other side that a beautiful fall day in this river valley is unlike any other. They like basking in the sun and not having to worry about winter and the lawn mowing and all the things that have to be done. I see the stones with the familiar faces as I walk through the St. Mary's Cemetery -- the people in the church pews of my early years. They still got that quiet way of talking and it is good to hear the voices of the past.

When I wander through the cemetery, their resting place, they ask me to say "Hi." More than a few invite me to bring a drink and a lawn chair. They like visitors to sit, smile, and listen to their stories.

Winters are warm 6 feet under and quiet more like the old days before the machines came and disrupted lives they say. The Indians were right, they tell me. Dead people buried. Death is supposed to be gentle, quiet and eternal. Till our forefathers, opened the graves, that was death. Our coming changed the life of dead people."

And the soft whispers roll.

Chapter 27

I'd gone to the Eagles Club and left through the back door. It smelled like a city alley. Steamy garbage, spilled beer and old cigarette butts. Anderson Rubbish trash cans waiting to be picked up.

You learned as much about living by hanging on around the three-entrance alley that made up the Morgan block as you ever did from the good teachers of Winona High. It was a land of cheap beer and for a buck or two the old guys would buy you a six pack. Schmidt and Blatz, Hamms and stuff you could buy for 1.99 a case. The smell of weed started creeping into those back alleys during the 60's.

As long as there was no fighting or mischief the cops would look the other way, figuring it was part of growing up Winona. Young toughs learned to respect those old toughs and the journey they took. You learned how to get along, get by, talk with old drunks and toughs that were more bluster than real.

There were always guys in the alley. Guys acting

tough, acting cool, out meeting dames who were window shopping up and down third. Always a tougher tough in the stones of old downtown Winona that the boys knew not to mess with.

"Hey man, you wanna hit?"

I stared at the guy. "Steve Thompson? Stoner Thompson is that you?"

He nodded his head. His eyes showed the years of living. His hair now white and long, unkempt from living outside and on beds which made a fellow more tired. I hadn't seen him in a good two decades. He had gone to Vietnam out of High School. We had shared the same teachers. Ray Kulas, Charlie Stevens and Lloyd Luke.

Many boys went to Nam and came back worse for wear or dead. It was an ugly war and an ugly time. Walter Cronkite would do the news and at the end of the broadcast the names of those no longer with us would be seen scrolling on the TV screen. Sad days and the boys and girls from the era lost much of their innocence, jungle fighters or not, far too soon.

The living came back with dark clouds. Friends and family saw the change from the boys who came home. Grudges from that war have been going on for 50 years. And if you listen long and hard you can hear the grudges letting go. The sounds of healing grow stronger as death creeps closer, ticking, ticking.

They all paid a price whether they stayed or fought or protested. Some had bum knees, some went to Canada and others followed a conscience. All ways of dealing with a war that made no sense. Nam was a horrible place. Stoner had enlisted like his father and grandfather. A family tradition. Went in as a boy, came out a man with all the baggage from seeing death up close and personal.

I hadn't smoked weed in a long time by now. Had made me fearful as a young man. But I wanted to hear what Stoner had to say. "Would it make you feel better, if I took a hit?"

He nodded and offered the joint. I felt myself going back. My body tingled and the aches inside me let go of my thinking. That pain, that pain in my throwing arm felt relaxed and the darkness and shadows I used to see were replaced with different light.

Stoner took a hit and began. "I started smoking the weed in 1963. The first times, I laughed. Belly laughs, uncontrollable belly laughs." His face got tight and contorted. "Then the laughter ended with the War. War, it gets to your insides, the hate gets inside you as you see friends lost, limbs gone. The politicians who brought us war, hang 'em high. The bastards."

He took another hit and offered me the same. I shook my head.

He carried on. "I was torn. I certainly wanted nothing to do with dying. And I couldn't see what we were there for. Just didn't make any sense. I had nothing against the Vietnamese. They looked different. I felt stirring, primal man."

His hands started moving with his words. "Grandpa and Dad were still carrying the devil's fruit. The seeds of hate the devil had planted as we reacted to the color of skin rather than the character of an individual. I carried a bit of that distrust Dad and Grandpa had inside them. And I enlisted because that is what my family did, my legacy. They sold us, the bastards."

"Who? Who sold you?" I asked.

His eyes narrowed and his voice became a tense whisper. "War Kings and politicians who found peace more uncomfortable than war. Rotted souls. Selling weapons of death. Aw Hanson, let me tell you I have to let go. It's unhealthy, eats me up. Makes me angry, tense. Life gets too short the closer you get to the last goodbye. What is on that other side and I'm thinking grudges won't make it easier."

"You playing head games, Stoner?" I asked.

He nodded, smiling. "Heard enough of that hope and dream dance they put inside you from the time you were born. How many of those dreams ever come out like you thought? My heart and my mind have been busted more times than I can count and each time I've gotten a bit more insight. I celebrated my 50th just a couple years back. I don't smoke it every day like I used to. No. But those War Kings, they are smart folks and know how to play the game. It is fear that they plant as they go about their business. Those seeds bear fruit. Fear is just one of the fruits, a horrible thing, like a cancer spreading. You sure you don't want another hit?"

I shook my head. I'd seen the seeds and fruits, the shadows, the darkness, and I wasn't sure I wanted to take another trip that way. Dead folks talk and talk. I was getting thirsty and that weed was goofing up my thinking. Stoner wasn't through talking. "Our politicians like to hear the pitter patter of dollars, no matter the hand from which they come. I fought and now fight the next war, the demons every day. My war was that Nam War and the fruits of that way of thinking still run through me."

"What do you say I buy you a drink at the Island Brewing Company? By the Acoustic Cafe just down the street from the Latsch building."

"I know where the Island Brewing Company is."

"4p then. You know anything about Jack the Cat?

"Cat that got killed behind Nate and Allys on Third?" I stood up. "Have you seen Cheryl?"

"Last place you'd find a classy lady is back here. But you said Cheryl? She is a bit uncommon, but I've not seen her. I'll keep my ears peeled. Jack, Jack the Cat? The coppers have been shaking down every two-bit creep in town. No news yet but eventually it'll get to us boys here on the back stoops of the Morgan Block. Only thing seen was a black Lincoln driving like a bat out of hell from the scene of the crime." He flinched a bit.

I turned to see who was coming. The Three Horseman of tomorrow. Goristenson, Sevanson and Koraleski. All in the early stages of becoming the men they are today. "I better have another hit, Stoner." I took a long hard drag and stepped forward.

Stoner Thompson Meditation

Let it out of my thinking. Release it from the place it has occupied in my heart, soul. Freedom from the constant barrage of information, misinformation. Noise, noise clogging my thinking.

Let it go, fly away, all the hate and anger and venom setting inside us. Thoughts which attach us to the emotions driving us. Let it go

Chapter 28

I've spent a lifetime working with crazy. It is what I do. My mind has been broken, shattered, cracked more than a few times. I've never stopped thinking. Hell, one look and you might crinkle your eyebrows and think some-thing is wrong.

I got little traces of disease running through me. A little Autism, some schizophrenia, and though the manic is gone, the depression waves its hand. That manic has been replaced by a higher level of anxiety as those synapses in my brain work in different directions. My body doesn't move as fast as yesterday.

He came out of nowhere in that alley. His beard was long and fuzzy. For all I know a bird could have nested there. He carried his thinking in a brown paper bag, and he talked with a bit of the drool. "How are you? Name is Joe," he said, nodding politely.

"Hanson," I nodded back

He started laughing. "I miss living, you know. I nev-er felt more at home than here, right here in this alley. An alley with old brick buildings. The heart of Winona. Just an old spirit out walking. We like to talk in the shade of the Morgan Block, just like when we were living. Waking, I'd feed the pigeons. Bright day surrounded by the brick. I'd stay cool. Then at night I would hear the nighthawks and that quiet filling the Winona streets.

"One night, I heard her sniffling. A broken heart sounds the same in any language, any barstool, any cafe, any movie. Lost love. I really can't tell you what I said, probably hardly a thing, but I listened. She came back to my stoop many times through the years.

"I always looked forward to her visits. All the years, I kept up with her comings and goings. She visited pretty regular. Her hair changed color but she always found time for Joe. We saw each other for the last time about three months before my passing. We hugged, knowing it might be our last. When I passed she was the last thing I thought of. She brought pleasure to me, one of the few things."

It gets quiet when time ends and I realized the three horseman were missing the fourth. Death, the face of the fourth horseman. I wondered if these boys were ready as I took another step.

Chapter 29

Another old guy started talking before I got to the next stoop. "That girl Patsy. I loved her. She lived over there." He pointed upstairs, right across the alley. "Above Morgan Jewelers. The neighbors all said it was the nicest apartment on the Morgan Block. She was young, tall and elegant. She was the most beautiful girl I ever saw.

"Every evening for thirty years I watched. I know, sick. I was a peeper. Not my proudest moment. I was powerless. An emotion filled me. I would think about her all day and every night. She moved with such cool, calculating grace. She seduced me and I never ever saw her undress. She had to know I was watching.

"At 7 every night I would go sit on my chair, pour myself a beer, and watch. Right here in the alley of the Morgan Block. 2nd floor apartment. I know, I'm not proud of being a peeper. She had class. My life wasn't always the best. Hard to make a living when you are drunk by noon."

I shook my head. "I didn't get your name."

"Max Dubing. Dubing. I was a ballplayer. Played with Julie Wera. Julie and I were old friends. He was a winner, and he played with an edge. The Yanks needed someone to keep Lazzeri and Ruth playing ball instead of being worried about dames is what we figured. Best team ever. 27 Yankees, hands down.

"Julie wanted a quiet life. Almost shy about being a pro. I think it's why he left town. He wanted to get on with living, have a family and kids. He wanted to be known as a family man. He thought it more important than being known as a ball player. Family owned an East End grocery store. Simple, humble man who just happened to be a fine ball player."

"What's that you were saying about Miss Patsy?" I pushed him to finish that story.

"Miss Patsy? Never met anyone like her. Seductive? You felt something when she walked. Every night she would mix two drinks. She would place them on opposite ends of the table. Glide over to her phonograph and play beautiful music. The sounds would echo through the brick alley. The bums like me, we used to sit on the back stoops drinking, eyes on her corner apartment.

"She wore dark sunglasses and smoked the long cigarettes. An evening dress, long, tall and elegant, never the same outfit. She carried beauty like no lady I've seen."

"Hey Max, you still talking about Patsy?' Debbie called out. "All these years. All that living, being dead for so long and you keep talking about a dame who didn't know your name. I think you should clean up your porch of those wine bottles. I thought you told me you were cutting back?"

"You'll end a conversation before it starts, Debbie. I have picked up my bottles. This is Hanson."

"The guy who talks with the dead?"

I nodded my head, acknowledging her.

Her blonde hair was piled high on the top, Bee Hive

hairdo. Her face was wrinkled, her lipstick red, and a cigarette dangled from out of the side of her mouth. She kept talking. "Pick up the booze bottles Max. They woke me up last night. There is no falling back asleep once awake the way Dickman snores."

"Dickman, I assume is your man," I said.

"He's my lover boy. Makes life worth getting up for. I start every day with a kiss on the cheek. You do know Patsy talked with no one, don't you, Hanson?"

I looked at her.

"Let me tell you, she was beautiful. Those dresses she wore came from Choate and places out East that you and I couldn't walk into. That Crystal was from Morgan's, not JC Penny. We all figured lumber money. She didn't have a thing in common with any of us. And her thinking? All you had to do was watch to see something wasn't right."

"Aw take it easy, Debbie," Max chimed in. "She had glamour. Can't you tell Dickman to quit snoring? I like sleeping under the stars. It's a shame a man can't fall asleep outside because his neighbor snores so loud. And I have cut back on my drinking; I'll have you know!"

"Max you just keep feeding yourself the same ridiculous lines. You need to mind your own business. Ever since Ethel left you, you been nosing in the business of others. You didn't make her feel like a lady, and now you're miserable. She walked out on you and you deserved it. We pay a price, ornery bastard like you."

"Why I oughtta..."

"You oughtta what? An old drunk like you, trying to beat up an old hag like me should be ashamed."

"To hell with you, Debbie. Like I was saying about Patsy, Hanson, two drinks every night and then she would serve supper."

"With whom?" I asked.

Debbie cut in before Max could answer. "Tell him Max. Tell him how for thirty years you took comfort in seeing Miss Patsy act out her ailments. Not anybody home, Hanson. It was all in her thinking. Every night she had dinner and a drink with a man who didn't exist."

"Shut up you old biddy! Hanson, I never felt the power of a women's love like that in my living years. I hope she found him, that man she saw, the man she loved. I hope they found themselves together on this side. Love goes beyond dying I tell you, beyond dying."

Chapter 30

I found myself wandering Morgan's Block when the dead from that area found me.

"It goes dark." The first guy I saw was as wide as he was tall. His arms and face, fingers and the old Y boys tell me his privates were just the same, nothing but hair.

"Mr Deerman. Stanley Deerman, you are looking fine." I reached out my hand and nodded my head.

"Do I know you?"

"No, no. Merle Hanson. You are the stuff of legends. You been gone how long?"

"Good twenty years. Yep, yep. Ya, know, this side is a bit different."

"People talk good of you, Stan. They got a smile on their face."

He shook his head "They used to stare, look away. You think, I liked that hair all over my body? Huh? Only

84

girl who ever talked to me normal, relaxed, was Mrs. Pomeroy. We would talk and I would smile. She made me happy. I didn't order these stubby, hairy hands or the hair coming out my ear holes. Some of the boys gave me a hard time, but they never got too close when they were talking."

"Pomeroy?"

"Come on Stanley." Another of the old boys put in his two cents. "Tell him about Mrs. Pomeroy. It was all you ever talked about when living. Never let anyone near her. She was your Queen! You followed her around like a puppy dog< Stanley."

"I'd do it again. Mind your own business Dickman. And on my Mother's grave, don't you ever say a disparaging word about Mrs. Pomeroy again. I'll break you in two. Words can't begin to express my deep love for the incomparable Mrs. P." Then he looked at me and whispered, "That's Dickman. He is married to the Hag, next apartment over. Him and I don't see eye to eye on nothing." He then raised his voice so Dickman could hear. "Dickman, envy is one of the deadly sins."

"Aw, shut the hell up. What's a heathen know? God is a Catholic."

"Methodist, you two pea brains," the man from across the way yelled.

"It ain't neither," the old hag said. 'It's Judaism. Hey, Sociology Boy. Yeah you, long hair, bearded, wire rimmed one, what world are you living in today, boy? What is your thinking on the subject?"

He stood up, "Well Stanley and Stanley, Debbie, Max and Patsy, I think the concept of God is far more abstract."

"Aw, youth nowadays. Gotta use the big words.

Make yourself feel smarter."

"It took one year to build that bridge in 1941. That was before computers and during the war. How fast can you build them nowadays," Stanley yelled.

"That old bridge speaks Winona. They built it during the 2nd World War. I like that bridge and the one that is half-way torn down next to it," I said.

"That was the town I knew and felt most at home in. Everybody knew me. Stanley Deerman. They had a nickname for me, they called me Chinky."

The student droned on, unwilling to let the subject drop. "What do you suppose the Japanese see as being, their ultimate being? What does their God look like, Debbie?" he asked.

"Damn kid is right." Another voice chimed in. "My roots go back to old Ireland before St. Patrick showed up. All my forefathers ended up over here. Didn't need no Catholic, Protestant, Lutheran, Jew or Muslim, Buddhist. Even the outlaws found peace."

"Patrick Finnegan, your brain is pickled. You make no sense. I've a mind to pop you one in the kisser."

"Would you all just shut up?" A woman on another stoop waved her hands like she'd shoo them all away. "It is the bottom of the seventh, and Sahn is hitting his spots."

"Aw, Mrs. Klute, we are sorry. Got the arguing disease in our bones."

"You let go of that anger or you'll end up like Miss Patsy."

"She was my grandmother figure, you see. She treated me with kindness almost like my Mama. Mama never looked away. Mrs. Klute just the first time. She would bake bread. No smell quite like the bread of the Morgan Street

86

Bakery. Men would stop on the way home from the mills and factories. She sent extra bread to Walt, Walt Neuman so he could feed the boys whose life had been turned upside down. This was my town, people without much, caring for people with less. Mama raised me right you see. Early on, she could see, early on, that I wasn't right. The old uncles used to laugh that I was born with a beard and mama worried you see, Uncle Herman, he was the family secret. He killed a man, who struck a woman in the old country. Spent most of his life in chains, locked up. Hair like a caveman and strong beyond strong. He had a hard time talking and reading wasn't something he did. Worrying that might befall me kept my mama from happiness."

There weren't many better places than the Morgan Block. Maybe it was the way the light filtered through the buildings or the feelings of life remaining and echoing through its walls. Winona's heart and soul.

Chapter 31

I still wasn't sure despite Stoner's assurances that I was going to get out of this mess without being jostled, but Stanley was looking out for me.

"Goristensen, Evanson, Koraleski you put a hand on him and these hairy paws of mine will find your neck. There is nobody stronger than Stanley Deerman." He pounded his chest.

The boys looked at me. "Got Stanley in your corner? Can't handle us yourself?" they said.

"On your terms? Not a chance. I ain't one for black eyes and scrapes on the chin. It wouldn't be fair now, would it? 3 on 1. Why don't you join us for a beer?"

Before anyone could answer, a new soul joined us. "Praise the Lord Jesus. May he lift you. Repent before the wrath of the Devil calls you home." His preaching voice rang clear as he sat on the Eagles stoop on the backside of the Morgan Block.

It had been a long time since I had seen Jesus man. Every summer he lived out by the Minnesota Maritime Art Museum. The land was part of the hobo jungle back in the day. He would walk into town and start preaching. By the end of the day, his hat would have a few coins, and he would buy the vegetables from the coins tossed for the boys living down by the river and tracks from Curran's Fruit Market. Being the bottle was the supper of choice for him like a lot of the boys, he often never made it to the Fruit Market.

He kept a small flask in his pocket. His suit was dusty, dirty and smelly. His thinning hair was a bit long, pulled back and greasy. His teeth were mostly missing. He looked and smelled like he hadn't bathed.

His eyes locked on me. "I do Baptizing. Baptized a lot of men in that Mississippi water. Yes sir, yes sir. You can always find peace when you turn to Jesus. Turn your life to Jesus. Amen. Amen. Rid yourself of the evil sins before the fires of hell burn your soul. Praise to Jesus, praise to Jesus."

"Any chance for me, Stoner, and Stanley to escape what awaits us?" I asked.

"Pray Jesus, pray Jesus. The good Lord, he has a place for you. Amen. When life falls on your head, turn to Jesus. I'll pray for you brothers to find the path to the Lord Jesus. God, he don't look like anything we've ever seen, brother. It's a great shining light. Far, far away. Can I get an Amen?"

88

"Amen!" Stanley responded. "I'll have my day, the preacher man says."

"The Lord's light shines through you, brother. Can you give a dime for the poor? Right here in the blessed hat. Blessed by Bishop Cotter himself."

I looked at Stanley. He had turned a shade of green. Stanley counted his days by his stomach and back in those days a dime still bought something. Nickel candy could be had, and Stan liked his candy. You'd often see him in front of Spurgeon's eating chocolate out of a small brown paper bag.

I stood up, looked at the Jesus man and asked if he wanted to tag along. "I'm thirsty, and I'd like to see how a good beer, a shot of Jameson affects your thinking. You ever try Stoner's medicine to fix what ails you?"

He put on his hat. "Are you buying? Are you Stoner? A pleasure to meet you. My name is Preacher Jon."

Chapter 32

I heard the woman's voice coming from a second floor window before I saw her.

"I come from a big family," she said. "All my aunts and uncles had fourteen kids. A couple of my brothers and sisters had big families. Life gave me no children. Jeb died serving the country. We had moved to Winona full of dreams and ambition. 1858.

"There weren't many things for a person to do after your husband died. Whoring, working in a saloon, folding laundry or cleaning toilets, baking, cooking, sewing. There were many widowed women living here.

"After the civil war, you see, young boys and old men were all that was left standing. Immigrants came speaking in a different tongue, holding on to the thoughts and culture of the old country. It's all they had. Farming needed workers, rails needed building. Lost our minds, sense of decency during those 4 years. Forged by the uneven hand of life, Civil War, Civil war." She shook her head. "Wasn't nothing civil about that war."

I looked up to the porch hanging off one of the old buildings. Big lady with a round face. Smoking a corn cob pipe.

"That's Esther," Stoner told me. "You get her going and you'll be here for an hour. You got to learn to talk a bit quieter on the Morgan Block. These walls are thin, and the brick echoes. Why just this morning people were talking up a storm at the Steak Shop. Mrs. Ozmun told them at least a dozen times just to shut up. A whole block away. Funny how word travels."

"You know we aren't quite right, in the head that is," Esther chimed in.

"Not right in the head?" I hollered.

"No Sir. I think it is the River and the opened graves. Made us think different. Not just those of us who got beat up by living, but those who made great fortunes have peculiar ways of thinking."

"Shut up Esther," someone yelled from the balcony a few porches down.

"What?"

"You find on the other side that the gate to dying isn't like you were thinking." Esther ignored the others.

"Now, I got his ear, Esther. Shut up, I'm talking to the young man."

90

"Perhaps, he wants to spend some time with a more interesting woman than you, Anna?"

"Oh Esther, you never stop trying. He is too young for you." Without even a pause for breath, Anna went on. "You see, I would have preferred, looking back, that Jeb never fought in that war. I never shot a gun in the fields of war, but I lived with that war every day of my breathing life. The wives and moms of war. Vietnam, Korea. Winona boys have bled on the battlefields of faraway places and mothers and brothers, sisters and aunts, uncles and fathers were left to deal with the shattered dreams death brings. I got a letter every week. Jeb wasn't one for writing and usually his letters were simple, just I miss you. Last letter I got was June 30, 1863."

I took her letter and read it aloud.

June 30, 1863

Dear Anna,
This I'm afraid will be my last letter. I'm here at a place called Gettysburg. The air is filled with gloom. The houses, businesses, bars and churches are all shuttered. The storm of war is just beyond the horizon.
I hear death calling, Anna. I pray I survive, but God is whispering that my time is ending. A town of women folk and old men, grandpas and grandmas all alone as their kin are fighting down south. Death, that's death calling. Lee and the south are just a ridge away. Gettysburg will be a massacre that people will talk about forever.
May our spirits meet again.
Love, Jeb

Chapter 33

I put the letter down. Her hair was pulled back scraggly thin, she rocked back and forth on the old rocker that looked to be a 100. She wore a flowered skirt and boots. Her hands were gnarled and her eyes showed life living.

"A person can hold out hope, but war wins. You feel alone and it sticks. Even to my dying day I held out hope that I would hear his voice, hold his hand again. That is what war takes from those left behind. Facing death as it came knocking, not wanting to answer the door. A good man, a good, good man."

My phone rang. The modern world driving the dead out. It was Cheryl.

"Meet me at Ruby's. Late breakfast," she said.

"I'm working."

"No, we are going on vacation."

"Who is going to cover the Morgan Block?" I couldn't just walk out on the old guys here.

"Call Chuck, Chuck Williams."

"Huh?"

"452-5454. He will be delighted. Those Morgan Block boys will enjoy Chuck's company. Where are you?"

"In the alley."

"Be there in 10."

Chapter 34

I gave Chuck a call. As usual Claire answered the phone and I explained I needed a replacement while I went on vacation.

92

"That would be great." She sounded pleased. "He has been all over me since I arrived. Chuck darling. Phone."

"This is Chuck Williams." His voice crackled into the phone.

I explained what I wanted.

"OK, you want me to do what? A live broadcast from the Morgan Block? For how long?"

"For as long as I'm gone. You know, you're a legend."

"Me? I just report the news. The legends in this town are heard in the streets and in the buildings."

"I'll be back in a week. Headed up to the Gunflint Trail. Going to head back to my younger days. See if I can still get one of those Zeb's Wild Mushroom Pizzas."

"Have fun. I wonder if I still have it. This is Chuck Williams reporting live for KAGE, 1390 on your radio dial. Live from the Morgan Block in Downtown Winona. Going to need throat lozenges and some juices. Hey Claire, I'm back working. Hanson, we will see you in a week."

I smiled, thinking of Chuck in my early days. I remember summer nights as I threw a tennis ball against the garage listening to stories and games of Winona. Can't beat those long ago memories.

They show up when they show up, the dead. Some I've met before and some were from long ago. They talk differently and I'm trying to listen, hear what they are saying. Sometimes I wish my world was like once upon a time. But the dead start talking in the morning and sometimes it is the last thing I hear before sleep. There are long days when Cheryl goes on vacation. They don't mess with her or at least they keep their distance.

"It's strange isn't it?"

"What's that?"

"Dead people talking. Many, many have heard the voices of the shadows, the past, you know?"

"What do you mean?" I paused, thinking. "What happened to the rest?"

"Locked up, doped up, killed, maimed, tortured. Words had meaning and if someone didn't like them in high places you ended up dead. Most folks hear the dead, sense the dead but keep it to themselves."

I nodded my head.

"In earlier times the church might have burned you slow. Authorities might have tried you for witchcraft and Kings, yes Kings might have had your head lopped off. Threats to their way of thinking. They would use the Holy books of the time and place to justify their inhuman acts. Threats to power, authority in the old days, meant dead. My generation might have put you in an institution. Before me, maybe a little shack on the back 40 with warnings for all the little cousins. 'His thinking ain't quite right' I can hear Pa saying."

"What makes you think like that?"

"Dying, dying changes how you see."

I sipped my beer. Nice flavor, nice ambiance, and people to talk with. Island Brewing Company. "Dying lets you see?"

"Like never before."

He wore an old ball cap turned a bit up. His eyes were piercing darts, his hands scarred and beaten. He talked like a truck driver. He carried himself like he had seen most everything and if the stories were believable about Second Street, he had.

"I mean you are dead. Right?" Sometimes I wasn't so sure about them.

94

"I've been gone awhile. Dead is okay, son. Dead is okay."

Chapter 35

It had been quite a weekend. Weekends in Winona are different. Life happening in places you never realized. Opportunity. I regained myself over the weekend. Saw a lot of friends. Life was back to being good. Me and Science Girl were back holding hands and my sanity was in check.

Dead people are exhausting. I was enjoying my morning smoke. Cheryl was back working and me editing. I felt heartened, emboldened by the strength, thoughts and feelings of our relationship. I felt good seeing I wasn't the only one having issues in my thinking. I needed a conversation with Dr. Jameson. I sat down, ordered one and noticed Big Daddy sitting on my right. Cowboy Hat, knee high white socks, nylon shorts, tennis shoes, and a Hawaiian shirt. "Big Daddy, how are you?"

"Fine Hanson, how are you?"

"They are all over."

"What's that?"

"The dead ones."

He laughed. "Me too, the old folks make me smile."

"It is so good to see you, Big Daddy. Can I buy you an orange soda?"

"I'd like that, Hanson. Can you shoot the breeze with me, Hanson? Can you, can you?"

"You think that's healthy? I mean, Big Daddy, I don't always think right."

"You think just fine. I understand you."

"You poor guy, but you never did think like other folks. What's that music I'm hearing in the background?"

"Beethoven's 110th. A sound quite unlike anything I've heard. You run into him while talking with the dead?"

"Beethoven?"

"Few places like Winona in the summer he says."

"Beethoven? Ludwig van Beethoven in Winona?"

"He is a lot more personable on the dead side. He tells me when living, he spent so much time fighting the demons, the energy, that he forgot to live. Tells me the kings got in the way of his composing. 'Make me look good, Ludwig.' Then he points to his chest and pats his temple. Here, here on the dead side he just starts writing music. Still reaching the soul of man. This 110th is his latest."

"Big Daddy, you got a way of thinking. What did you put in that orange soda?"

"Quit joshing me, Merle. Isn't your girl coming?"

"In her time, it is a poor thing but a good thing, our relationship."

"What do you mean?"

"Being able to talk with the dead don't make me any money and let me tell you, her hands are full. Bless her little heart."

He started laughing. "I bet she loves it, certainly not bored."

"No, not by the look in her eyes, bored she is not."

"You still searching for the title of your next book?"

I got up from my bar stool. "I like this music. Captures the spirit of this town."

"I knew you'd get it, Merle."

"Good advice Big Daddy, good advice. We'll be seeing you."

96

Part 3 The Dead Take Up the Story

Chapter 36

Hey, While Hanson's on vacation, I'm taking over, at least for awhile. Us dead folks planted a few seeds in that Science Girl's mind and those of you who know her, know that once her mind is made up, not much will stop her. My name is Scooter, Scooter McBain. Bill White, publisher of the Winona Republican Herald woke me up, 4 in the morning demanding I cover this Morgan Block story.

"Mr. White, you fired me just last week," I told him.

"A misunderstanding."

"Mr. White, I write what I see and hear. Sometimes I hear and see things about your country club friends. A spade is a spade after all."

"I run this company. I own this newspaper, and I damn well have the right as its owner to print what I see fit."

Bill and I often shared a drink. We would head to the Park Brewing Company to hash out the day and set the headlines. There was little doubt about which party Bill believed in. I believed in the little guy and sometimes our worlds would clash.

The boys in town liked to see us argue. The town was full of agitators trying to get the two of us going. Just a part of my life he was, helped me with my identity, but he made me feel like Billy Martin as he kept firing and hiring me.

My left arm was four inches shorter than my right. I walked upside down, sideways. Struggled most of my life with balance. Fell down more than a few flights of stairs, never rode a bike. But I did one thing in life well. Write. Scooter McBain, though you got to dig through some yellow newspapers to find my name.

"But Mr. White, I won't write for you about the Morgan Block unless it is unedited and is my byline." I drew the line. My story, my name on it.

"It is my paper." He raised his voice.

"I'm fully aware it is your paper. I also know circulation dips when word gets out that you've fired me again. This TV era isn't good for thinking. These aren't newsmen. Just a bunch of pretty faces, all shiny and polished. I want a regular guy, giving me the news. I'm tired of smiley faced journalism. Readers want the same as me."

I heard him grumbling, mumbling, moaning in the background. "All right, twenty-dollar clothing allowance."

"Screw that, I want a bar tab paid for every bar in Winona. You want a story about the Morgan block? I can do that, but those are my terms. That is where the stories are. You fire me again I'm going to open up tabs in Wisconsin, and you know those folks ain't right over there."

"All right, all right, deal."

"Not quite." I grinned. "I want Mrs. White to make me one of her rhubarb pies.

"Mrs. White? My Mrs. White? You want me to negotiate her making a pie?"

"Yes. I know I could call her up and she would be

delighted to bake me a pie. Dare has soul. But when you get around to telling her about my firing she'll extract a pound of flesh. Dare always liked me needling you, gave her ammunition for the arguing back home. She takes delight in Shakespeare, you know. Legendary Lamberton negotiating skills. So yes, a rhubarb pie and I'm confident she'll get her pound of flesh."

"You son of a bitch. I can only imagine what this is costing me, McBain. But just 2 bucks at every bar. I don't know how you can drink that nickel swill."

"You ever been poor Mr. White? I know boys who would have been honored to drink all the liquids in your medicine cabinet. Those boys who used to live down by what is now the Museum. They'd come in the summer and leave to find a nice winter spot for in the fall. No town like Winona during the summer months."

"I can't imagine how the bums lived like that. Place to place, no possessions. Disowned by their own families."

"Some stayed, got over the hump, became fine citizens. Lived on virtually nothing. Life you see Mr. White isn't all about you. I'm guessing that Mrs. White reminds you of that quite often. You get set in your ways Mr. White and that doesn't work. You know history after all and not just the official version."

I could almost see steam coming out his ears and I knew I had him. That was what Bill and I did at that Park Brewing Company now gone. Argue, back and forth. We used to be a town like that, cheering on the underdog. The guy who stepped up after he had been written off. Rich folks used to see to it that being born on the other side of the tracks wasn't an obstacle. It was in the grade schools where the poor kids got to see and dream of a better life, side by side with rich kids.

Bill gave in. "All right, all right your terms, now Rod Hurd and Ed Allen down at the radio station are going to want to talk with you. You can bet your bottom dollar they will not let Mr. Williams off his sports beat. They might ask you, if you know of anybody, who might be able to talk with your friends. They are a tough nut to crack."

I looked at my watch. Time to head over to the KWNO building across from the girls Y. Maybe stop in at the Sunshine Bar, have a burger and a cold beer and wonder what Hanson was up too.

Chapter 37

When Hanson went on vacation, some of the rest of us took up the slack. My name is Stoner Thompson and I'm reporting live from the Winona Athletic Club in Winona, Minnesota. This is my first work since Nam. The war messed up my head, my stomach, my way of seeing. I passed in 87. Gave up on living. They wanted to hook me up with tubes. No get up and go left in me. Gumption gone. Said to hell with it. That damn war took a lot of my heart.

"Say B Brian, can you pour me a Jameson?" My bartender is almost as crazy as me, just in a different direction. My kind of bartender and he pours drinks right here at the Athletic Club on Mankato Avenue.

"I tell you this bar has a way of talking. Dead folks telling their stories. Dead people, dead people do enjoy living now that they are gone. I need a hit to change my thinking."

A female voice came out of the radio. "Stoner, Don't forget you are live. Watch what you are saying! This is a live broadcast from Ocooch Mountain Music."

"Sorry Miss Braveheart. B Brian, my personal bartender, tells me his grandmother and grandfather met on the dance floor when they were just twelve. I'm just wound a bit tight, first day on the job you know. My mind is going too fast."

I heard a whooshing noise over the air.

"Did you just inhale?" asked Braveheart.

"Oh, I forgot. Hee, hee, hee. Live, right? Mankato Avenue, where the Irish and Polish can share a spirit. I'm headed to Stooges next."

"Stoner, Stoner, Stoner you must have been one hell of a guy living. Stoner, brought to you by the Moore Motor Company, located at 260 W 3rd. Where Studebakers are kept purring."

"Tonight we got Rollingstone Steve, Jake Ilka and the Heavy Set. We got the Society boys and special guest Emil McAndrew. Jay Epstein might be stopping by. They are serving up Ice Cream at Nate and Allys, Blooming Grounds has Stacey Hughes and the Congo Cafe has those Jazz Boys. Life in downtown Winona feels good."

"Playing at the movie houses we got Casablanca, Cool Hand Luke, One Flew over the Cuckoos Nest and Citizen Kane. I'm guessing, the percentage of marriages still together that found their love at the movie houses is off the charts. When love starts with hand holding and Chocolate treats you got yourself a healthy relationship. Brought to you by the West End Theatre and chocolate store. Where love starts."

"And when the hand holding gets old stop over to

EB's corner. Buy yourself a refreshing glass of Schmidt beer. This is Butch Wessin. You'll see my chair when you walk in the door and you'll find more characters than you can shake a stick at. EB's Corner, where good people meet."

"We got reporters all over town reporting on the comings and goings in our fair city. This is Braveheart, live from the home base on Third street in Winona. It is looking like a decent crowd down near the corner of 3rd and Franklin, Sportsmen's Tap and Broken World Records or is it the American Legion and the No Name Bar. Life gets confusing, the older I get. Old people, young people, sharing stories over a beer and a laugh."

"This is Bic, bartender down at the Boathouse. I'll be discussing the early works of James Joyce and what life must be like being a character in a Dostoyevsky novel. I am here every night pouring drinks and watching people eat some of the best and finest food in all of Winona. Our food is shipped fresh to the little restaurant right along the Mississippi.

"I'm joined by Mr Bo Munro, President of the Midwest Music Festival and Music Store Communications. How are you Mr. Munro?"

"I'm fine, proud to be a host for such an amazing endeavor in such an amazing town. I couldn't do it without the tremendous support of this town."

"Hold on Mr Bo. I got a report coming in from Ruth's Restaurant. You are disgusted Stanley?"

"Me? The whole town is not happy. They can't hit, they can't pitch, they can't field. The baseball boys aren't happy. Fit to be tied. Al Smith, Earl Brugger, Max Molock, Boobie Hargemsheimer and Eddie Spencer. The Twins are sucking, just bad baseball. A summer with bad ball gets a bit long. A waste of beautiful weather. The Merchants Bank thermometer says 75. That is perfect weather. Those Texas cowboys sweltering, 110, 120. They just aren't right in the head down there I tell you. No place like Winona. I'm sitting here with some of the boys."

"Some of those boys called you Chinky. Are you all right with that?"

"I'm just happy they remembered me. But I like Ruth's Hash Browns. Food just don't taste like it used to. All the old haunts have gone away as the people have walked away from what was. Barneys, Kewpee, all gone. The Varsity, Dairy Bar, Chief. Fried onions and sliders at Charley's. Time eroding our memories. I remember beautiful girls walking up and down third. Always been only one girl for me, but in the spring of the year, the winter coats would come off and a man could feel like a man."

"This is Cheer down at Farrell's Barber Shop. Chinky Deerman was the best customer. Every Thursday morning 10 am. I never saw a man whose hair grew so fast. Hair all over. Chinky told me once he stopped trying to be clean shaven by the age of four."

"I tell you Braveheart that George Orwell wasn't too far off. The kicker is people starting to fear what isn't there. That FDR had a way of talking that made sense and you listened. That early radio caught people's attention. Helped open minds to the outside world."

"Now Cheer we don't want to turn this into AM radio do we?"

"No, no I suppose not. It hasn't worked too well. But Chinky with those stumpy fingers was never meant to be a watchmaker. A scissors in his hands was going to lead to blood. Some folks are just not meant to be surgeons or watchmakers. I was one nervous man clipping his nose hairs. Do you know how strong he was? He could have busted me in two. But Stanley, Stanley was a tender heart. I miss the old boy."

"These guys get talking and I lose track of my advertising. Bo Munro and Grippen will be getting on my case. That is Morgan Block Stanley brought to you by Ruth's Restaurant and the fine grocers of Winona. Liefeldt's to Prondzinski's. Libera's to Riska's and Bambenek's. I can taste a Tushner's Hot Dog like it was yesterday."

Chapter 38

Winona has always been a town of characters. Is it the water, the bluffs, the river or just an odd mix of people who settled and called it home? The names change as time passes but one constant has been plenty of work and odd lots who listened to their own drum.

"This is Stoner Thompson reporting live from the mighty Mississippi. Back to you at the Mid-West Music Store."

"Stoner will be reporting in a little bit later. The Stoner road trip is brought to you by C. Paul Venables where they service what they sell. Head on down and drive away in a new Cadillac from the good people at C. Paul Venables."

"We've hired on Patty Parsnip down here. Let's ask her about what restaurants are serving for lunch."

"Miss Braveheart. This is Patty. My food reviews are brought to you by JR Watkins where the best spices can make ordinary food a night of celebration."

104

"It was one of those hot days last week. I had forgotten lunch and I was running late. My friend Betty Panzinski had told me about Ocean Sushi located in the mall that once housed Tempo and Montgomery Wards."

"Now Betty is as often right as she isn't but I heeded her advice this time and stopped in. I put on my sunglasses, sat down and looked at the Menu. Choices. Salmon, Tuna, Godzilla Roll, Winona Roll. Tasty, tasty. Sixty some menu items. The wasabi was hot, pure, and woke you up. The avocado and crab and all the combinations made for a delightful lunch.

I decided I was bringing my husband, Elmer. He was the one who got me started eating different foods. I'd have never eaten sushi if I hadn't met Elmer's brother, Sidney. I love Elmer but Sydney is sizzle and Elmer plop. Brothers. Sydney he lives up in St. Paul with his darling wife Estelle. He takes us to these restaurants every time we go to visit. I mean I can't even pronounce some of the things on the menu we've eaten from. Elmer told me that I best soothe Sydney and his ego or he'd become a pissant the rest of the weekend. Just ask Sydney and he'll make your selections.

We walked into this place. I just followed, up there on Mears Park in St Paul. I think he got me a fourteen, a seven, a twenty-one, and a nine. He tells me it's gourmet and my palate is about to undergo a sensual explosion. I looked at Elmer and he just shrugged his shoulders. He'd eat anything. Raw fish, I thought and said a Hail Mary. Sushi.

It was in my head that aversion about raw fish eating. Maybe it comes from eating smoked carp and catfish, bullheads. Sunnies. Person wouldn't be seen as right in the head eating raw fish. Big, big catfish, bottom feeding. Eat them raw, not a chance. A drunk Elmer would eat anything, but even he drew a line with big bottom feeders.

Sydney has class and a lighter heart. White linen and candles every night of the week. At home we eat on a gray linoleum table. Elmer, he stopped living once he got hooked on my noodle casserole. 7p the TV goes on and by 8:30 he is dead asleep. Don't even make it to the 10 o'clock news. There has to be more to life than that. Dying before you've done your time. I remember those nights when we stayed up past midnight. No more. Brain dead by seven.

"A good man but in these last number of years I got left I don't care to spend it with a dead man sleepwalking through life. Any suggestions on how to get Elmer out of his easy chair can be dropped off at the Winona Post. Attn: Dear Patty Parsnip. 64 E Second. Winona, Mn 55987. Responses may be read on the air and names changed to protect the innocent, the guilty and the easily offended. Back to you Braveheart. And I now love Sushi. I feel awake, recharged and refreshed when I'm done eating."

"That was Patty Parsnip reporting. Brought to you by the cooperative effort of the Pizza Boys Barth and Perella who in competition have been serving the Winona Communities taste buds for over 50 years."

"I got a phone call from Don, Don Nelson, a Famine Foods believer who seems smarter every day. He said Stanley is right about food not tasting like it used to, but the reason foods don't taste like they used to is because of the chemicals. The microbes of good soil get killed by those chemicals they put in the ground. Builds up over the years, Lost taste. No wonder so many kids got short attention spans."

"Is that you Stanley Deerman? Say what?"

106

"I'm down here at the Steak Shop on Third. Washing dishes and trying to pick up the latest ball talk. All the legends come walking through that door. Moose Krause, Ken Wiltgen and Ron Ekker stopped down yesterday and talked with Gordie Addington and John Kinney about center Paul Plachecki. Six foot seven. Been watching him for a long time down at the YMCA." Stanley lowered his voice, almost whispering, "Moose was the AD at St. Mary's then Notre Dame. Ken Wiltgen is the great St. Marys basketball coach and Ron Ekker coaches at Winona State. Stanley Deerman listening to some of the great basketball minds in the country. That's what makes this town great. You know Bravehart I miss the old high school gym. It just felt like Winona. The new gyms just don't feel the same.

"Somebody has attracted the attention of some of the roughnecks in town I tell you. The Lake Street gang and the Dickson Brothers were whispering over in the corner and that's never good. Can't be a good thing getting Fahrenholtz and Dinger collaborating. Something is going down. Always vigilant, signing off. Stanley Deerman."

"Hey, this is Spike Malone, down at Hal Road Lanes with the news. The Nose on the Alley report. Big news this week isn't all the 500 and 600 series being bowled here in town. No this is the week where Federal Bakery takes on The East Side Legends from Peerless Chain. There is no love lost as these two local bowling powerhouses have been eyeballing each other for the top of the Professional Division the past month."

"With just a couple hours left before the bowling starts, I am hearing even money bets can still be had. Come on down to Hal Rod Lanes tonight and watch some fierce competition. I'll be back to talk to you next week. This is

Spike sounding off."

"At the Mid West Music Store this week we have Yung Buck playing Thursday. Midwest Voltage playing Saturday. On the walls of the Music Store is the Art of Gina Favano through the month of July. She can paint, really paint and the prices are good. A gift for somebody who no longer fits in a box store. Things are happening in downtown Winona. Stay tuned here for more activities as they get announced. We'll also hear from Pretty Girl and listen to some new releases of local musicians."

Part 4 The Vacation and Back

Chapter 39

"She was a pretty girl. Not too tall, thin, little sparkle in her eye and a smile on her face. We had to share tight quarters as she had her hourly smoke. Me working, she surviving in the world of psychiatry. Yellowed cigarette smoke hung from the ceilings and walls of the psychiatric unit smoking room.

"What's your problem," Cookie girl squawked. We are out here on the Mississippi River, one of the most beautiful valleys in the entire world, on a beautiful summer day and you are talking about smoking in a closed psychiatric unit? Are you nuts?"

"I think so. Don't you think, Dick?"

"I think that might be selling you short."

Science girl chimed in, "He is nuts. Dead people talk to him. Frankly I'm a bit worried that it's contagious.

"This young lady was the best storyteller. She had 700 hundred stitches on her body. Collected them like some do tattoos. Done it herself though its roots carry a sad story."

"Cheryl, are you hearing the voices?" squawked Cookie."

"Small shadows, small remembering, small feels. I

think he is rubbing off."

"If you listen you can hear the dead folks talking. They'll tell you the river dying isn't for everyone. The river gets you and considers you forever theirs. The dead spend another lifetime in the water of this river and they laugh and play, carrying on and hopping aboard. The weather is great they say."

Dick started laughing, right from the heart, short kind of laugh, that had a way of growing.

Bright Eyes said, "Oh yeah."

"I'll have another," Science Girl said and Cookie lit up a cigarette.

Captain Tom kept the boat straight as he followed the crooked river that carried us to the Bays End. A beautiful 4th of July just upriver from Winona as we started early on our midnight cruise.

The river and its slow running lift the tension. The kinks and knots inside me leave. That healing river water will chill you out and wake you up. It runs through us.

Chapter 40

On the boat, Dick was looking at me. Staring straight at me. I was feeling one of those moments.

"What kind of medications are you taking?" he asked.

"Just blood pressure pills. Went into see Dr. Heise and he tells me he has never heard of a person talking to the dead."

"No Haldol, Stelazine, Thorazine?"

"Nope, I haven't tasted that cocktail in nearly 40

years. It would knock me out, stupefy me just the same as it did back then. Felt like I had two hundred pounds wrapped around my neck and shoulders. My thoughts moved so slow I could count them."

"That slow?" Dick said, as he rubbed his chin. "You do know the original Dr. Heise has been gone for 50 years?"

I nodded my head. "He examined me. It's my disease you see. I get to meet his sons the next time I go in."

Good people in this town.

Chapter 41

Tom kept the boat straight.

It was a small unit, 16 beds and the door made a real crisp click when shutting. Each person carried around their way of thinking. Doctors and nurses sat behind the safety glass, feeling the piercing eyes of people whose clocks ran on different time. I never felt right sitting behind the glass, preferring to blend in with my mates.

"I bet the nurses liked working with the guy who the schizophrenics identified as one of their own," Science Girl said.

That's why I love my girl so much. She just blurts stuff out because I am dumber than a tree stump quite a bit. She startles me and each day I realize how fortunate I am.

My fellow boatsmen bring stories out of me. Trigger something inside. Last time, we were in close quarters I saw dead people flying while sitting in church. People affect us in different ways and these folks are as good as it gets.

"We used to talk whether in the smoke room if they were on precautions or out on the floor. The walls were stained nicotine yellow. They would bite those cigarette filters, right off and smoke them right down to the last strand of tobacco. Trying to get a buzz or a release from the thoughts they had going on inside their head."

"They liked those camels, I bet," Bright Eyes piped in.

"Don't enable him," my girl said. "Relax," she added as she patted my knee.

"Thank you," I said to them. They showed me their inner thinking.

"I'm no longer banned. Pour me another Gin and Tonic," Science Girl said.

"Cindy had 700 stitches, scars on her body. Cut herself, razor blade. Many, many times. Never hurt a fly. She told me everything about what started her cutting. All these years later I think of her. The river shakes it out of you."

"Look at the bluffs, feel the movement of the water, Dear. Is there an island we can drop him off at, Tom?" Cheryl asked.

Cookie girl started laughing.

I settled down. The river bouncing and the greenness of the bluffs can settle a restless soul. The cabins tucked on land touching the river were filled with happy people, families together. The waters of the Mississippi filled with fast boats and barges and pontoons and kayaks, all leaving the problems they come from. We locked through the dam.

"Hey Buddy. You remember me?"

"Aw Diane, of course I do. How are you?"

"Better, much better. I stopped the cigarettes."

"I'm so happy for you."

Diane used to visit us on the unit once every four months or so. She would stay for a few weeks, slowly retaining her identity. Her problems had started at a young age. Daddy had tried to teach her stillness with the end of his cigarette.

"That was the only release I ever found," she said. "My insides felt nervous, more and more pressure. My apartment was spotless, my life well organized, my meals planned. I would wake up, exercise, and stretch out the kinks. Yet deep down on my insides something deep down, started taking over. I was 14 when I started taking a cigarette to my own arm, just like my daddy first did when I was three. A doctor told me once the burning was the trigger and that my body released endorphins or some fancy name."

We used to have to restrain Diane for a few days. It was gentle and she readily accepted the help. She would flail at unseen objects, demons nobody saw excepting her. You learned a lot sitting in that smoking room hearing life lessons.

I could hear the pleasant sounds of the Bus Boys as we reached Bay's End. The setting reminded me a bit of that garden party song, and I saw happy, friendly faces bounding to the gentle sways of boys playing the music we love. We danced to the setting sun and remembered old friends and times long ago where a tree once stood and the dance floor was dirt.

Chapter 42

After my vacation, I felt fit to find Winona again and visited Dad.

"Seven years," I said. "You've been gone 7 years. What have you to say for yourself?" It was November, a bright sunny day where the sun was warm. The wind told you what was coming. A beautiful day for walking about Winona.

He sat smoking his pipe, rocking on the rocking chair outside his new home. He looked around and said this is the American dream. I noticed the American Flag swaying.

"Your guy lost," I said.

He nodded, saying, "It don't mean so much on this side. We don't need governing. Anger and drive, they leave when you step on over. Money don't make a difference over here. The big stones of the necropolis see in a different light. That is just a man and his ego wanting to be remembered." I told him the grandkids still talk and that they have a smile on their face when they do.

"My golden years," he said, "were the best of times. Seeing grandchildren grow into fine adults and being part of that is what mattered. What's in the backpack?"

Science girl had packed me a backpack with all the fixings. Bloody Mary's, Coffee and some Jameson. "Drink for us" I said, thinking it might take the whole bottle to get over the demons of tribalism we carried between us.

I was feeling good. The hair on the back of my neck wasn't standing. He was an old school Republican who defended that way of seeing his entire life. I had left the party of my forefathers and our relationship drifted. Politics and

114

Fox News. Limbaugh and Hannity. We stopped talking and grew more set in our ways.

We finished that bottle we did, and as we let go of the things, I felt a lifting. Time heals all and there are few things better than letting go of those hateful things that weigh us down. Peace, my friends.

Chapter 43

"Being dead is quite comforting. For many of us, it brought relaxation. For the first time, the first time in a very long time a comfort fills you. That sense of place engulfs you. Your head and your body are one. Mind isn't going in eight different ways."

I looked over to the newcomer. He seemed familiar but I wasn't placing him.

"Paul Nelson. Father Paul."

"Cotter Paul?"

He nodded and continued, "I liked the sound of life. God gave me a good ear and for that I'm appreciative. Every kid has goodness as his identity, and I sometimes think we have forgotten that. We are losing kids, and that's not a good sign for tomorrow.

"It was hard for me when the marijuana entered our culture. I saw it as a dark cloud. I saw kids change because of it. They became guarded. I thought it was the pot, but as I thought more, I started seeing the issue in the light of guilt. Guilt works through you, like the river. Hard letting the guilt go. We teach our young to follow the law, part of most cultures, certainly our town."

"Nothing wrong with that, is there?" I asked.

He frowned. "Guilt can ensue after breaking a law but what happens if the law is unjust? What is justice, Hanson? Guilt is an attachment. One of my priestly functions, my job is to help ease the guilt, let it go. Winona kids get raised with a strong sense of right and wrong. God gave me a window, you see. People are dimensional."

I scratched my head and asked him to tell more about justice.

He said that justice depends on where you are standing. "So much justice is an eye for an eye," he said, "forgetting the basic scripture of turning the other cheek. We don't know how to do that, but it is one of the tenants of Christianity from my seeing.

"I tried to let God's light shine through me, but I saw those young people change. It's hard to hide guilt and that gets instilled in kids as they smoke. They cover it up and instead of being open, they become closed. A form of rebellion, I suppose, to the parents and the culture that says no. A path, a journey to adulthood for some. The beginnings of lost identity. But I loved the smell of burnt leaf, and it does take away some of the pains of living when you get old."

I nodded.

He said he would spend one Saturday in the confessional booth a month hearing the tales of woe. Those reflections of life he carried with him he said. Hard letting go of the secret stories.

I nodded again, a bit in awe of this most decent man.

"The kids' seeds, they didn't fall far from the tree. Some parents like to pretend now and then, but kids are often most like their parents and grandparents. There are exceptions, and a good teacher hears those kids. I was a teacher to families from both sides of the tracks."

"Standing up for injustice is what Catholicism was about. I went to the Catholic mass."

"Survived?" he asked.

Still standing I thought as the sounds of the Bus Boys entered my soul, settling my being and like that, he done left.

Chapter 44

In Winona, the townies would slurp their beer and listen to country music. It was a path filled with hardship, broken relationships and battles with the booze. A rocky road and a beer and a burger could make the journey a bit less bumpy.

Folks were smiling, lightly nodding their heads keeping a step ahead of the devil himself. Life moved slower in the bars of yesterday, work had its proper place and folks, even the bums went to church. The Catholic Church was right downtown where the grocery store now sits and all the faiths with their beautiful stained-glass windows were close. It was a town for walking, talking and benches under shady trees.

In the back corner of the bar, restaurant you might see two men playing chess. Down in the next booth you might see two guys arguing over Marx or Shakespeare and Schmitz and Schmatz sat in the corner arguing Beethoven and Bach. It was a town where people liked to talk. It took pride in its schools and teachers were the best. The old Prussian and Pole sat sipping Vodkas wondering how their families could have so hated each other in the day.

Me? I liked the bar where I could usually find eight to ten broken, battered and twisted minds. They were a good lot, once you got over the nerves and they started talking about how life kicked them, knocked them down and how they had pride in their standing.

I turned to the guy on my left. "Nubs, Nubs Breeden, how is the pitching arm?"

"Shot to hell. The riser don't rise, the drop don't drop and my neck has a kink in it from turning as another ball finds its way over the fence."

"Nobody better than you, Nubs." I lifted my glass to him.

"Yesterday, you are living in yesterday. I've been training somebody to take my place. Fast Jimmy Hengel. Kid has the tools, best stuff I've seen. Makes a softball dance. Hard though." Nubs had eyes popping out of his sockets which burned bright from seeing things in places most of us never reached

"Hard?"

"Rollingstone, Minnesota. When you are born and raised in Rollingstone, you laugh and talk different. You got Guenthers and Kreidemachers, Speltzs, Hengels, Kalmes, Hoffmans, and other families who have roots back to its founding times. Luxembourg. Enough kids from each family to field their own ball team. That town sticks together, and Fast Jimmy plays town ball."

"I'm hearing that the Green Terrace boys have some players."

"Between Ernster who can pitch and those boys who can fly, us old boys feel like we are moving in slow motion. The ball is past us before some of the guys start swinging.

118

Lang's, Johnny's East Side and the Black Horse are still trying, but unless you got a pitcher you stand no chance."

"You still driving the Cadillac?"

"1943. Slow and steady. Keep the oil changed and the spark plugs fresh. Slow drive. Try and keep her under 20. Bought it from my boss down at the Box company. Over 20 years. Purring like the day it came off the sales floor. Got to make things last. Money mostly goes out faster than it comes in."

Red Nose was seated to my right. He was milking his afternoon beer. He didn't get going and wake up till a bit later. He would wander into Lang's here, and more often than not the yellow cab would drive him home. He worked the night shift and those boys have always had a funny winding to their thinking. He lived in the Harmony Hotel, down by the bridge. A life alone.

"Judge took my license away," he told me. "Said I couldn't hardly walk, much less drive. A man without a car doesn't have much standing. I can't get away with driving. Cops in this town know my habits, my patterns. Winona cops are tough. They might give me a break because my brother was a cop, but I wore out that welcome long ago. I can't sleep without a drink and drink without money from work. Demons, my head won't rest. Hey! We aren't on the radio or anything are we? I heard about you, writing down all the stories." He shook his head. "Maybe it don't matter. Hey Madge, can I have another?"

The Dame nodded her head, her scraggly skin, wrinkled and hanging low, rouge patted cheeks, glasses, and a smoke dangling from her lips. Her breasts hung comfortably on the bar. "What are you staring at, Hanson?" She hissed as she spoke.

"Your beauty, Miss Madge."

"My ass, you are trying to write a story. You figure I'm an easy target. Well in my day you wouldn't have been able to afford me or my girls, you bum."

"You don't want to be messing with Miss Madge, Hanson," Red warned me.

"You are just saying that, Red, so she buys you drinks."

"Now Hanson, you are disrespecting Miss Madge with that arrogance you got in you. Madge could hold her own with anybody. A walking legend she is," Nubs said.

"Madge is, huh?"

"Let me tell you something; she kept her eye out for folks needing help. She was one of the best. You are talking about good people who'd give you the shirt off their back. Survivors. Madge ran a stable of girls who wouldn't work for anybody else. Another example of a strong woman coming from Winona. Surprised you didn't know."

"Hey Hanson, you think you are better than us bums?"

"I got no interest in fighting. Miss Madge. Just here talking to the best people in town."

"Miss Madge, she outsmarted the lawyers, she did," Nubs piped in. "They don't talk about it and in the long history of this town that doesn't happen so often. Ran her own whore house down there on second. She owned it." He squinted at me. "You know, I've been looking at you, and you aren't right in the head."

I looked at him puzzled. Nubs Breeden telling me I was crazy. Issues yeah, but crazy? This was coming at me from a different way. "You say I have what?"

"Issues, you are really messed up in the head."

"How so?" I felt a bit tense. Hank Williams Sr. was playing on the juke box.

"You can make sense out of our talking. Most of us have a hard time putting words together, and you seem to have a way of twisting our words just right. Is that what they call messed up or what?"

I took a deep breath. I've found a home where others thought in backward, different ways, where the living meet the dying and the rivers meet the bluffs. I figured I was okay. Nice to be living around such fine, fine people as I sipped my beer.

Chapter 45

It took me some time to figure it out, but I finally latched on to the idea of writing down the stories of the dead. That put a whole new pressure on me. A few days later, I was at the Athletic Club trying to beat a deadline. The phone rang. Alty.

"Hey, I'm wondering when you are going to write two more columns? Deadlines. What am I supposed to put in this paper of mine?"

"Want ads, advertising. Do a comings and goings piece. Do a fishing report or go take a peek at some cows and tell us how they are doing. Say did you ever touch a cow?"

"How do you keep a job?"

"I got the best boss in town. Now you go crawl in that hot tub of yours, relax. Talk to that tree that overhangs the river. Your chapters are coming. Oh, and I'll be needing a day in August."

"Who says you'll still have a job?"

"Maybe not, but a day in August."

"Let me write this down. What date?"

"Doesn't matter."

"Doesn't matter? What do you mean?" Have you been drinking?"

"Tools of the trade. Doesn't matter. No destination on my day off. Make plans and then have it rain or be 110 in the shade, everything has to change."

"Doesn't matter?"

"It doesn't matter. I need a separation. Regain my identity. Doesn't matter, Monday through Friday."

"You're nuts!"

"It is why I work for you. Who else would hire me? Tells me you got some understanding. I got mental problems and some days you need to just get your brain organized, relaxed. That is why a Tuesday or midweek off day is kind of nice. A different energy you know."

"Energy? Never thought about it."

"See what you miss when you worry about other things."

He started laughing.

"You poor guy," I said.

"What do you mean?"

"When I start making sense something must be wrong. A schizophrenic getting something right. Thinking. Oh, and I met up with Al. He says Hi. You want to talk with him?"

"I don't hear voices like you do. Are we talking the same Al? Scooter Al?"

"One and only. That was a weird visitation. Never felt anything like it. Open casket."

"Now that you mentioned it."

"Damn funeral director."

"What, do you mean?"

"Al had a happy kind of face. Stern looking in that casket. Can't remember Al that way. I mean he is right next to me here at the club and he is still laughing, just like he was before dying."

"I can see why you got upset but sticking a pin in him like you did, to see if he was faking it? A little above and beyond, I think. Does he remember the pin?"

"You want to talk?"

"I'd like to. That would be something. Al's last gag. Talking from the beyond. I don't believe it. I know, I know, look at what I'm missing. A way of thinking."

"Why would you think or want to think any other way?"

"I have to get an assistant, just to talk with you. I like to keep sane."

I took a look over my shoulder and at the two bar stools next to me. Seemed like hundreds, hundreds of people wanting to talk. "You'll have your pieces by morning." I sipped my Jameson, felt my nerves settle and began to write as they talked.

Chapter 46

"The world is nothing like it was."

"Hey, Al. I used to get surprised, seeing dead folks. Not anymore."

"I want to have a drink but the bartender isn't listening. Thinking about other things he is. See how he handles those bottles, something running through him. You know him?"

"Little bit, beautiful wife and kids. Good guy, he just thinks he is Q."

"Q? From the Next Generation? Star Trek fan?"

"Not so much Star Trek. Hey Stink."

"Hanson."

"Stink still hangs here?"

"Daily."

"Gone 25 years. You know those Trekkies I always thought were a bit more astute and so would be aware of a parallel world. You know that pin hurt when you stuck it in my hand."

"Something wasn't right, you know. I told the boys Al wasn't dead"

"Nick."

"Hanson."

He was laughing. "You should have been in my shoes, seeing, watching my own wake. Living like we did makes for great stories."

"B. Brian, a beer for my friend Al." I nodded to my left.

"Oh, how long has he been dead?"

"Long enough."

"Listen as long as you pay, I'll serve, but I will not take part in your delusions."

Al shrugged and accepted the drink I paid for. "Kids miss a lot of things while thinking about something else. I suppose my presence would disturb their reality if the premise of the dead living is part of the equation."

"You still liking Hedy Lamarr?" I asked. I was starting to feel a bit out of sorts. A different feeling.

"Naw, that was Burmie that had a hard liking towards her. I preferred Myrna Loy."

"I'm guessing you liked Mrs. Robinson?"

"Oh shit, I gotta go."

Chapter 47

"Oh, that bartender is cute. He walks like a man I might be interested in meeting with. Sharing a drink." Something was oozing out of this boy, A vibe, a flair. Something running upside down in him.

Feeling my townie roots I asked him, "Where you from?"

"Chicago. Living up here. Winona is a different world."

I chuckled, looked around the bar, and said, "You can say that again." I told him I miss parts of city living. World is growing too fast.

"Privacy is hard to come by for a guy like me. Chicago has only a couple clubs. Chicago cops are a bit rough around the edges and they don't much like guys like me. I'm a friend of Chester's. Name is Alan."

"Hey B. Brian. This is my friend Alan. He's a friend of Chester B."

"Folks leave me alone. Some of them shoo away their children like I'd hurt a child. The last thing I would do is hurt a child. You don't fool me, Hanson. You are a writer, an observer. That twisted mind creates stories, develops characters, dresses them up and then presents them to an unknowing public. We got your profile."

"You have me profiled?"

"George Orwell, he saw a lot of things. It is coming. You are living in an algorithm world. You got no idea how much the mechanization and computerization of life has messed it up." He lifted his hand, settled and quietly said, "If your mind, Hanson, doesn't hear quiet, doesn't hear the sound of a creek, birds chirping and frogs croaking your barking up the wrong tree, missing life. I call it zero state."

"Zero state. How'd you get your talking? Where'd it come from?"

"Where did what come from?"

"Reason. Your way of reason."

"I spent a lot of time hiding."

"From what?"

"Myself, others."

"Hey B. Brian." I lifted my hand. "A grasshopper for my friend Alan."

"Chocolate covered or green?"

"Lime green."

B. Brian looked at me. He and I don't see eye to eye on some things. This was one of those instances he couldn't venture into. Talking with the dead is a learning place. You can do it any time of the day. My meditation. He just won't walk down that path. Closed mind.

"The thing is B. Brian," I told him, "You remind me of Q. Different camouflage, but he thinks in a different direction. A little nasty, kinkiness to his thinking."

"Don't be messing with my intellectual Super Hero," he replied.

"You know I think a little Jameson might do you good."

Alan spoke up, "I always felt as safe in Winona as anywhere else. I could come to this town, relax, get away.

Not much companionship, but folks mostly left me alone. I was gay and in the 50's that meant a deep closet. That bartender is so, so cute."

I had taken a psychology class at St. Mary's University once. "Tell me how did repressing your true identity affect you?"

"In many ways I guarded that life. Put it on the back burner, tried to hide it. It comes down to this, Hanson, when you can't express what is inside you, when you can't express yourself, you aren't really living. It is a process. You feel an inkling, an inkling as a youngster. But all these outside things say, No. A forbidden fruit. Institutions screaming NO! And to the biggest institution, God made us different so we could smile, laugh and express love. As I aged, I had a bit of that courage in me and I'd say to my old friends that knew that I was gay that the good Lord was looking down at how you treat the loved ones, the special ones, the ones that think different, act different."

"Your mama must have been pretty special, raising a son like you, Alan."

"Rest her soul. Growing up, growing up was hard, rejected by the whole world. Friends were hard, very hard to find as I kept my story."

"It must have been messed up, seeing reality which was different than what you had inside you."

"Threw myself into work. Non-stop, hours upon hours, denying the reality of who I was."

Just listening to him made me tired, so tired. I asked B. Brian to call me a cab.

Chapter 48

B. Brian had a Jameson waiting before I could even think about leaving.

I looked at him. "Yeah, I can feel it. Losing my mind as I see beyond seeing, being different."

He shook his head with a worried look. "You don't get paranoid?"

"Whispers, shadows and God himself talking. I found a way."

He started laughing, then looked at me, and began rinsing the bar glasses.

I heard a voice on my left. "You have fun, but the young man can see. Everybody tells him the dead are gone but he just might start seeing the dead if he let go of the things that chain him to his controlled state. Letting himself see when the brain says no way. You think he can handle it?"

"He might but most of us folks headed down that path get locked up, put away."

He paused, savoring his beer, "Hanson, can you leave our daughters alone?"

"Have you looked at your daughters? They are beautiful. East end girls got life in them. Dead spirits don't follow a map. Let's just hope the rhubarb survives the storm." He looked at me, a bit perplexed. "Keep talking, there is a meat packing plant not real far from here. Some of the boys, I hear, are talking about sending your mom a package of fresh catfish."

"I didn't get your name."

He shook his head, cropped hair on top of a big skull, knobby face. Strangely he spoke with a quiet voice,

"You'd butcher it anyway. Ski, call me Ski."

Polish last names are long and filled with unusual letter combinations. Grzybowski and Jazcewski, Prondzinski, Czaplewski, Lubinski, Literski and at one time those east end homes were filled with kids who slept nearly on top of another. Dzwonkowski and Drazkowski.

"Back in the day this place was classy. Bartenders wore ties and polished shoes. Every night men and women would bowl downstairs and stop at the bar for a nightcap. You can do the churching thing but much of the heart and soul of the Poles was seen here in this building, right here on Mankato Avenue."

I gave him the fuzzy eyeball.

"Wedding dances. Old poles, young poles gathered upstairs, Ate, drank and danced. Dance, dance, dance to the polka. Can you hear? Sweat and drink and dance some more. All day and night. Marriage was a celebration, a beginning, new life for a Polish heart that had grown so dark from the generations of oppression in the old country. The dark heart weighed heavy on the old Pole."

I could hear Doc Schultz singing Red Sails into the Sunset.

The faceless man on my right spoke up. "The best stories of long ago came from here. If you got good hearing, the stories still echo in the walls and the woodwork. They used to talk about how the dead would like Winona. Our bodies, hearts, and minds lay quietly in the echoes of the past, I remember old man Gostomski saying just those words.

"Even today all these hundred and some years later at night when the skies say goodnight I can hear the weeping tombstones of the old country. They lament how the dying generation has forgotten who they are and where they came from. A lost identity as they forget where Grandma and Grandpa first saw each other, met, snuck a kiss in the coat room while those that were watching danced the night away. They too got married, had children and bowled as the years passed. Right here under one roof."

"Tombstones crying?"

He nodded his head. "It was how the times talked. Our language, that which we spoke, was lighter and used symbolism to get meaning. We had an attachment to living. A lack of the classics, I tell you, in our schools today. Everybody in a hurry, going nowhere."

"You sound like you've read the books of the past?"

"I lived not far from Diedrowski and we would spend evenings talking on his porch. Every night I would walk the streets and wave at my neighbors. We knew how to talk all the languages. Why Diedra himself knew 17 languages. A poet at heart who could howl to the moon. Largest Polish newspaper in the country right here in Winona.

"This town was full of walkers." He shook his head." These old houses heat up in the summer. Now you must remember what it's like with no air-conditioning. No TV. Family might have one car. You would wake up and want to get outside, away from your brothers and sisters. Time alone was hard to come by in a house packed with people. Sitting under shade trees and on porches. The river kept us cool. Swimming and fishing kept us from the sticky heat."

Ski spoke up, "Back in the day a journey west of Mankato alone meant a whole new lot of ruffians and their neighborhoods you would have to pass through. Part of learning, always in this town was navigating the streets. I tell yah another thing, Grandparents and parents didn't used to complain about the teachers like you do nowadays. They respected learning and those that taught. Learning lasted forever in the happy ones."

I noticed B. Brian staring.

He said, "It's raining out. Go take a walk, clear your head. I'll have a Jameson waiting."

Chapter 49

"Walking in the rain. I was walking in the rain. Splish, splash, cooling my feet." I can sing when I'm walking in the rain. Nobody listening so they can't hear how badly I sing. Some guys sing in showers and others don't. But walking around in a rainstorm like I do gives a man a chance to really break loose. "Like a Rhinestone cowboy, out on his horse in a Star Spangled Rodeo."

"You best be saying your Prayers. The devil will be sowing his seeds in that thick skull of yours. The lord Jesus has his hands full with the devil's fruit." He joined me out of nowhere. He had a woolly, frizzy beard, nearly halfway down his chest. Flat brimmed hat and a long black, dusty coat. Blue eyes that danced as he talked. He walked without an umbrella and his clothes didn't seem to get wet.

Rain, even walking in the rain. Dead people can't leave me alone in paradise. "What do you mean, intruding on my relaxing time?" I asked without stopping. "Raindrops, raindrops, can't you feel the raindrops cooling you, relaxing you? Let your mind think, be free."

"That devil is smiling as God's tears fall on your closed mind. The good lord is unhappy in the thinking you are spreading that he is a hateful person, seeking revenge. That devil sure did plant some seeds in your thinking. Name is Silas Richter."

"You ever find hell? I disagree with your assessing,"

"The good Lord spared me that experience of hell. I never thought death would be like I've found. It's a special place."

"Where'd you come from?"

"I was a bum. Rode the rails. Spent my life preaching in the hobo jungles of this country. The men who rode the rails had some real demons in them. Seeing and hearing things nobody else could. I tended as best I could to their spiritual need. Made it to Winona every fall. No prettier place in the world. Always wanted to get out there on the river, that lazy Mississippi river. Had a fear, a fear of swimming, drowning, not being able to breathe, being helpless." We stopped at the Zesto stand and even though it was raining, we sat on the side bench. Shared a moment of pleasure. We both liked chocolate.

"I always liked Winona. Deep thinking. The Masons are serious in their thinking and the Masons while believing in a God thought the interpretation of that God was left to a person and his own way of thinking. I guess that is why in Winona, all the faiths seem to have a place because they talked about the things that really mattered. Lot of Masons in this town and their way of thinking ran strong. I was fortunate, I guess. Never felt any hate coming out of the pulpit or the people sitting in the pews where I grew up. Mostly, people gathering, sharing a communal feeling.

"You think we should head back? That bartender of yours is probably wondering who you ran into on your rain walk. You know, you got to watch that whiskey drinking

132

and hope it never turns bad."

I looked at him.

"Once you get a taste of the bad whiskey, it slips right into your pores. It starts tasting better and better, taking over your thinking, your control. You get the bad whiskey in your blood and life becomes far less pretty."

We walked by Prondzinski's Grocery on Fourth Street, and I thought about stopping in to see if they still had nickel candy and baseball cards with real gum.

"They don't do any butchering in back anymore either. Wrong generation, Hanson. Sometimes I think you were born at the wrong time. You sure are messed up."

"Well, yeah. I think a person who talks with the dead should be considered a bit messed up in their thinking," I said.

He chuckled. "Never thought I would get to talk again. Kind of nice."

"Any stories of hell on that side?"

"Not a trace, not a trace. I've been gone over a hundred years and I've yet to find hell. The bright light of dying is the first thing that hits you. Not a mean bone in anybody's body on this side. You do get a yearning."

"A yearning?"

"People and you miss what was. Even surrounded by all the wonderful things that dying brings. You feel a yearning for people. You feel, but you lose touch when you step on over. Best to get your hugging done now. Eternity waits."

Chapter 50

One day, while I sat in the Mankato Bar, Shive showed up. He was ready to talk, and I got set to listen.

"I used to fish down there on Shive road down near the Sewage plant," he said. "The sheepshead were always just a bit bigger than the ones you pulled out of the lake. I thought they were tastier but I'm not sure if eating Shive Creek fish was healthiest for me. Three times daily. Year round. Every day, all day. You like a bit of variety in your eating so I pickled, fried and smoked the fish. Not easy. Lots of bones. Someone once told me, that might have been my problem."

"Eating Fish?"

"No. I don't think it had anything to do with eating fish all the time. Seems healthy to me but Snot, he once told me he thought those fish out near the sewage plant short circuited a person in his thinking. Then he'd say I was never much in school, implying the sewage consumption got in the way of my thinking.

"Snot?"

"Long last name, so we called him Snot. He died young, good man. I never much liked school, you see. You wouldn't either if you got your fingers whacked by Sister Cybill. She'd get mad at me because here I was in the second grade and I couldn't spell my last name Pretarekabobolinski."

"How'd you get the name Shive?"

"I fought for it. Mikey Ears and I went to the Washington School. Near Kolter's Bicycle Shop. I was in Second Grade, full of myself so I went up to Mikey Ears who was in fourth grade and was called Shive. Told him that there was room for only one Shive in Washington School near Kolter's, and that it was me.

"Mikey Ears took the cigarette out of his mouth, stuck out his tongue and put out his cigarette. He had a carton rolled up in his T-Shirt sleeve and put the now unlit cigarette in the box. "Punk' he said, "Tonight under the big green stands of Gabrych Park. 7p. You best bring your Mama to pick up all the broken pieces after I'm done with you."

"See, though I couldn't hardly spell, I could always talk, Hanson. As long as I had done some thinking before starting to talk. I'd be okay. I went home, grabbed my cane pole and tossed in a line. Time for me to do my thinking." It must have been 15 minutes, hardly a nibble which was rare in Winona when I felt a tug and a strong pull. I thought catfish right away and I had one heck of a time bringing him in. I kept worrying he was going to bend my pole enough to break in half. I finally landed him."

"He sported the long whisker that would numb you if it got hold of you and I was worried about him stinging but I got the metal stringer through his gills, wrapped the stringer around my bike handle and headed home catfish tail dragging."

"Tommy Boy," I hollered. "A drink for Mr. Shive."

He poured the beer and brought it over, staring at me and saying I needed to show people respect or he'd be haunting me from the grave. These are good people who frequent the Kato Bar," he said.

I nodded and Shive started right up talking about his big catfish. "It had to be forty pounds," he said. Evidence he cried that he indeed was Mr. Shive. "I rode that bike all through the East End. Never felt so proud. I brought the catfish to Gabrych thinking Big Ears might realize I indeed was Shive. Not everybody can haul in a catfish weighing 40 pounds with a cane pole, much less than a kid who weighed maybe eighty pounds dripping wet. Old Shive pummeled me. Then, soon after he met a girl and wanted to be known as Michael. I remained Shive.

Chapter 51

After Shive finished his story, I sat there enjoying my Bloody Mary. Tom was still bartending. Mankato Bar on a Sunday Morning.

She had a wide, broad face and she oozed kindness. She waddled as she walked to the stool. Her butt cheeks flopped over the edges of the bar stool. "My name is Janice," she said. "Died in 1928. Had the gout bad. Told the Doctor to put me under. Was tired of living with pain. I figured I'd deal with God later. I had enough."

She turned to Tom and asked for a Fallen Angel. Stumping Tom was no easy task but after hesitating a bit he poured the gin, squeezed the lime juice and added the bitters and Crème de Menthe.

He presented the drink to Janice. "A fallen angel for a fallen angel. Thanks for showing up in my bar."

"We left everything. Left our homeland to come to this country where we were free to breathe, free to express ourselves and free to vote unless you were a woman. We couldn't vote until 1920. I voted for Mr. Cox with my first vote. Considering President Harding was nothing but trouble all these years later I think I made the right choice. "Not a lot of hope for Polish people in old Prussia. America was a chance and to a man who worked hard tomorrow looked better. I liked the old church. You could feel the beat of the Polish Heart in those pews. Shoulder to shoulder we sat listening to the words of our priest. The St. Stan's church captures our heart but the Polish heart beat strongest in the old one."

"Big Red is a bit intimidating."

"I can understand that. It is a Basilica after all, a monument to not only the Polish vision of God but to the people who came here, little or nothing in their pocketbook and built a monument to worship in. Little houses all chipping in. Those people had heart."

"I been inside, the colors overwhelm me."

"The Polish kept themselves pure. You should have heard people talking when word would get out that one of the children was dating someone other than a Pole. The party lines lit up."

"How did you make a living?"

She looked at me. "I raised eight kids in a small house not far from Gabrych Park. Between sewing and cleaning and cooking and gardening, who had time to work? Bill wasn't going to change a diaper or help teach them to read. Keeping those kids out of trouble was a full-time job."

I took a deep breath and sipped the Bloody Mary. Just enough bite to keep me alert.

"I just don't understand what you are all so mad at. You got yourself shiny cars and big houses. And still you complain. It's greed that's causing the problems. You just want more. That devil's seed can't be satisfied."

"People got their beliefs."

"It's the devil's fruit," she roared. "A full blossoming, the folk of your generation got running through you. You kids got no idea what real living is. You know what I miss most?"

"No, tell me."

"Kids out riding their bikes, fishing poles hanging out over their front wheel, ball gloves on the handlebar. Baseball cards and colorful plastic things attached to wheels. Riding a bike with no hands, hot shots. People out talking, getting along."

"You think you can stop time?"

"I am the fallen angel," she roared.

Tom had a disgusted look on his face as he stared at me. "Let the Fallen Angel talk, Hanson. She's seen things you can only imagine. Death, you got death all wrong you know."

I paused. Tom had a way of talking that always made me reflect. A good bartender, a better man. I often worried often about the machines in our living and how the faster we go the further we grow apart.

She started right up like she could see my thinking. "Those machines get right inside you. Faster, faster they go. Ain't never enough time. Wanting to be elsewhere. You've forgotten the things that matter. They've filled you with noise, taken away your quiet, disturbed your sense of place. Our bodies need quiet to reclaim, recharge ourselves. Always going, little white noise filling your mind. Damn machines are driving us nuts. Those machines are rolling right over who we were."

"Herman Hesse. What was that book? Yes, *Beneath the Wheel.*"

"Never much of a reader. I learned Polish first and I was stubborn enough to want to live my life with my native tongue. You all don't understand English too well either."

138

"So how did you get your learning?"

"My eyes and ears. Listening. That is the thing about dying. Over here you see life different. You see change through time. Gives you a chance to start seeing in a different light. Besides, I knew most of all I needed, at a real young age."

My Phone rang. "Chinky. Chinky Deerman? You got a sponsor for your Ocooch Mountain Music Radio Show? Tushner Hot Dogs. You mention them three times in a half hour, yeah, yeah. Six hot dogs Stanley? Living heaven."

Chapter 52

I sat down with Stoner. Science Girl and I were headed to Duluth and the North Shore. We were sitting in the Old Kresge Café.

Stoner spoke up right away. "That girl you got, has to be a saint, putting up with your messed up way of talking. You don't make any sense sometimes. Blind as a bat."

"You aren't the first person to say that Stoner." I gave Stoner my phone number and I said we'd call when we got to Duluth."

"I hear they're putting Chuck Williams on the Morgan Block," he said, shaking his head. "Chuck is the best there is but he don't..."

"Don't what?"

"Talk our language. I mean we aren't right in the head. You want a hit?"

"No, no."

"The boys would be honored but their words come out scrambled. I mean a microphone in the face would send their minds going in a million directions. Poor Chuck trying to make sense out of Stanley talking. He talks like nobody else. That wouldn't be fair."

"Argue, argue, argue. Hag, Debbie, Dubnik, the whole neighborhood would be arguing from their 2nd floor back porch. The Morgan Block was the greatest asset downtown Winona had."

"She was in rough shape before she died. 'New is better' was the way of the talk. They took that wrecking ball and with it went 80 years of good stories and laughter coming from the cafes and bar stools. Gone. The heart of downtown Winona, who we were and are, sits covered by a faceless Shopping Mall and a High Rise. I feel sorry for today's kids. Us dead folks remember when the entire block was lit up, windows open and you could smell the food and hear the sounds of Winona. Not part of a kid's way of thinking. Can't see it."

"You have a bad night sleeping, Stoner? Get up on the wrong side of the bed? Blaming kids for not being able to see what we tore down. The great cover-up pretending we were pure. Disturbing to my way of seeing."

"I haven't had a decent night sleep since Nam. Never quite been able to shake the experience. Sticks with yah so I found myself early out walking today. Stopped at all the old places. The Main and Charlies. Sat down for a beer at The Eagles Club. It's amazing how quiet this block has become at three in the morning."

"All great towns got a cemetery in it and Winona did. Back part of the Exchange Building. Small church and a cemetery. Lest we forget the Indian mounds. This is sacred land, Stoner."

"I'll give you a call. Tell you how it went."

140

Chapter 53

I like to drink in the morning. Wake up slowly. Let the day settle in. Scare away the demons which mess up my sleep.

The Athletic Club was built in 1931. The Polish wanted a place to gather, celebrate their new lives in a new country, remember the old country and the people from whence they came. My dry throat and the Athletic Club serving cold beer worked together.

B Brian was my personal bartender. My beer was waiting, warmed for twenty minutes, room temperature, before the golden water filled my insides. Brian thought I was nuts.

I conducted no business before my first beer. By 10:15, there was a line of dead people waiting to talk. B Brian just shook his head.

"Hi, my name is Jeannie LeBeauski. You the writer, that talks with the dead?"

"Yes. How long have you been dead?"

"Getting on fifty years. Dying isn't all like it's cracked up to be. It ends. You can feel sorry for yourself or you can stand up and get on with living."

"Living while dead?" I asked.

She took a large drag from her cigarette as I stole a look. Her red smudged lips and her painted face with the wrinkly skin and rouge applied to her cheeks showed a life lived. I nodded at B. Brian for another drink.

"Tough day at the office? First one went down pretty fast. What is that like?

"What do you mean?"

"Dead people. Talking with the dead people," he

said as he put the beer in front of me.

"Tell him, if he opened his mind to all that is, he might learn a few things."

"Jeannie says if you weren't such a blockhead."

"Jeannie." He shook his head and walked away to fill Blue Nose's bottomless glass.

Jeannie said, "I spent my early years peddling my wares down at the National Hotel on second. That was where I met Jack. Railroad men worked long hours, long days and all men need a little love. We got hitched. I worked with Teddy and Elmer down at the Hurry Back as I grew wrinkles. Rackem Teddy. Art Cunningham was a good boss and after my Jack died they got me a place on the third floor of the Williams Hotel. Walk to work."

"Downtown Winona?"

"The Hurry Back. Best years of my life. I remember using a microwave for the first time. What a mess. The boys laughed." She got kind of quiet and then went on in a low voice. "Miss the old boys, the young kids. Wishing they realized dying ain't really dying. Whatever happened to that cute little Reed boy?"

"Started talking with the trees, grew a beard. Darling wife."

"I always felt respect from those kids. They had fun with me but at the end of the day I felt their respect. You meet Joseph yet?"

"Joseph?"

"Dywan. Joseph Dywan. The guy sitting next to me. He is kind of quiet until the singing bartender shows up."

I looked to my left. The chair was empty. I wondered how many other things I wasn't seeing.

"Been gone over a hundred years. Drank himself to

death while living. At least that is what he tells me. Never met him while living."

"B Brian," I yelled. "Give me some of the Irish!"

"A good day for the demons eh?" He was laughing as he poured the Jameson. "You affirm my belief that even those with a screw loose, have some purpose."

"Joseph likes the singing bartender. Frank Sinatra, Don Ho, Elvis, singing the songs of a different era. He says he pours a mean drink."

"I got little energy left, dealing with you and the dead. Singing? You are insane. Who is Joseph?" I accepted the drink from Brian and closed my eyes for a moment as the first swallow burned down my throat.

I heard a quiet whisper and the seat was no longer empty.

"Music, music, can take you to another place. A better place. The sound of glasses meeting and good cheer. The gentle tones of a piano relaxing the mind from a tired day. Working, working all our living years. Name is Joe. Jeannie got me out of my shell."

"What a kind thing to say, Joseph. To think love exists on the other side. Different generations finding love." Jeannie giggled.

"I was dead by thirty, Jeannie. Drank myself to death. Never left my Mom's house. Started drinking when I was eight. Never stopped."

"I'd like to meet her, Joseph."

"You know how life is on the other side, Jeannie. Never know who you might see. I ran into her once, shortly after she passed. Not sure, I will see her again."

"She must have been a fine lady."

"I could have done her better." A single tear rolled

143

down his cheek. He wore a hat with Winona Coal on the front. His wearied skin seemed to echo that of his love, Jeannie.

I nodded my head as B Brian poured me another. I felt the quiet of the dead people leaving. The chairs are now tattered, the walls seem dim, and the laughter and smiles that used to fill the Athletic Club have gone to a different place as those still yet breathing have forgotten the roots from which they came.

Downstairs men bowled and upstairs people celebrated life and marriage. I slowly sipped my Jameson thinking about Jeannie and Joseph and all the other good people in this town. I nodded my head and wondered who was next.

Intermission

Chapter 54

The judge placed the blue pill just under the tongue. "Just under the tongue," he said to himself. "A good journey. My choice and to ashes I must go, so only my spirit remains."

He found it was rough, those years where his mind and body had started crumbling. He'd kept the little tab in a safe place. Assurances had been given that time wouldn't affect the potency of the drug. He felt he had to say goodbye before he left.

His mind had dulled. His beliefs were crumbling. Feelings cropped up that he had not felt since young. Awareness finds its way as he realized the judge was no longer in charge, the smartest man in the room. Time gets everyone.

He had come from a family of immigrants, teachers, and professors. The best and brightest all the way through. Catholic, educated in the classics and history by Jesuits with a conservative bend. He'd been the brightest guy in the room."

He lay down on the bed and spoke to the empty room. "My heart was America, and it was fueled by a mind that didn't rest, didn't stop." His heart had responded when young, but then like all things it began to wear out. Faster, faster it beat as time inflicted its toll.

The voices of the doctors echoed in his head. "Judge, Judge," they'd said. "You must exercise, eat well, lose weight. Take these pills; they will help."

But he'd thought of himself as invincible as a young man. "Hardly," he whispered, as wisdom flowed through his bones. "Think, think my Noni, as I let go of my living family. The sounds of the old neighborhood brought me pleasure. The smell of Italians eating together gave me warmth."

He sighed and made himself more comfortable. "I had a good life. I got to use my mind for its entirety and tonight I shall go peacefully into that good night. No Bible, no gun, no righteousness, blocking my thinking. I hear Bible thumpers saying it is a choice of God. I say to them how I wanted to live was my choice, my responsibility, and in my last remaining days it is again my choice as I prepare for dying.

"Hypocrisy shows in my face as I start stepping through the curtain. Choice to live, to love, to die, to marry. Choice rings through me here in Nowhere, Texas. I hear the ancient tomes of old Catholicism. No, no they cry as I take my last breaths peacefully, calmly."

He covered himself, put his head on his pillow and got ready for the long, long nap. He didn't know what awaits but he put away his shields, his armor, and his thoughts. He closed his eyes and gently placed the tab beneath his tongue and started his journey.

Part 5 Memories and Thoughts

Chapter 55

I sat in the bar, nursing a drink and remembering.

She made us take off our shoes and line them up. Organize our shoes, straight line. Raise your hand. Miss Reiter I hate to tell you all these years later I still don't line up my shoes.

In first grade, Miss Pennell worked on our reading. She was very tall and reading, the teaching of reading, was her life. She ended her illustrious career running a reading program for Winona State University.

I fell in love with Miss Dunlay and her way of inspiring. She had wrinkly skin and white hair. She had some Old Winona in her. We would take a walk, and I remember the old sidewalks that told the story of an ancient past. The old houses creaked their own stories and not wanting to break my mother's back, our minds kept a moving.

Miss Foster. She made us learn how to spell antidisestablishmentarianism. It was a way of working our memory skills and the sounds of that bouncing ball got us on a roll. She made me believe that by spelling the longest word in the English language meant we could do about anything. I'm guessing Opal is smiling, thinking about that kid who made that word the idea behind a paragraph.

I remember reading the Boxcar Children and the Chip Hilton series. Dick and Jane. Grade School was a happy place, where the burdens of living took second. I remember feeling hot in Mr. Brook's math class, being it was after lunch and playground.

I look back and wish my old science teacher had planted the seeds of curiosity. I was close minded about that scientific learning. It took Science girl to get me to realize that science is tomorrow.

I look back and I wish I would have had a crazy, alive art teacher. It took me a long time to express myself and art has helped. Color and letting go has been good.

I was a good math guy who ran into a teacher who used a pointer stick that he would whack across desks. My mind froze. I stopped progressing in the world of Math. Just the way I'm wired.

I had a music class from a short haired, big glasses nerd like character. I couldn't sing, dance or play an instrument but I could understand the rhythmic paces of composition. A good teacher opens windows.

I remember Henry Hull, extraordinary teacher at Winona State. He would come over to Phelps Grade School on the WSU campus and give us a lecture about milling and I couldn't take my eyes off him. He was a real performer. He had a long, grey beard, and he walked with a cane. As he talked history, we would shake that cane. The old chalk board grew dusty as he wove his tale of Winona and its history, lumber and milling.

Teachers are performers. Activating the imagination of a child is what the good ones do. It is not easy learning how to dance with the mind of a child. They come from all directions and backgrounds. A lot of the kids sitting in

148

the chairs have been listening to family members telling us how bad our schools are and is it any wonder some of our students are jaded about school and thinking and learning. We like to blame teachers for kids not reading, learning and yet as a culture we don't read much anymore. We also have a tendency to read things which reinforce our thinking rather than challenge it. Kids learn many things in the background noises of everyday living.

Little sounds, I remember little sounds from the time I was very young. I started to like sitting in churches when nobody was there. It was quiet and I tried feeling the energy of a church. The best times were spent reading the sins left behind. Some weeks were more intense.

I haven't been to church in a while. Noise, sounds, people. I found peace outside in the woods and I don't think my God has any problem with it.

The big water of the North shore takes me somewhere else. The lake is deeper, the rock harder and the myths greater. The wind bites you. The sun wakes you. You'll feel yourself rising from deep within. Some ancestral kind of thing I thought as I finished off my Bloody Mary.

Chapter 56

I got to thinking about Betty and the way she faded. Alzheimer's does that. It gets people looking and thinking and back to talking and sharing some of the times. I was there and they tell me it was a nice day for walking.

Betty drifted in and started talking. "I would have liked to say goodbye as people should but trying to put words together eludes us with the disease. It hurts me not to be able to remember a name and still feel the love inside. Not remembering changes everything and pretty soon you even start distrusting your own self.

"My mind started going quiet before things were noticed. I struggled with my concentration, becoming distracted by any little noise or somebody talking. I sometimes noticed that I was leaving things unfinished and the stove still on. I had always liked a clean house.

"I put spoons and forks in my bedroom drawers and hid my money. Sent some to the preacher man. Those familiar faces will find it someday I suppose but I can remember my Dad hiding his money under the floorboards and I'm not certain the kids would look there. Strange, how you lose one part of your memory and yet you can think of things from a long time ago.

"I could hear you talking and the pleas to remember who you are. I don't remember as my mind stopped thinking like that. After a life lived and filled with the sounds and smells of that life, it's quiet now as if I am returning to the womb from which I came.

"I loved you, but words were not to be. I like the quiet. There I can feel the small traces of love I once had. Names and faces I can't remember but I can feel the warm hand of the man I love. Early on I said things I should not have said as I was angry, mad and confused. I lost the things that mattered most. I lashed out at those I loved. I can't remember how regret works but I think it belongs here.

"The day is coming when I won't be able to walk as my mind can't tell my legs to go anymore. My body will stop working and I think this is not a way to live. I want to go gracefully into that good night with peace awaiting me.

"I will be there watching over when it's all said and done, like it's meant to be. I'll be with my old family, hearing their voices and sharing the stories of a good life while looking at those whose time has not yet come.

"I can hear the bells of the next life from a different place. They seem nice and are telling me that is what life is. It has been a good life and I thank you all for sharing the journey that brought us together."

She drifted away as quietly as she'd come in.

Chapter 57

I was headed to Mike McAndrews book opening. Faces of Port Townsend. The town was fast asleep. I had a thermos and smoke. I went looking for a place to sit and watch a town wake up.

I thought about putting some Jameson in my coffee as I looked for a place. I thought about Sirens and the Pour House bars. That's when the whispering started.

I slept in that old rusty bucket of a boat. Clear skies. The air felt fresh. The heat had lifted. I could breathe. I was having my morning smoke out walking about. The early light.

I take a trip; I let my thinking go. I tell myself as I roll out of the driveway no thoughts of home for a week. Let go of the attachments to living I carry in my head. Those mental connections we have to place. Vacate so I can look at the world fresh when I return.

"Welcome to Port Townsend. Up kind of early," he said. "I like the sounds sound and smells of dawn. Seagulls and baking bread. A release to my being.

"Drums, my drum sure didn't beat like most folks. I saw light through a different prism. All these big Victorian houses, relics of an old army post. A lot of myth on the streets of Port Townsend. They don't change easy but with gray hair comes wisdom. I hear those myths strongest when that sun starts its daily dance. Dark. The town's sounds dampened by the deep Puget Sound."

"I like the quiet. The noises of living have done put us on edge. I tell you it doesn't let us let go of the energy we carry with us. I could breathe at three in the morning."

"Yes, sir, I heard dead folks could talk to you. Seeing is believing."

"From what I hear stepping on over wasn't what you expected?"

"I'm still shaking my head at the mere thought of being able to talk again. We first started hearing that Mike McAndrew had a friend who could talk to us dead folk and of course, believing was something else. You got a line of dead folks behind you if you haven't noticed. Don't let them scare you; they just want to talk. Some of them don't look well."

"You are fine storytellers, you dead folk," I said. "A shame we've stopped hearing your voices, the tones of those who were here before us."

"Today stopping tomorrow. Getting in the way."

"A soft mingling of memories. Faded laughs and tinkling glasses. What a warm, comfortable place. Nice brick and brick has a way of talking. Closed I see."

"You'll find locked doors can't stop dead folks. You can't leave Port Townsend, you know?"

"Oh?"

"Well, why would you? Life is and we see our fingerprints all over the people left behind. The living faces of Port Townsend make us dead folks proud. Tell them Thanks."

I saw a flickering light, mutton chop sideburns and big black Orbison glasses without the tint. He laughed and said he would see me later.

Chapter 58

Back in the bar, I ran into Lucille again and gave her a nod. "Well Lucille. It is always so nice to see you and Tommy out and about. I must tell you that you have to be the most elegant person in this bar. I now understand why Tommy beams like he does."

She patted the empty space next to her. "Let me tell you, we have what is called undying love. You carry that way of thinking about love ending at the tombstone and you'll find a much different answer when you get on over. Tommy says so."

I gave her a little peck on the cheek and told her she might be the sweetest person I know. I asked her about Stanley who was sitting at the end of the bar with Dave and Carol Fratzke. People and dead people shoulder to shoulder. What a great bar.

"You've made Tommy jealous, kissing me on the cheek," she said. "There is no touching in the land of the dead. And now a passionate night of love awaits me. And Stanley, we are all a bit worried. Fame finally found Stanley and that opens up a whole new can of worms as the seed of the devil works its way through his being. Stanley was one of a kind.

"I always liked Port. A stronger wine. Makes me laugh. Dregs of the barrel we are, my Daddy said. Then he'd smile and say that dregs, people dregs are the best kind. I think you got a bit of that in you, Hanson. Psst. I must say, I still think you got a bit more of the crazy in your bones than me. Cheers."

"Why Cheers." I lifted my mug. "Would you and Tommy like a Port?"

"Oh!" She fluttered her eyelashes.

"Bobby Rutkowski. Two glasses of port for our love birds." I had noticed a guy in the corner. Never saw him before. Decided to go see what he was made of. I asked him where he was from in my townie way

"New York," he said. "though my learning was done in the South, my appreciation for language, all nurtured in the traditions of southern hospitality."

"A tobacco man?"

"Life fell right for me. My daddy was a cotton dealer with strong ties to the old ways. All the way back to before the civil war."

"This town, Winona, has always provided perfect camouflage for those who think a bit different. 'Fit in' is what you hear coming out of the single-minded chambers but us broken branches beautify the river valley. What brings you to town?"

"I'm a writer. I work for the NY Times. Mr. Ochs, the owner of the paper said I had stepped on some toes, but I'm right. The Yankee team lacks grit and heart, underachievers. Winning has gone to their heads and when a ball club has no heart, you don't win. They are a sinking ship and George Steinbrenner, the Yankees owner, didn't like my commentary. He advertised and wanted Ochs to fire me. Mr Ochs sent me to the hinterlands in search of a Yankee heart. I'm searching for Julie Wera's heart. He was the glue that kept the greatest team ever assembled from imploding."

"Julie Wera, the ball player? A lot has changed in the East End. Julie he went to work up in Rochester. He became a butcher in a grocery store called the Piggly Wiggly. Gone now too. I think. His parents' grocery store got sold to Old Man Riska who drew murals on his garage and operated the swing bridge on the Mississippi. Gone and the old ballpark lost its identity when the big green stands came tumbling down. All the old dreams that came tumbling down when the Green Stands of Gabrych Park fell. Julie Wera's heart made him who he was."

Chapter 59

"Hi Stanley. Something bothering you?"

"I could use Mrs. Pomeroy. She was always so gentle and kind with her talking. Helped me through my toughest times."

"Dead people work on their own time it seems. What seems to be the matter? Mr. Grantland Rice over there says you are an American success."

"I'm just nervous. I get to judge the rib contest at Big Muddy Brew n Que. I got a horrible problem when it comes to eating. I can't stop. It'll be all over my shirt and my beard. Everyone will make fun of me as messy of an eater as I am and then I get nervous and start talking a million miles an hour. Pretty soon I'm frustrated and well you know."

"Come on Stanley, there are not a lot of living people who can see the dead and those of us who can, could care less about that barbecue on the front of your shirt. I'm guessing you'll be saying it's the best meat you ever had."

"Now wait, wait Hanson, I don't give up my love of Tushner's or Ribs from Ruth's, just because some guy from Kansas City is saying they are all the best. I'm guessing those boys with all their fancy cookers and spices couldn't top Ruth Ribs. I wish I had gotten the secret to their tasting. One reason I like the local samplings at Big Muddy Brew n Que. You don't suppose Ruth Behning died without revealing her sauce and rub?"

"Could be, she was a good thinker and probably kept it between her ears. Otis gone as well?"

"I'm thinking Otis must have juiced them somehow. Otis never moved too fast. He was the finest slow cooker one could imagine. He'd get to cooking those ribs. All those smells getting ventilated straight outside. Best advertising in the world. He cooked those ribs slow."

"You are a star Mr. Chinky, a star. A man people look up to nowadays. Why that is Grantland Rice over there and he wants to interview you. You got poor Lucille worried and I'm even hearing rumblings that you aren't handling your fame. Don't be losing your identity."

I'm guessing I'll want seconds. I'll keep my pinky out. Time to be a star."

"That's right Stanley, show them style. Stanley Deerman, style."

"You think I'll make it?"

"They'll be calling you Hollywood."

156

Chapter 60

We were fortunate to grow up in the time we did. But now, hardly a week goes by when someone I knew isn't leaving. More traces of yesterday gone. I found a place near the back of St. Mary's church and settled in for the service. "Come on. Tell them dead isn't really dead." The preacher was gyrating and preaching about some heavenly place that was all light and I was trying to understand what he was saying. He kept repeating himself like a broken record. I'm thinking they pulled him out of the Nursing Home. He was older and it seemed like the forgetting disease had started.

The voices of yesterday started my thinking. Dead folks and their ideas and talkings bouncing off the walls. I tried ignoring the whisper, but dead folk don't rest.

Old friend Frank was talking in my ear. Cheryl, Dick, Julie, Tom, and Joan were sitting near. We were paying our respects to a classmate, friend. Mary King. The living and the dead together, here in St. Mary's Church. Winona, MN.

I heard Frank whisper, "It's about soul. It's what matters on this side of living."

I looked at my friends. All caught up in their own thoughts about life and living. They were listening to their memories. Cheryl had a twinkle in her eye and a little bit of a smile.

"Mary will like it over here," Frank kept talking. "The burdens lifted, gone. It's like floating in air. Your thoughts are released. Free to follow yourself, your heart void of the Devils seed which fills the living. Too many things blocking thinking. Our thoughts and drives get shackled to the

157

past. Chained, imprisoned in a box."

"You never talked that way when living," I said out loud and felt the sharp elbow of Cheryl.

The whole church was staring. I heard a couple rows back that God will have him in hell and Old lady Scarfish looked angrily down that mountain of a nose between her eyes from across the aisle.

The old priest, all wrinkled and disheveled, continued with the death mass. He must have been 90. He kept mumbling Latin. Mumbling over and again the Latin words no longer heard often.

"It's not bad over here at all," Frank whispered. "The stress is gone."

I told Frank to hush and Cheryl stared.

Tom mumbled to tell him hello and the folks behind me were telling me to shut up and respect the dead and her family.

"That Hanson was spoiled in his upbringing," I heard.

The old priest came walking down the aisle staring at me through his fuzzy eyebrows, asking if I was all right. I lowered my head. I heard Frank say something about taking the rap. Then the priest said I had interrupted the sacred words and he wasn't certain if a person got a second chance to Heaven without the sacred words. He'd have to start all over and he wondered if I was happy.

I asked him if he had a key to unlock the gates of Heaven.

He raised his fingers to the sky. "The gates of Hell await you and your kind. Questioning the inner sanctum is a short path to Hell," he bellowed. Then he mumbled something in Latin as he trudged back up to the altar.

Frank mumbled something about ancient myth and that it felt good seeing old friends gather. Cloudy days have got their own way of bringing light.

Science Girl and I walked down the steps after the mass. She asked, "Who were you talking to?"

When I said Frank, she said no kidding. I did too. I kept my mouth shut. Not wise to say you hear the dead. They'll be locking you up.

Rest in Peace Mary King. Rest in Peace.

Chapter 61

Charlie Downs used to sit on the stoop selling old newspapers. He was kind of funny looking, with narrow eyes and a round happy face. He spent much of his day watching the buses and he told me he liked the Greyhound bus driver hat. The drivers always had a kind word for Charlie.

Charlie made money selling day old newspapers to anybody who had a nickel. He would make the rounds, visiting lawyers, businessmen, and bankers, filling up the front basket on his bike with their old newspapers of yesterday, reselling it the next day. Everybody liked Charlie. He was at the restaurant every day. Everybody knew Charlie from the Eagles Club to the Labor Temple. He liked Chicken Nuggets and Ketchup, Orange Pop. And he would smile like there was nothing better. Charlie made us smile and look.

The boys who gathered at the Kewpee were rough-necks, hoods. They smoked Pall Malls, wore white T-Shirts, and used Brylcream to shine their hair-dos. Success would come to these guys through work, hard work, and while they were still young they had some learning in front of them. Those boys liked teasing Charlie, but I would have hated to see what they would have done to somebody who hurt Charlie.

Charlie's mother: Ruby's story:

My name is Ruby, she said. Worked the old trade down on Second for thirty years. Lot of folks don't remember me, being there is a fine singer by the name of Ruby walking these streets today, but I gave more than a few men their start. I still walk with the bowlegs. I was four foot three and had an ugly, block face. Ugly as sin is what folks whispered.

They were right. I wasn't much to look at. I had once thought about joining the Carnival. I had roots in this land. My parents had a small farm up in the Coulee and I was an only child. The last in the line.

I never liked the little schoolhouse. We had a teacher who thought girls were supposed to be dignified. Boys would be out rough housing and we had to stay inside practicing cursive so we could get a job taking dictation from men who tried to sound important.

I never let go of the anger towards men. Most of my life people would look away. You learn to deal with the rejection. Only place I felt comfortable was at the Kewpee Restaurant on Third.

I set the terms of our talking quite early. I told them I came from a long line of uglies when I came to the restaurant. My family had never amounted to much and I was the last one standing except for Charlie. God had a way of ending a bad line I told myself.

I told them to look me in the eye and most would look the other way. I told them I was plain ugly and wanted to know what their excuse was for being so miserable. They mostly shut up and we eventually became friends.

Turns out, they were good men, a little rough around the edges. I worked the Bar in the back for Ed Rivers. He was a good guy and saved me from working the Carnival. Not many jobs for an ugly-as-hell old hooker and Ed never treated me with any disrespect.

To Charlie how I looked never mattered. I was his mom after all and then like now having a baby at 45 sometimes caused problems. He just liked feeling part of a family and the Kewpee had that kind of feel. I kept Orange Pop in the bar just for Charley. To be honest, I wasn't sure of his father. The last years of hooking have gotten blurry. Everybody seemed the same as I closed my mind to the actions of my ways. I'm just grateful that Ed gave me a job after Governor Stassen shut down Second Street.

Charlie wasn't able to do a lot by himself when young. Many folks thought an institution was where he belonged. I heard their voices. He was my only son and had someone tried to take him I would have fought with all I have. Charlie was raised at the Kewpee. We had the backstairs apartment just above the depot office. Ed said he could hear Charlie moving around and everybody chipped in with changing diapers and raising a young child in a restaurant. It took Charlie awhile to get going but he started helping with dishes when he was 7.

I was getting up in my 70's when I noticed Charlie slowing down. I thought the weight gain was just his slow metabolism but I learned that most folks like Charlie never made it past 30. Just the way he was. He died and I was not far behind. He went down, eating the chicken, drinking the orange pop and most of all smiling.

I remember the night of the wake. I was all dressed up in my mourning black not thinking any would show for Charlie. But I was wrong. You find the heart of Winona many times on the grayest of days as the visitation line at Burke's Funeral Home ran around the corner.

Chapter 62

They were all there for my book reading. Proud, like Hanson men tend to be. They all had their canes and they sat near the back of the bookstore across a long bench. They were filled with pride as I started my talking.

These were the dead faces of my Republican roots. They fought for their country and farmed their land. None of them had ever written a book and a man expressing his opinion was at the heart of their America. These folks carried that flag of honor as they went through their day.

A book that questioned their way of thinking was at the heart of their better America. They were never afraid to argue and being they now can't talk I wonder how they resolved their differences. I nodded my head as they found their seat. I could feel the energy of them being there and of seeing them. They asked for milk from the dead waitress. I could tell by their eyes it was time for the show. I sent a note to them thanking them for being. It is not every day dead people show up for a book reading. They, like the rest of the folks, were watching and waiting for the talk to begin. I mumbled some words and got a bit off track. My spotters gestured, and I found my pace.

I read stories of dead people, old priests who might have been, and dreams crushed on the fields of death. Pretty horrific except for some of the other dead folks who showed. They were happy to be remembered and thought maybe there was still hope for us all if we remembered our history. I felt good when the talking stopped. The night wound down and we all said goodbye, living and dead.

Old Grandpa Hoagie stood waiting just outside the door. His long white hair stood in contrast to the dark sky overhead and I could hear him saying to keep on writing, knock down some walls of ignorance. He said if I got too high in the britches him and his grandsons would put me in my place. I heard Harry Chapin singing *Cats Cradle* and as I turned they were gone

Chapter 63

The NRA has us believing that government is going to take our guns. I don't know what they have been drinking, but they have stopped making sense and need to take a deep breath.

The gun manufacturers like the NRA and the way they help their business. The National Rifle Association is a tool that helps those manufacturers sell guns. They even get folks believing that the guy in the White House has the gumption or the resources and money and people to take that gun of your grandfather. You wonder if this way of believing is another sign of America's decline.

They get people too believing that a gun is needed to take care of the shadows. Our ancestors faced the shadows, often without a gun, because they believed that reason and hope built this country. Not everybody carried a gun in those good old days.

The old church used to talk about man and his sins. They used to talk about Pride and Greed and Envy as not being a good thing. The church I was raised in, Catholic, called them deadly sins and we sure do carry a lot of that in our civility. That old church got some things right. Lost America.

The man who wrote that Declaration of Independence, Thomas Jefferson, read the old books. Even the thick ones written by the old philosophers like Socrates and Plato or the great minds like Bacon and Locke. He read so much more than a few folks wondered if he was all right as a child. He preferred reading to hunting or playing rough housing.

Jefferson's father made his living as a surveyor and Monticello, his plantation, was from the estate of his bachelor uncle who the family helped take care of in his waning years. Thomas Jefferson inherited his wealth and land from a founding family. The Randolphs.

Thomas Jefferson believed in words and ideas. The history he read asked real questions about man, his role, god, free choice and matters of the conscience. Jefferson had not seen much freedom in the world of his reading. He dreamt of that day and in America he saw that possibility though he didn't free his slaves. Of the more than six hundred people he enslaved he freed only ten.

Money was not something Jefferson was much good at making. Though he had a plantation and slaves and an exquisite book collection his finances were in disarray. Old Tom was a poor businessman and died mostly broke. The government bought his extensive library collection to start

164

the Library of Congress. Tom continued to read his entire life wanting to learn about as many things as one man possibly could.

Thomas Jefferson thought ideas should be the force in the ways of our living. When he put pen to paper, he was saying goodbye to kings. He wrote those words of freedom. He borrowed the ideas of those before him, men who had lived their lives within the shackles of repression whether in Greece or England or France, Of course he copied the words of John Locke in writing the Declaration of Independence. He made freedom the basis for America.

Jefferson of course had slaves and his second marriage was with a beautiful woman by the name of Sally Hemmings. It was said Sally brought a smile to the over studious, serious Thomas Jefferson. The first Mrs. Jefferson was a Randolph and a might serious, the boys at the Gadsby tavern once told me. Sally Hemmings was a mixed-race slave related to the first Mrs. Jefferson.

Jefferson had read of kings who ruled by force. He saw the limits to that way of life. He dreamt in America that reason would be the ray of light that guarded against rule by force. All those books he read formed the way his thoughts and history, philosophy his teacher.

Jefferson walked to sort out the old words of the old books. All those little insights from the great men of the past made him think and he would reflect as he rode his horse in his later years. He thought about his slaves and the hypocrisy of his own living. He would marvel at the wonderful world he lived in and shake his head at those who see guns as a solution. He would remember the words of John Locke who wrote of a man stealing the goods of another through the use of force. He would smile as he thought of the right he wrote about, and how the use of that right was not always right.

Chapter 64

"It is not like the old days. Back then it was mostly working at night, quiet, cutting a few wires, hitting the guard over the head and walking out the door. Person could make a good living. Plenty of buyers. These young guys tell me that is the most difficult part, the selling of stolen goods. Nobody is buying and the cops got it covered. If I was living, living today I'm not certain what I'd be doing."

Winona was full of characters and the downtown was filled with coffee joints and smoky bars. News traveled fast in this little river town and you knew who to trust and not. I was a writer and no matter how Officers Mugglecroy and Hillski tried squeezing me for my sources, I knew my rights.

That guy over there, Freddie Bogofor, was a classic. He would get caught. Like those snowmobiles. Stole them and tried burying them on his property, went out, got drunk, and told everyone. Got a year, I think and a lifetime of fond memories in the eyes of the boys sitting in the stools. I was in the old G and D Bar across from the Red Train Depot, Downtown Winona.

They were a different bunch and many of them have polished and perfumed themselves up nice now that they are living the golden years. The bartender had hair like Elvis but a 3.2 joint on Sunday morning was one of those places where a man finds stories. Men who had seen life from the other side of the tracks and slept with window

166

panes cracked in the cold of winter. Some of those boys sat upon the stools, reflecting on a life of living.

It was one of the things we talked of as we drove through the memories of my Aunt Glen, last in the line of Marvin and Mary Gale's children. We talked of Mikey Tyson and boxing matches, movies in Utica and courting, watermelon seeds and old friends. Sad days and a lifetime of overcoming. Uncle Dan and his best buddies.

"I wasn't the best of Dads. I couldn't provide very well. Beer grabbed me, clouded my mind," the old guy told me. "You don't grow up to be like me. Yah love your family with all you got."

He was sitting next to me. Old cap on his head. Grit on the cap and under his nails, inside his head, a way of living setting in his bones.

"I lived in Lewiston," he went on. "I come down here on Sundays. Family visit and most bars were closed on Sundays. The Rustic, Stockton then here. Sometimes even sleep it off upstairs. City says no but Dan figures a buck is a buck." He laughed. "You should hear those walls talk."

We went out driving looking for the sounds of her youth as we left the G and D. We talked over breakfast at Bonnie Rae's in Rollingstone. A nice breakfast and the right level of chatter. Felt right at home and didn't see any staring that sometimes happens in a small town. My hash browns, eggs, and bacon were priced fair and tasty. The cup of coffee was hot, fresh and timely.

A lot of the memories have been torn down. The old school, family home and Grandpa's house out by the Fremont Store have seen the wrecking ball. My grandpa was a hired hand who moved his family from farm to farm. Grandma had passed on in '62.

We stopped by the Fremont Store and took a peak in. What a remarkable living history. The old general store still standing, looking good and the big old tree providing shade for as long as the store has been there. We drove by the second Fremont store and I heard the back story wondering why Dad had blocked the telling of the story behind that store.

We drove through Enterprise, saw an old school and the creek where a young boy died while swimming with two friends. They had been warned, it was said in the pauses and reflections of remembering, and I wondered about the cross one bore.

We visited the gravestones and met the preacher man and his six children. I visited my uncle who had missed a turn in Kalamazoo, Michigan, and I could hear the stories of time gone past in the old stone yard.

The sun shone, and the air had a touch of crispness to it. We visited the war monument, looking for engraved stones next to the Grimmelsbach barn. Out here somewhere was where the pool was, and I wondered and remembered what early dying can do to a small town.

We learned so many things as we walked back through time. A day remembered as I signed her book. An enjoyable day and the Three Queens were still smiling as we rolled into Winona.

Chapter 65

She laughed when she told me about some of the things Judge Buck had left behind in the attic where she rested her head. There was a real spiritual movement that spread through this country after the war. She liked Bill Windom and said he would have been a wonderful President.

She said the Civil War did things to men and this country that tested us. We struggled and grief hung over the country like a dark cloud after the fighting stopped.

She pointed to an old bum sitting on the other side of the park. "It was the war." she said. "It broke his mind and spirit. Couldn't hardly carry on a normal conversation but he would work for his keep, rake a yard, or paint a room."

She told me he heard the voices of the dead and said that she felt for the poor boy. He wasn't alone. Those days, it seemed like there were always a couple men around town wearing the jacket they wore in the war. She was staring at me with those sparkly eyes and said she hoped I would come back and visit. I nodded and walked towards the bum.

I sat down next to him. Told him I was a brother from a different war and that I liked the quiet of the night. I liked to see the light of the shadows and the dark. I told him I could feel yesterday and that we shared a kindred spirit.

After a bit, he started talking. "We come back in the spring and leave in the later fall. The streets are full of the dead people living in the beauty of this valley. It's a place where spirits echo off the bluffs and the river water. My name is Cy Barnes. A beautiful sound."

I let the man talk, thinking his journey had taken him a few places mine never had.

"I like seeing life when it wakes. The first greens, that fresh rhubarb. Dutchman's Britches. The tastes, the air, the sounds of life happening. Young people outside. Joyous sounds of children laughing, the only light I heard while living.

"Those were tough times post war. Dark clouds. We figured this was what life after war was about. A gloom. The faces of the dead etched on the living faces of time."

I sat on that bench hearing Cy talk of yesterday. This park is a place like no other where yesterday can be heard from those that walked it, rode horses and automobiles through it. They come at different times and hours of the day and night. They say, no the money didn't help. They take a deep breath, bow their head and say answers are different where they now live.

The big houses surround the elegant old park with the fountain in its center. This was the place where the wealthy rested. It had been a long time since I had seen those boys and their wives. I wondered how Mr. and Mrs. Huff were getting along.

We would talk just about every night. I was a writer and Windom Park was one of my spots. The houses and the mansions stand, but the people who lived in them, built them, now lay dead and the park is different than it once was.

Cy sat on the bench beside me and whispered, "I was doing a little yard work for Mrs. Huff and mentioned to her that she would benefit from a Southern Climate. She replied that Henry would never allow that. She said, 'I detest the dark grey skies of winter and this house is haunted. He built this house on Indian mounds. You can hear the spirits. Right down to the lumber. Henry hears them too, making him mad. They got to him. Made him crazier. He couldn't sleep. Someone was coming, and if you knew my

Henry, everything was about him. Finally I divorced him.'"

I smiled, nodded my head and continued listening to Cy.

"I liked Mrs. Huff. She wasn't much for heirs. Salt of the earth kind of lady. She spoke her mind, standing up to her husband, Henry. He paid a price when she got angry. I was fortunate Henry and the Windom Park Boys always liked me. Winters in those houses were hard with the sounds of deep quiet that come from the good lumber. I remember talking with William Windom one night while we sat under a nice October sky. His roots were in his Quaker upbringing and they didn't believe in War. Pacifists, he called them."

I felt the breeze blowing through the leaves as we listened to the splash of the fountain. "Did you ask William Windom about that Dakota War of 1862?" I asked Cy.

From out of the gloom, William Windom apprered. "The Quakers and the Mennonites were not much for fighting." He glared at me. Windom had this round face and some long, fuzzy sideburns. His cheeks blushed red. "I am Secretary of the Treasury. Who are you?" He glowered.

"A living man who can talk to a dead one. Not many like me around," I told him.

"Trapped in the cry of freedom never hearing those who lost the freedoms they once had. Never entered my thinking. Hindsight, hindsight says I am sorry," Windom said.

I could hear the cries of the Native people as the wind blew and the sun set. Searching for the quiet place where they used to rest. It is late and I want to close my eyes to the park and the emotions it holds.

Cy nodded to the fading form of William Windom.

"He was as smart as any man I ever met. The Lumber and Rail boys thought so too. He was 28 when he moved to town. He and all his neighbors would meet out here to talk about the world. The old first ward park became Windom Park.

"I got along with Henry Huff as well, even though I fully understood how bad their relationship was. Henry, by the end, was crazy just like Mrs. Huff said. That last decade before he left, he would bring a bottle that he stored under the tree where its rumored his children once lay in the depths of death. He said the wine in the wine cellar was the finest and I swear the spirits found their way inside the wine. He started hearing more voices as he drank.

"By the end Henry was thinking people were out to get him. He was right and I told him so. He moved to Chicago. I always stayed a bit longer than most before I headed back south. And I always worked for Mrs. Huff. Their divorce was well chronicled in the local newspaper."

I stood, needing to walk more.

Cy put up a hand to stop me. "It just wasn't me, that thought this way. Huff liked to get into the faces of people. Little Prick is a name that fit. Still, he was good at what he did. Made himself a fortune selling and parceling the land in a boom town.

"Now, Winona in about the year Huff built his house had 1300 steamboats stopping at the Levee. They brought supplies to Winona and people headed west for 40 acres and a better life. It was a crowded place and lots of money changed hands.

Cy let go of my arm, and buried his face in his hands. "My mind was shot from the war. Scrambled. Money had little meaning to me. The war had taken that greed out of

172

me. I was already seeing the spirits. They never did leave me," he said.

I left him to his thoughts and said to myself, "I am not alone."

Part 6 Speakers Among the Dead

Chapter 66

The end is close as I huddle under my blanket on the warm last days of living. My children stop by all business in their demeanor, dollar signs behind their thinking, actions. My nurse keeps me breathing as my talking has already left me.

The kids and grandchildren ask the stories behind the paintings that adorn the walls of my dying place. What do you think, Daddy? 5 million, 10 million, more? I wonder what will become of them as their way of thinking crumbles under life itself. Buy more, cover up the ignorance of the price one pays.

My Grandfather, you see, made cannons and armaments, good, good money though peace could make for some lean years. It was then we started planning, orchestrating the wars, finding some cause, some meaning that would turn young men and women into blood lusting animals. Manufactured war, the seeds of my guilt.

Took near dying before I realized the things that mattered. By then it was too late to save my children and grandchildren from a life with no meaning.

The business, it still stands, no longer a family business but a corporation with locations in the Cayman Islands, Switzerland and the British Virgin Islands. Tax Havens set up to avoid taxes, paid for by the schmucks who pay taxes so I can stir up the fears of the masses from my boat just off the shores of Greece, lining my pockets, weaving the web of deceit. Another seed sprouting guilt as dying knocks and corruption shows its ugly face.

Life starts slipping and becomes clear as you look at those footprints of your past. Tender love, family, and laughter are what matters and can't be bought. Bombs on the heads of innocent children. I still smell the gunpowder on my hands no matter how I wash. Guilt runs deep and I feel the calling of the gates of hell. Actions and not just hollow words and righteousness keep us from those gates the old preacher man said.

Those wise old professors said there were more important things in life than a pile of gold. I finally nod my head with understanding, a long time to capture the meaning of their words. I was headstrong and my Grandfather's money made me know best. I'm wondering if my father had these same thoughts as he passed into the dark side of living.

I once dreamt of greatness but now I see crying mothers, wounded, dead soldiers and children without fathers. I see revenge filling souls, forgetting to turn the cheek as the smell of gunpowder gets inside our thinking, corrupting our very thoughts.

Life ends and the dying begins as the child seeks the revenge, the justice that feels right but is oh so wrong. My guns, my guns have helped bring them to this point and the blindness of revenge clouds judgment.

That is good for business and will keep my children

and grandchildren comfortable living long after I've left. But that certainly doesn't make it right or the smartest choice or ease the burden of my dying.

I like to read the old books. My father and forefathers sent me to Oxford and the best schools that money could buy and urged me to read to try and see life for what it is. I did some not so bright things and learned from those mistakes. The great books show man at his worst and best, dignity with meaning.

The boys and I learned our lessons, put them to use. We bought newspapers and filled them with lies. Television networks and men who for a buck would do anything. Can you hear me, children, now that I can't talk?

We made bad guys out of nice people hoping all this fear and righteousness and revenge would go to the next generation while lining our pockets for generations on end. I see the gates of Hell just down the road, close, getting closer. Starting wars became easy when interests got threatened. We threatened everything just to sell a gun or a rifle or a tank or a missile. Some of the boys got the sickness of loving war; loving dying is not a healthy way. Can you hear me, children?

We never went hungry and money at least in our business is a seed of evil. Once we found out that bombs in the wrong hands or that well-written words could move men, we knew boys would die and governments would buy the best guns they could get. The drums of war make dealing with the governments of the world seem an honorable venture to those who don't stop to think, realizing fear is driving us. We work with all the governments as cash has a language of its own. Some of us sell weapons and others oil but we know as long as fear lies in the minds of many then we can sell it.

Sometimes I think about how I earned all this money and I feel guilt. My dream is to die on a park bench feeding the pigeons. I want to wear a black hat and an old overcoat and grow a long white beard. I want to die with nothing in my pocket and walk with a wooden cane feeling no fear or guilt for what I have done. All the money in the world, but I can't die like I choose because the money hunters, family members fear my giving away the dirty money which fills my mind.

Lord knows I've spent most of my life pursuing more money not much thinking about the lives I trampled. There are benefits to old age, being as you look back you start to see what is really important. Some folks will never admit they are wrong, but I see now how blind I was. Wisdom is indeed a gift of the times.

Those trampled lives began to show up when I slept but I now hear their voices in the shadow of the day, behind me and in the other room. They have begun to make sense and they don't let up. I think about Dante and the gates of Hell. I feel what life is to become.

Take my money I want to scream and save my children from the dirty money that is mine. That money means another house or a larger yacht for them. I would settle for an hour of fishing at the end of a dock with a young child and telling him the nursery rhymes of my grandfather. I was not so wise when young and I waited too long to talk. I now see, but no longer can be heard.

My children looked at me like my mind was gone when I told them I wanted to give it all away. I told them it is evil and it gets in your veins. It clouds your thinking and makes one think of I, a less than noble act. They scoffed and then shortly after, their Doctor gave me a shot.

I told them more life is lost as the circle of grief of the trampled soul breeds brothers who like us do not turn the other cheek. They didn't listen and forgot the wise words of the great books. Some day they will hear my words like I now hear the words of my grandfather. They too will burn in hell as the swords of the ages wield themselves upon the heads of men. I wonder if my grandfather is watching as I take these last breaths knowing each time Hell seems one step closer and I can only hope the burning fires let me remember his dying wisdom.

Chapter 67

I was mighty proud to see the Blacks march through Selma. Our towns had been run by sheriffs and judges and good old boys for as long as we could remember. I felt a little sheepish. I kept quiet as my Daddy told me it was best to be quiet or you'd end up battered and bruised or maybe find yourself dead. Southern justice had an ugliness to its being.

My daddy owned a newspaper and businessmen would stop advertising in it if he wrote about life in the South like it was. He is gone now, but I still feel his sadness at not being able to write about how life and its people could be so mean. Living in the South has always been a bit different. Almost like the heat and humidity did something to a man's brain.

Great writers come from the South. All those repressed ideas they said as I talked to them. I met Faulkner, Williams, and Richard Wright. They talked about life itself.

I met George Wallace before and after the shooting. He was a markedly different man from that bantam rooster know-it-all he used to be. Still a bastard but he no longer thought he was God on God's green earth. I never felt so good in all my life as when Southerners showed him there was a better way. A little humility helped George a lot.

Dr. King had a vision. It was rooted in that better way and while he knew his Bible, his understanding of people was what made him who he was, faults and all. I was honored to have shared this earth with him.

John Lewis, he was afraid of nothing. He knew boys with billy clubs would enjoy nothing more than whacking their club over his head. He was not afraid. Front of the line. He spoke in his walk. Facing the ancient hates his whole life. The hate and the racism never left. John Lewis kept marching his whole life. Never blinking, slow and steady. An American hero.

Only 1% of black folks could vote in Dallas County, Alabama. The sounds and actions of repressed living could be seen in all parts. We were all a bit afraid to talk as Billy Bob was on every corner looking for things that weren't of his believing. That was the law of Dallas County. A way of life.

Women folk could be battered and bruised. The courts had no time nor inclination. The boys would snicker and say she had it coming. That and the KKK was man at his ugly best.

I heard about the Klan and knew they walked amongst us. They could make life miserable for folks helping the Blacks, folks like me. They thought the North was full of people with too much feeling for the others, though most of the Klan boys had never crossed the Mason Dixon line. For them, reading a book was unnecessary because they thought they knew right and wrong. I guess their daddies had beat that into them and that was all they needed to justify their actions.

Everything was separate right down to bathrooms and the corner cafe. Even if you were a white man, you had to keep all to yourself or you'd be looking for work or your child would get beaten by the bullies. Those were hard times in the South.

Years later, I would get together with some old friends and we wondered if some of those old deputies were a result of their parents being close enough cousins. They were mean bastards without brains in their heads. They put a lot of men in jail and separated families just because their skin was black. That judge would often twiddle his fingers, think about his next bourbon, come out of his slumber and yell out, "30 days, guilty as charged."

I look back now and wish that I had shown more strength and dignity. Dr. King had shown how a quiet peace could overcome the worst of man if even for a moment. As time passed a lot of the hurt has scarred over but the festering of man at his worst seems to be on our doorstep once again. The voices of the 60's, Dr. King, John and Bobby, Malcolm were all taken early by the gun.

I remember walking back from church Sunday mornings listening to my Black brother singing, thinking to myself that they had a wonderful spirit to their words. Daddy liked walking that couple blocks out of the way too, though I never realized he liked the sound of that choir.

I'm getting near the end and so when Dad and I sit down to talk I'm guessing we'll relive those early years. I look forward to that.

Chapter 68

They called me Mama Closser. I left when it was my time. I had the best kids and finest husband and those were the last pictures that filtered through my mind. I took a last breath and saw Dad worrying and the kids talking with heavy hearts at a life leaving.

I thought my life over when a spirit took me. A powerful, swirling journey. Dark and light swirling through time. Shades of life shown anew. I forgot my hands and bones and the ache they carried. The jitters stopped and my hands felt light. My insides felt alive. Home, home.

Eternity. A grand place. You hear laughter, you see the weight of time. I hear the gentle laughter and warmth of old stories. I feel the love of the people I've left. I see but I can't touch as yesterday is beyond my reach.

I hear a loon from far away and I feel the spraying of water and the joys of family. My heart remembers what once was. All the children and grandchildren tug on my heart. I start thinking of Al and how it was nice seeing him join me in life beyond the seeing.

I learned through the years that time moves different for each and trying to sleep when the kids were still out can make for the longest nights. I prayed and counted but would not rest until everyone was home and safe.

The house was big and as each one moved out into being an adult, I felt the quiet of your leaving. I would walk through the house dusting and cleaning. Remembering the joys and laughter that make a home. A good life.

I remember my old people telling me that children must find their way. Finding themselves wasn't always easy. You give them love and plant seeds of thinking. They may stub a toe or pound a finger. Give your children and grand-children all the love you got.

I miss card games and laughter. Children and grand-children. It is nice here and the temperature is right. Not too hot or cold, and I feel light. Like water skiing or crack the whip.

Dad is now with me and we listen to the sounds of your lives. We come and go and then find ourselves some-where else. We feel good and happy. The flowers are like fresh air and we walk. The headaches of living were never bad and now things are good.

We'll be moving on. Dad is getting restless, and he is still adjusting. I think that is the spirit talking, telling us to move on. Till the next time. I can do it all.

Chapter 69

This is Stanley. I'm down here walking the streets of Downtown Winona. Looking for old haunts and places which kindle the memories of yesterday. I went to see the fish tanks in the back of Kresge's and found a parking lot. I looked for Delilah behind the counter and saw more of the same.

I kept walking thinking I might head to the Hurry Back and shine a few shoes. Say Hi to Jeannie and Art and old friends who called me Chinky. The building still stood but nobody's home except for us dead guys reliving the chuckles. Jeannie, aw Jeannie.

I headed over to the Post Office, waving at Shot-gun, Frank and Nola as I walked. I saw old barbers who practiced the craft. Nola was smiling, her shop filled with the colors of living and then a building now looking for an identity where the Post Office once stood when I started smelling the grizzled meat.

Winona, Winona I tell you, was a town of great smells. The smell of the Federal Bakery and places where a guy could get a steak that didn't cost an arm and a leg and everybody knew you when you walked into a place. That wind, that wind, numbing as it whirls its way through the empty lots where buildings once stood get cold in the winter.

This whole area changed. The Masons moved out on Fifth Street and the girls Y went up in a puff of smoke. The Landon Mansion no more and the new post office smells like a backroom deal. I walk by the auditorium I think of Gordie Addington and John Kinney, Chuck Williams and that feeling I got when I walked into that auditorium for the first time.

The lines are lighting up, Stanley. Callers all wanting to tell their stories about the auditorium. Some guy named Bump says that he remembers his first visit to the auditorium and the immense size of the building. Said he was in the 5th and 6th grade when he walked into the auditorium for the first time. It is magical he said, makes a person feel part of something bigger, better. A cause worth living for.

This is Stanley Deerman, a guy just happy to have a job with a quarter in his pocket in search of the best hamburger.

That was when Newt pulled into the parking lot of the Shirley M Wright Library in Trempeleau, Wisconsin saying that Ocooch Mountain Music Radio Hour is not like anything else.

Chapter 70

This is Stoner reporting for Ocooch Mountain Music. I'm sitting on the steps of the Winona Public Library. I hear the voices coming through the marble. Books and authors clamoring to be heard.

I'm enjoying my morning smoke. I wish you were all with me just taking in the sounds of a city coming too. Being nuts has benefits, hearing and feeling things others don't. Us townies have always had different ways of seeing." "Four in the morning. In the old days I'd be just winding down from a night spent out enjoying the times of our living. My body don't work like that anymore. I think I'm gonna buy me a cane whether I need it or not and shake it at the demons and gods I carry in my thinking. Growing old, spitting and kicking all the way through.

It is the waking time of day. People waking up, heading to the bathroom and I hear mamas hollering, put the toilet seat down when you're done. Kids covering their heads wanting that eternal ten minutes more. The noises of living surrounding me.

The sun is just waking up. Mr. Bauer has his reading light on in the house where a gas station now stands. You can hear the sounds of a city waking. Cars and trucks starting up. Dawn where light shines different. All those years, all those years ago when I thought I knew all.

"Stoner, Stoner. This is Braveheart. You can't be getting high in the morning, going on the air and reminiscing about all that's wrong. Our listeners want to start their day on a good note."

Not so sure you know what people like hearing. Sometimes you young folks miss things. Like you are living in a different place than me."

"You'll scare away our listeners. People need to be told how happy things are. Modern journalism 101 and ratings are bad enough."

My heart has been broken so many times by life itself that I only know one way to talk. Life and death, what else is there? You see, when you forget about us broken people, cracked people you forget what living is. Life gives us fortune and not so much. We lived in the apartments in the brick buildings downtown and worked in the small shops. These were home and the restaurants and stores were where we spent our money and made our friends. We watched the kids after school, walking downtown, spending their nickel, dimes and quarters and looking in the store windows at things they couldn't afford. We watched the kids and could see trouble and smarts from a long way away," Stoner said.

The brick buildings were monuments, stones of our learning. Downtown was a school of its own as kids learned the streets and a way of life. When that school moved out by the lake the heart and soul of a town was torn from its roots and downtown cried as a once great history got buried in the yellow archives run over by progress. The roots of a great town shaped by rivers, bluffs and buildings built by hard working men whose grandparents came from all corners of the world.

"Stoner, that's deep. Can we break for the morning report from Stanley? He is sniffing out the smells of Bar-B-Que down by the Levee. I gotta pay the bills."

"Peace out, Braveheart. The sound of children will soon be echoing through the alleys and buildings of downtown. What more could one want a clinic, a school and a bakery all within walking distance? I can't wait to hear

Stanley around the smells of good bar-b-que during this weekend of Big Muddy. Until tomorrow, this is Stoner signing off from the steps of the public library.

Chapter 71

"This is Stoner, Stoner Thompson, back again, reporting for the Midwest Music Store Radio Show here in Winona, Minnesota. There is sadness all around like nothing I've ever seen or felt before. A spectacle, an event, a tragedy, and a future not looking good. And through that prism of time that death brings a chance to see for oneself."

We were space cruising along that Wisconsin side of the river. We didn't have much for plans, wandering through the coulees looking for some dead folk. It doesn't take too long and before you know it, you'll come to an understanding what those Coulee people mean about there being no better place to call home. Newt was driving. Science Girl and Cookie were listening to Stoner's every word

Stoner had grown quite famous. It was an unusual thing to be able to roll through time and now that Stoner had made it to the other side he was liked and beloved by all. A true tribute to a Vietnam Vet who came home carrying the baggage.

I could hear him inhaling over the air and I thought Braveheart down at the station was about to start yelling at him for inhaling while broadcasting. There was a seriousness to his voice and I prayed he would find the fortitude to see this through. That FCC threatening to turn off the radio lights, as I heard Stoner take another hit, can be stressful to an owner and his thinking.

186

"I've been hearing about this Jesus fellow since the beginning of my learning. Prayers and church sitting and little bitty desks. Everywhere I turned I saw the faces of God in thought and building, hard to find places where the God thinking hadn't pervaded living." Stoner mourned.

"He's lost it," Cookie yelled and Newt started chuckling.

"Stoner, this Patty Parsnip out here at the Anacabee Cafe in downtown Goodview and that weed you smoke has you talking in circles. I remember your generation back in the day. Lazy, didn't know what work meant. That marijuana stinks, I tell you. Smell it from a mile away. Skunk, smells like skunk and burning leaves."

"I tell you if Elmer were half together he'd be tearing you a you know what. His thinking has just about left him. Just a bad case of forgetting. Only way I can get him out of his easy chair is to mention food. He has been lumbering his way to that kitchen table half brain dead for years. Food, shovel. I've tired of my own cooking and so we go out."

"What did you and Mr Elmer do last evening?" Stoner asked.

"We went to the Sky-Vue out here in Goodview. Watched *Cape Fear*. I love Gregory Peck but that Mitchum gives me the creeps."

"Did Mr. Elmer hold you tight during the show?"

"I wish, but the next thing is he started groping me. All over. You know, Braveheart, how men can be. Just a little touch and they start thinking. A women's touch can get a man to do about anything. I was scared after all. Mitchum was pure evil. Made my skin crawl so I moved closer to Elmer. I thought I could find safety in the arms of

Elmer, instead I felt a grope.

"Some mornings he doesn't know my name. He needs three cups of coffee just to get going and then it's not very fast. Losing your remembering is a hard thing. What's a person to do? We have been married 52 years this October. A good life, a good life but when the thinking, the memories start going, time changes. I can see he don't like being confused. He gets frustrated and starts yelling. He is still strong as an ox. He doesn't know his own strength and I worry. Getting old is hard.

"The thing is I was talking to the owners and they seem genuinely happy here at the Anacabee Cafe. Not some plastic smile trying to sell something on TV. A Caledonia girl and a beautiful daughter. Anacabee man, her husband was telling me how his relatives come from Belgium and Luxembourg and then Ireland or somewhere like that. Oh gosh, remembering names is getting harder by the day."

"What are you and Elmer having for lunch Patty?"

"Elmer, Elmer he was all set to do a Philly Cheese Steak. I think he may have changed his mind though. I'll just have to decide for him. He just can't get anything right sometimes. He is talking, carrying on a conversation with the stools on either side of him.

"Elmer, Elmer what are you doing. Too-da-loo Elmer. Ohhh, Oh Braveheart, I don't know what is worse losing it or watching another lose it? I got both. Elmer, who are you talking to?"

"Patty, its Leo from the Grocery Store and Joan Pryzbylski. What a great restaurant. Any person living Goodview way in the 60's and 70's knew these two people."

"Elmer, Elmer, Elmer there is nobody there for you to talk with. Can't you see? The stools are empty. Are you seeing things that aren't there? There is nobody in that stool."

"Look, look Patty, that's Frank Matejka reading the sports page at the small table. Look. Frank Matejka over there reading."

"Now Braveheart, I like their mashed potatos, beef gravy. It's so much work to make them from scratch for the two of us that I usually order him some. I don't have to worry about him choking. He just inhales that food. And he puts ketchup on them, along with lots of gravy and pepper. Their chicken is crispy, juicy and tender to the bone. The best part is no dishes, pans and utensils to wash. My hands get so dry from the dishwashing that it's nice when I can keep my hands out of the hot, soapy water. Elmer once had the most seductive hands. Slow moving and pretty soon I'd have goosebumps all over. A hard working man with soft hands was my Elmer. I just wish he'd wash some dishes and pick up his socks."

"How old are you Patty?"

"I'm 72 and Elmer is 74. Met at the Cotter High School on seventh. Oh, those were good times. Father Nelson, oh I loved that man. We got it together, the forgetting disease. Oh Elmer, Elmer. There is nobody there. Hold my hand Elmer, hold it and don't let go. Let's hope we don't start forgetting the same things at the same time. This is Patty Parsnip from the Anacabe's Little Kitchen in downtown Goodview."

"Give my best to Elmer and take care of yourself Patty. I sure do hope that one of Winona's most charming couples makes it home safe."

Part 7 Walking Winona

Chapter 72

I like walking through the neighborhoods. Spring-time, snow dripping, melting down and the air smells fresh. I remember friends from the days of my being young. Simpler places when time moved a bit slower. It is hard to find quiet in a town that works hard.

I visit the churches. As many as were in that neighborhood you can tell our ancestors were searching for something more and better. You felt it from East to West. The little houses and big houses, both spreading the gospel of a better tomorrow.

She lived her whole life in the same house except for two years spent in Minneapolis she said. Never married. Moved back home, began working as a librarian at the school out her back door, Phelps. That was my Grade School.

Winona Senior High School was nearly out my front door. I got my first degree at the college of my Grade School, Winona State. Not many folks can say that she said.

She is one of the folks who come back in the spring. She had on a floppy hat with a multi-colored scarf that covered her wrinkled neck. Her eyes twinkled as if life had dealt her a flush. She walked happily with her head a bit tilted as if listening.

"Eccentric," she told me. Loved the Theater. New York, New York. Times Square and all the great plays. She said spring always made her realize the hardness of winter. Such a release to feel winter leaving. The neighbors would be out and about talking with the students who had a bounce in their steps.

At night, in the Summer we would sit out on our porches cooling off with a drink and letting our worries flitter away. These couple of blocks would get beautiful, quiet. Haunting like. We were surrounded by churches and schools, businesses and history. It was a bit like listening to Wall Street on a Sunday morning. Just a different kind of quiet.

As a child that campus and those backyards were my playgrounds. We knew the maintenance people and the professors were parents of our classmates. We would play hide and seek and there are tunnels running underneath that Phelps school.

Some of us went to Madison, some Central, some Phelps, some Cathedral, some Lincoln. The town's forefathers saw the wisdom in the big view. World class are the people of Winona she says as she goes.

I remember my own time growing up. Dating a girl, going to Prom all had meaning to my life. Helped form who I became. Part of my history, sense of place. I like to feel that when I walk through the neighborhoods. I run into people, special people, like Elsa above. It is hard to find the spirits in the noise and the new buildings.

This was a couple blocks that had a feel to them. You could feel the people who lived here once upon a time. I never knew, really knew the folks who lived here in this neighborhood growing up. Except for Hollywood. I thought he was headed to the big screen. And a pretty girl who I went to prom with.

A writer like me needs shadows to write in. Places where time stops. Old neighborhoods not run over by todays quick fix. Old barns still stand in this town. I hope the old buildings are still standing 100 years from now when our great grandchildren walk the streets looking for the remains of who we were.

Chapter 73

You can feel the spirits as you walk the school halls and work with the kids. Their hopes and dreams have been shaped by living. Hard to get away from the death they've seen but they got a spirit that is making their forefathers proud.

They have seen life in all its ugliness. The highways have long swallowed the citizens of this town before their time. Time ends far too soon for far too many.

They have a resiliency at their core. Get on with living or let it run you over. They suppress those feelings of anger, grief, denial as the lifting music of Amazing Grace gets played at the funerals of fathers, mothers and cousins. Brothers and sisters.

These school years give them time to learn, to share, to live. You see as you walk the school halls how in a small town we are all connected. Poor kids, rich kids. Families with Dads and others not. Getting on, carrying on. Learning, learning that life doesn't have to end in such a heart-breaking manner.

From the waters of Enterprise to the gun, death has happened too soon. It happens enough and death becomes part of the myth of living in Lewiston. Hard living at the foot of fate. It becomes a self-fulfilling prophecy as it happens again.

Letting go of the myths that tie us to the place of pain can break the cycle of death. The winds of death are like a black cloud hovering over this small town. Letting go of the pain which reminds, ties us to the place is freeing. Not that death ever gets beat.

Schools give kids a chance to succeed. Break away from the cycle of death. It shows on the football field and in the choir and art classes. Engaged youth can change for the better.

Doing things right seems to be a spirit running through the halls whether at the Elementary, Altura or the High School. Parents and Grandparents can hold their heads high as kids learn and teachers teach.

In small towns, school and community run hand in hand. Together they can overcome the evil spirits which fill our insides. I see the gear heads carrying around that state championship trophy and I see good things happening. A commitment to doing right in a world gone amok. Break the cycle and support your school.

Chapter 74

I needed to walk. Talking with the dead was wearing on me. Felt the tension. I headed toward Madison Grade School, knowing the sound of children would take me back to simpler times. I crossed over Broadway, waved at Kay Dunlay and could feel myself relaxing. Preston, the new owner, smiled.

I heard the sounds of children, the pitter, patter of feet and I felt young for a bit. I saw mothers waving good-bye from the front of their porch and I saw old people taking their morning walk, listening to the sounds of yesterday. They are happy and pleasant as I walked along.

"You close up that Madison school, there won't be a grade school left near the center of town. All gone. Cotter and Cathedral, Phelps, and Lincoln, Central and the Jr. and Sr. High. All gone."

"Well at least Cotter went to a place where the lumber and walls speak. That new Middle school, all bells and whistles, but the walls don't talk."

"Let me tell you something, Jerry. Small towns know what happens when you take a high school out of it. They die. I don't think it's wise to abandon the core of our town."

"To be honest, far too many people and places have left the downtown. Not only the schools but downtown itself. Quite a legacy."

"Springtime. I can start feeling it. Beethoven and Shakespeare and sounds of music and whimsy will be heard in the streets of Winona soon. Town gets quiet when the colleges leave."

"I like Shakespeare. Such good people. Spending their money all throughout the town. Such a refreshing mix of characters."

"So many things to do."

I heard all these sounds of a neighborhood as I walked through yesterday.

"Hey, Billy!" a young man yelled. "The Dodgers left

194

Brooklyn. Get a new hat."

"Come and get it, Mike." Billy challenged. "I heard Grandma Carlson chewed you out for running across her front yard," he continued as Mike bounded across the street. "Did she call your Mom?

"No, I think she just likes yelling. Gives her meaning. You hear Ray got caught smoking? He's not sure who squealed but he'll be looking. He has that temper and he'll be looking to take it out on someone."

Billy nodded his head. "I felt the wrath of Ray before. He came after me and I threw a wild punch. Right spot, wrong time for Ray. Right in the nose and blood splattered. He left me alone after that and of course if you got on Darcy's kickball team you were safe. Darcy ruled the playground."

"Darcy? Who is that?" I asked.

"Well," Mike said. "She comes from a family of brothers. Don't mess with Darcy. You mess with her and then you would have to deal with the Brothers. Not that Darcy couldn't take care of herself. One of those life learning experiences as you made your way to school. You learned things about life when you walked to school. You rubbed elbows with rich kids, poor kids, bullying kids, smart kids, dumb kids, and the old folks walking and watching. That mixing, meeting each, that's a real part of who we are."

I was feeling better. Just walking through the neighborhood made my heart wake in the sounds of yesterday. I heard the school bell ring and saw kids running. I was thirsty and wondered if Steiny's was open. They make a nice Bloody Mary down Solvay Way.

Chapter 75

"I wanted to find my own space from early on. Just wanted a place of my own. It is how we rolled back in the day. Now don't get me wrong I wouldn't trade my upbringing for nothing."

I was talking to Bonnie, sharing a cup of coffee. Late afternoon and the townies were just waking up, getting ready to spend another night partying until the wee hours. Seems like yesterday.

Bonnie stirred her coffee. "Life has gone on so fast sometimes I have to let it out. I've been thinking inside my head since I was that child looking in the window glass. I saw big buildings and took the elevator up and back down again in that Choate building. A big city in a small town, when all the buildings towered above.

"We all didn't come from the lap of luxury. You can see some nice homes of people who made it big but when you want to see some of the character of this town you go drive down by the tracks and the river. You see the small houses we came from and listen to their stories and you begin to understand what life is about.

"Everybody used to talk with each other when they came downtown, and it wasn't just about business or the weather. Our family is what we got, but life hasn't always been topped with a cherry. People walking downtown on the burial grounds of those who first lived in this valley knew the pain living can bring. You could hear the past on every corner when you listened to what the old timers said.

"I could look at the picture window and see boys through the reflections as they drove from Franklin to Johnson and back again. I saw a nice car or a movie poster and thought how nice that would be. That would be a better life. It was a big deal for some to have a bedroom of their own."

Bonnie always got me thinking. I suppose we are all a bit crazy in some ways. You live in this town long enough and you hear about everything. Some of the folks will tell you that spirits walk this town. People found their way to the churches and if you sit in the pews and listen you can hear the echoed thoughts still bouncing off the marble and the sleek woods.

The fires take away a bit of our history each time they happen. We probably don't know who built the building or the many types of business that building has housed but at one time that building housed a man and his family's dreams. More likely than not there are still kinfolk in town and family being what it is, folks never quite leave no matter what.

It is that kind of town that makes you want to stay or come back home. All the families got stories and skeletons, no matter how big the house they come from. Some things never get to the paper instead people pray that this shall pass. That river water runs through us strong.

Growing up in Winona meant you thought for yourself. It was how we rolled and finding our own path was how we moved. The cops knew, the parents knew, and most of the neighbors knew.

Our schools were good and while some chose to listen, others heard the music of the jukebox while finding that path. We had prohibition busts and tunnels and women of the night who were part of who we were even if they came before us. We knew our history, warts and all. Part of who we are.

We forget some of our roots and time doesn't help us with that remembering. The good feelings and the good things that filled our hearts and mind slowly harden as the descent into age closes our minds. You lose that old, relaxed smile, as life twists and turns like the river.

We carry the memory of a life lived as we go about town. All the old stores are mostly gone and the places where we bought clothes and dreams have moved out to large parking lots and owners who gather our money and send it to money counters in a faraway state never causing those profits to trickle down.

For some, they could dream of a better life as they looked into the display windows but in Winona, they, with hard work could buy that dress or pair of shoes. In Winona there was opportunity and a better tomorrow.

There are gift shops and artist studios and consignment stores. You can fix your computer and like the old days you can meet the owner and find out his window on the world. You won't find that service and story at the big box stores.

You might find a vase the Morgan family had on their shelves once upon a time or you might find a coffee cup like Pa or Grandma used to drink from. You might find an old fishing pole like the one you learned with, that you can hang in the garage and remember Grandpa and how a day out fishing on the river was as good as it got. For a man who has everything there is art to be bought and put on the wall or the shelf.

You might find a clerk who is also the owner. You might find a fresh muffin and not one shipped from a distant place. There are few things finer than the smell of baking bread and that old Sunbeam Bakery filled the streets and alleys of Winona with the smells of bread baking. It was a sad day, when fire struck the bakery and the town has never smelled the same.

The old town grew older and some of that money died and moved away. Life sped up and money rather than family became the driving force of what we do. We joined our separate clubs and did our church and lost track of our neighbors.

The old town was built on people talking from all the walks of life. We saw differently but we were a town filled with reasonable people who moved forward and made things work. History told us we made mistakes. We weighed the decisions we made.

We used to walk to work, saying hello to those who crossed our path and making sure the older folk were getting by. Rich and poor shared the streets and even Mrs. Watkins liked to listen to the birds and think about her dead grandson as she tried to forget the pain that comes with money.

Time made us busy as we scrambled to make a living and trips downtown became less frequent. We followed and heard the stories of bad parking and nothing to buy until only college students called it home. The sun set and the welcome mat got rolled up as our town saw better days. The walkers and shoppers who filled the streets when Winona got along were hard to find between Johnson and Franklin.

Those old memories were part of our life as we tell the stories to our children and grandchildren. We look back and realize there were a lot of smiles on our faces when we hung downtown. We'd do about anything to be young again or even show our grandkids how great a town this was. That downtown and our grandchildren now see the empty storefronts wondering what Grandma and Grandpa are talking about.

We shared coffee, stories and sweets in the old buildings that fill the town. TV was none and radio, newspaper and party lines were how we got news. It seemed like time moved slower back then, and we all felt a bit safer and healthier.

Many spotted the man they married as he drove up and down third through the reflections of the Choate window. For some you could hear Chubby Checker, Elvis or Hank Williams playing on the car radio as you began to think about your life.

You ran into all sorts of people downtown. You ran into folks a bit off and others a bit uptight. You laughed and thought about the next time. Downtown was full of characters all living the broken dream.

You laughed your fool head off when you heard some girls rolled through the Hurry Back when it was a club for men. The boys never knew what hit them and women all across this country started knocking down the wall of ignorance. Stay-at-home no more as there was a life to be lived.

Our town took pride in the successes of our children. Everybody knew everybody and there were party lines on the telephones which to the news of their goings, their celebrations, and their failures. We no longer know that neighbor and everybody is the same as we grow set in our ways.

We can tell you who owns Target or Walmart or the other corporate faces along the Highway but we have no idea the people who own the small shops which have begun to reclaim our downtown. They hold the memories of our past and sell the goods which can bring us back to the times when we were happiest.

The sands of time change for no one and the stores and bars that we laughed in have been replaced. Grandpas walked into an old bar and shared a cold one with a younger person just to see what he or she was thinking. That was how we rolled.

They are mostly memories now as we have lost a few friends. We are left with the memories of what once was as we recollect our past. We see a couch or a dish that reminds us of what was important in our lives and we start to think back to simpler, happier times. Mom had a serving dish just like that and they don't make them anymore.

Parts of downtown are showing the signs of life. You get down to the east side of downtown and you see people walking in and out of stores hawking memories of a time gone by. You don't find Walmart on third because their products get bought a few years later at a garage sale if they last that long.

You might find an old friend or a new one searching for the past. You can sit with an old friend sharing a beer like days gone by and it is as if you are 16 again, laughing free and happy. Good friends and old brick buildings make us remember what life was.

You drive through the town in the day hours you notice the town is bustling as people are out and about. Out-of-towners see Shakespeare and Beethoven, Bluegrass, movie and music festivals. This must be quite a town, they say, when people gathered. There is only one Winona.

That downtown is a legacy for a group of people who sat and watched its decay. It is easy to blame government or others, but we have been taught from the time we were young that responsibility is ours. Downtown was part of who we were, and it is a shame what we have forgotten.

Chapter 76

People would cross diagonally through this park getting to and from work, school. They would sit and talk or walk and talk. And the kids, well, it didn't matter how much money they had. They were kids and they ran and played. Neighbors watched. Always a safe town where friends were met in school and remained friends for life.

"Look at these houses surrounding Windom Park. Huge for the times. This was nothing in the 1850's. This was a town built on Indian Mounds. Oh, the rich boys knew it and on Sunday morning they would be reminded of their errant ways. Some Sunday mornings that Organ would roar that hell awaited those filled with the deadly sins. They felt the spirits but weren't about to let go of the power and money."

"When you can't see it, it's hard to act upon. You talk of seeing dead folk and they'll lock you up."

"C.F. Buck, believed, he did. Judge Buck. Lived in the Green house today. Had a place along Lake Boulevard too. One of the early Winona settlers. He had a wit about him, but he indeed saw the dead. Had a son who was a lawyer too," the old bum said.

"Judge Buck?"

"I got his diary. Mrs. Tweedy across the street asked me to clean the attic and this was tucked up underneath a loose floorboard. Showed it to her and she said it was mine for keeping. Said Judge Buck liked to walk in Woodlawn.

Spend all day out there sometimes."

"Judge Buck, talked with the dead?"

"Yes," he said, pulling out an old, now yellow paged book. "October 7, 1902. Visited the grave of William Sanborn. My good friend Bill said hello as we walked. We walked and talked, sharing ideas when living. I was deciding whether to bring charges against the son-in-law in the Kuhlman corner shooting. Back in the day, a son and his father had a cigar factory where the coke plant now sits. They never got along, always fighting and one day they brought out the pistols. Leg shots only.

"After all, Huff and his men took to shooting at Bill when we were young. Bill brought a calm to my thinking and it is reassuring that the veil of death didn't stop him from weighing in. Family didn't want charges brought forward, but it seemed to me a person needed to be held accountable for his actions."

When I shared this excerpt with Mrs. Tweedy a few years later she laughed. Cackled more like it and proclaimed Judge Buck always thought different. It is what made him unique. He was one of a kind. He would want his insights known and talked about. That was old Winona. He loved the characters that settled in this valley. Nothing left to chance with Judge Buck. He left it, thinking a poor man still had a chance.

Back when time was slower the park echoed wealth and greed and power. Money oozed from the houses and the people who lived in them. Rich, powerful folks lived around that square and the devil found easy pickings, as he planted the seven deadly sins.

"The rich people, they could send their kids to any school in the country and when they reach the right age they did get sent to the best schools. But for grade school, they kept them here. Let them hear the stories of this town and the spirit that runs wild. Stayed close to their family but the stories of this town stamped Winona on their hearts." He took a swig of something from his paper bag and offered me some. "Look at these houses. Railroad President, Banker, Judge, Treasurer of the United States of America. Lumber Baron. Peerless Chain. Land man, lumber. And you know what?" His eyes weren't quite right in his head. They were glassy and ran a bit deep. Blood shot and tired.

"No, no. What?" I asked.

"They sent their kids to the local schools. They believed in common man schooling. They wanted their children to learn from our humble roots. In a Winona classroom, you could find a millionaire's son eyeballing a girl from the other side of the tracks, working side by side with a child who didn't have a pot to pee in."

Chapter 77

"Hanson, you are late." The voice came from nearby as I walked across St. Mary's Campus.

All these years and the quiet, gentle growl of the old man still raises the hair on the back of my neck. Max Molock. The face of St. Mary's Baseball.

"Your hair is getting near your shoulders and you've grown heavy. You were never fast, but now you move like a sloth. You wouldn't be playing for me. How many times do I have to repeat myself? Preparation."

"Aw, Max. My goal was already starting to see a different finish line than yours when I played. Moving in a straight line? Me? I moved like I pitched. My fastball couldn't break a pane of glass. I threw curveball, curveball slider, and slower. I mean you were right. An exceptional coach, teacher, man you were, but my mojo ran in a different direction."

Max shook his head. "I saw your life crumble. Shattered dreams. I wasn't sure where you were headed. I am a bit surprised to see you. Just in a completely different direction to get where we are. How old were you when your mind went?"

"18, couple months into Freshman year. It's a strange emotion that works its way inside. Shadows everywhere you turn. Your insides start feeling completely opposite of what they once were. You repress those emotions and before you know it your thinking is upside down."

"You did throw a nice curveball and your thinking was like a flaky lefty. Bill Lee. You were all twisted around. I always figured it was the Marijuana, the drugs."

"I think it was inevitable. Probably got that schizophrenic DNA in me. And Max, I won't be sliding on that gym floor anymore. It's hard getting up what with these old bones I'm carrying in me. Never reached base anyway. You carry old ways to the other side?" I asked.

"I'm dead, but life carries on differently than I thought. You are late; we've been waiting. It took you forever to realize you had the gift. You got a couple teachers who've been waiting. Practice at 3, so get a move on."

I smiled as I thought about those early days of losing my mind. The middle of the campus is looking a bit different than it once did. There is a plaza covering a field of grass and beautiful plantings and flowers line its walks. Illustrious graduates hang on flags reminding people today that they once walked the beautiful grounds.

"You pick the right flowers, the petals, the grasses and you can dry them and use them as tea,"Brother Charles said. "Even help your nasal passages. Keep you regular and some of them can lower your temperature providing you prepare them right.

"To know flowers, plants, is an understanding of life itself. You get to see life and death all in one year. The Earth would have lasted forever had us humans not shown up. Consumption, greed, lust, envy. You living folks are full of the deadly sins creating hell on Earth.

"Pollinators, we need more habitat for pollinators. Too many chemicals being put into our ground, destroying the function of natural plant cycles. Poisoning and starving the birds and the bats. Forgotten our place. Consuming the green earth."

"Brother Charles. Brother Charles Severin. Been ages since I saw you. Never had you, but I watched. Thank you."

"How did you find your way here amongst the dead?"

"I'm not sure science can understand. Not that I was much of a scientist. I think it was more between my ears. Chemicals though. It has to do with the processing of in-formation. Data."

"What did you eat, exercise? Your metabolism is dif-ferent. Are you saying altering the chemistry in our minds can change who we are?"

"Why, yes sir. You are right. Most everything starts in our head. Good, bad."

He asked how I found the oneness that allowed me to pass.

"Pass?"

"Pass into the world of us dead folks!" he cried. "No time! Waiting a long time for the answer to that question. Life. Plants live, die. Every spring. Perennials take a rest, recharge. You folks don't understand that people need to relax. I found that peace in the woods, in the churches, and in my students."

"Everything working. All working. Mind, body, Brother Charles. All the ducks in a row. Just a different form to my living that others find strange."

"I miss the students. It's powerful seeing a young person and his or her mind begin to see. There are so many things blocking curiosity. Easy answers, religions, politics, social standing, on and on. Can't do this, can't do that. So much more than memorizing is what real schooling is. Now move on. Dr. Conroy is waiting. Hurry. Let the boys, excuse me students, know I'm still learning. It is a nice place. All those students will see me soon enough. Learning to be a bit more patient on this side," he said while bending over studying the grass. "Oh, don't keep her waiting."

I am 62 years of age and yet even today my heart beats faster and my mind starts wondering what I have forgotten when I hear her name. She demanded the most. Frankly, she scared me. None of the easy answers which so easily flow from a young man worked with her.

The live voices of Larry Luttmers, Gabriel Fagan, Bill Crozier and Pat Costello still echo in the polished, marble halls of the school on the edge of town. Living voices, their words ever more meaningful as time passed. Insane, insane as I remember the crazy thoughts that ran through me back when I was young.

I saw Brother Peter ambling by, dressed in his suit,

lifting his hand and saying, "Welcome back. Tell us your story."

"I'm here to see Dr. Conroy," I muttered as I climbed the stairs. She had encouraged me to write, to express myself, and she let me know anything less was not good enough. It took me a long time to accept the wisdom of her words.

Her shoes were that of a nun. She had a bit of the old strictness to her. Never married. Entirely devoted to teaching. She was at the right school. She received her degree in Greek and Latin at St. Theresa's right down the hill. She received her Master and Doctorate degrees at Columbia University. Relentless she was. Getting me to think in the days of losing my mind was never easy.

She invited me in and when I told her my name was Hanson she immediately corrected me. "I remember my students. I want to know how you did it."

"What?"

"Break on through."

"Huh?"

"You have the ability to talk with the dead people. You still don't get it? Do you know how remarkable the gift you have is? How, how?"

I put on my serious look. Even today talking coherently is at best a 20/80 proposition. She'd be on my case, and I'd be hearing it. Suck it up, Hanson and I heard the sweet voice of old friend Cush who I thank for her confidence.

"My synapses never slowed. All these years, a million miles an hour. Never stopping, never resting, connecting ideas, thoughts, language, motivations. All the things that are part of living. The classics, the languages, the inner workings of man. I know. I know there are better paths than that which I followed but you have to play the hand you are dealt. More pleasurable, less hurting ways but those other ways didn't get me to you now did they?"

"No, no they didn't," she said.

"Those old languages had their roots in guttural sounds. Right back to the caves. Language development. Evolving, getting us greater and greater insight as we clarify what we are seeing. They are the basics of our English language, all language in fact, comes from the people, our ancestors, whether they are Japanese, Sudanese, Persian, or Hispanic. Languages have so much meaning and nuance, rhyme. You find words say nothing in isolation. Words by themselves are nothing. You find throughout History, absolutes crumble. Beat your chest as hard as you want, Dr. Conroy, bad ideas crumble, no matter your beliefs and effort."

I heard the voice of Father Fabian saying something about the unexamined life. I had thought enough for one day. "Dr. Conroy, may I come back?" I asked. "My mind is worn, tired and needing rest."

"I want something in writing," she said, "so I can study, learn. Ask questions."

I thanked her for not accepting the easy answers. "I'll be back," I said.

I left her office and felt a burden lifting. Dr. Conroy had followed me, been part of me for nearly 40 years. Seeds of my conscience.

I put on my 1970's ball cap and bounced down those steps two at a time, needing air and a chance to breathe. My Steamroller was out of my backpack and working by the time I made it to the meditation pool. I saw Bolton and Brannigan, smiled and yelled, "Bolton, Brannigan you Chicago guys don't know what you're missing."

Home at last, home at last, and headed toward St. Yon's.

Chapter 78

"Hey Buddy, how you are you?"
"Well as can be expected."
"Looking good."
"I try."
"You got style, Pirate man. You got style."

He smiled. It is people of all kinds that make up a town. All towns got them. They might have names like Jimmy or Stevie, Lucille or Sally Mae. Some never had a full deck, others faced the onslaught of life. Got kicked in the teeth at a young age or sometime during adulthood. Life is a peculiar thing in a river town. Characters, souls and spirits. Part of our collective myth, our inner psyche. You used to see them all up and down third and on second and down by the river. Under the bridge and out by the museum when it wasn't there yet.

"Hey, Stretch man."
"A good day, Sir."

They come from all walks. From the big houses to the small houses in the East End. In river towns they are family and part of us. The very fabric of life as it happens. A walking museum.

Down by the river you might talk to a quiet man. It is a gentle talk, 15 minutes with a character that reminds you of Chance in Being There. All in this river town. And then there are the regular folks.

"Norb, Norb Thrune. A long time."

"Hanson, I thought you were dead. God must have spit you out when you showed up. Then I heard you came back and that you could talk with the dead. I've been shaking my head. I always thought you'd end up on second or third or under the bridge. Not right in the head."

"I never stayed on homeless drive, outside with nowhere to go. Oh, I walked, tiptoed, trampled, through insanity but never faced the night sky with nowhere to sleep. I walked the streets and bridges of life gone awry."

"Didn't think you'd ever be back," he said. "It's a bit like war from my experience. War changes men. So does the psychiatric unit. Life is never the same."

"I have. I was in Spokane. Met a lady who changed me."

"They'll do that. Mrs. Thrune was like that. I couldn't keep my hands off her. 16 kids. How did she keep us together? I'm searching for her. My love grew as our golden years grew gray. I hear you met a bona fide witch?"

"She had a wrinkly nose and a wart. A big fat wart. White flyaway hair and a black pointy cap. I was terrified. She had these black pointy shoes. Scared the bejesus out of me. I shook when she spoke."

"She talked?"

"She did, but it was more like a howl. Talking to another spirit."

"Well, come on what did she say? I don't have all day. I'm going to have a beer with Butch."

"She pointed her finger and raised it to the sky saying the devil had my soul. A short path to hell awaits you," she cried. It was crooked and bent and her long fingernail pointed to the heavens above. "Hell will enter your soul," she said; then she pointed straight at me with her eyes ablaze. "How could you forget a lady like that?"

"Well, did you see hell?"

"No, she wasn't quite right, though the journey made me wonder. Haven't been to the gate yet."

"You're messed up in the head and you ain't dead yet."

"Yes, the rumors are true. You ever hear the voices, Norb?"

He wrinkled his nose and forehead contorted like. "Never thought they were real. Kinda thought people could just turn them off. Never thought they were real." He shook his head.

"Voices, the quiet ones will get you thinking. Those whispers of self-doubt start circling inside your thoughts. You can't see any of these voices. They work in the shadows. They whisper. Took me a long time to realize it was just dead folks talking."

"No, never heard the voices. Too busy I guess to think sometimes. 16 kids will do that."

"How did you keep your sanity, Norb?

"Just faster and faster, trying to keep one foot ahead of the bill collectors. Sixteen kids would have starved if I didn't keep going. Opened another gas station. I was fortunate, I didn't fall apart when living. Wired lucky. Never enough time to hardly get to know my kids. Let's share a cup of coffee some morning. Cheers to the dead ones and the live ones that can see. Oh, and tell the kids hi."

Chapter 79

When I visited the Eagles, the place felt different. Morning, afternoon or closing. There were drunks, crazed drunks and regular people sharing stories about life and living. People who found comfort in a dark bar, with little to no lights.

At night it got dark, real dark on the backside of the Morgan Block. The regulars were all hunkered down for an afternoon of socializing. Meyer and Czaplewski, Rinn and King, Tust and Porter. Good people sharing life at the Eagle's Club.

I saw Lawyer McGill in the back booth.

Before I could talk to him, Roman Lubinski touched my elbow. "Listen buddy, stay away from my daughters," he said.

"Roman! I wouldn't do that to you or certainly them. Mess up another person? You did a fine job raising them."

"You ain't right in the head. I miss my kids. Can you get them to open their eyes so they see we are still with them?"

"You know how it is. People got their minds all made up."

"Not my kids. The wood creaks mean Grandma is visiting. Raised them right."

"Not looking to argue, Roman. Just looking to keep one foot in front of the dead and a nice glass of whiskey helps."

"You sure got problems. Like I said, stay away from my daughters."

"It is a crazy thing, isn't it?"

"What's that?"

"Talking with the dead."

"Oh, I wish more had it. I been yearning to talk for a long time. You don't see the same over here. Runs through us dead folks. You'll never run out of stories."

"I'm finding that out. Gets hard to tune you folks off."

He nodded his head backwards. "Judge McGill has been looking for you."

I could feel Roman leaving as he said those last words. Just a moment of quiet, then he was gone.

"Mr. John, looking for me?"

"What mess do I need to bail you out of, Hanson?"

I looked around and whispered, too quiet to be heard.

"You want me to get a restraining order issued? Dead people are talking to you and you'd like Judge Buytendorp to stop it? Stop the dead?"

I nodded my head.

"I never heard such nonsense, Hanson. Lubinski is right. Stay away from our daughters. Lock you up and they'll strap you to your bed, dunk you in cold water, zap your brain or worse yet make a little snip in the front part of your brain. I'm guessing a little snip will take care of the dead problem."

"They do that in Rochester?"

"Yes, yes. There used to be a Dr. Freeman who traveled the country in a work wagon. Big letters: Loboto-Mobile on its side. Met him once and I didn't much like him. He had an all-knowing, prickly kind of personality. Used an ice pick, right through the nasal cavity. Drove from town to town, institution to institution. That is what got the Kennedy girl."

"Rose?"

"Yep, Old man Kennedy, just couldn't handle Rose and her outbursts. She was filled with the Irish demons their old folk said. I mean look at you. You indeed are full of something. You've a hard head and you can't do nothing without thinking. Dead folks have been waiting forever for you to open your mind. There are no courts I've come across on the dead side. I do run into judges every so often. Judge Sawyer is well but he and the others can use a bit of levity in their lives as they stare into their footprints."

"I'm not understanding."

"You get on the other side and you get to see. Walk in the shoes of those jailed. Sometimes it ain't pretty."

"I'm learning. I already talked with Dr. Heise. I spoke to the mother of Doc Tweedy. Fine lady, That green house by Windom Park."

"Judge Buck's house."

"One of the early Winona judges. He was a probate judge and knew all about the rich folks of this town as the families played the game of getting all they could. He was wired a bit different. Ants in his brains, couldn't sit still. He might have liked you and still put you away if you broke the law. I mean if I were wearing your shoes, I'd go quiet on mentioning dead people are talking."

"Strange legal advice. You looking to get paid for that are you?"

"Money does you no good over here. Keeps you away from living. It's like a mental crutch you need to get rid of before you start really living. Like your eyes get opened for the first time."

"That sounds like a bit of unconventional thought to me, Lawyer John."

"Listen, I love this town and a little bit of strange thinking has always run through it. It's the river, the river, I tell you."

"It gets inside you, messes with your thinking."

"You kids have lost that attachment too. The spirits are still running through town. One side of town to the other. There's a bit different thinking that goes on. I'm telling you, when they opened the graves and built the town on a cemetery they interrupted the natural attachment of life and death. Got our thinking upside down."

"You had a way of thinking, Mr. McGill."

"I tried to practice law just the same. Damn hard sometimes to battle the machine."

"I do hear things. Whispers, from you dead people."

"You really do wake up when you get here. A real brightness. You are blind no more and a spirit fills you. A fine spirit, we got ourselves, a fine spirit at the core of who we are."

I nodded my head. Lawyers always thought a bit differently. The good ones anyways and the bluffs and the rivers always had a way of talking to the best and brightest.

Part 8 Family and More

Chapter 80

   She left us a few years before she actually died. The forgetting disease got my Granny as she slowly forgot the things that once connected us. The names and places she once knew became overwhelming as the feelings and the mind began their different journeys. She tells me the other side is a relief and she feels whole again.

   I was young and she told me that the birds carried the spirits of the dead. Oh, she never told me directly, letting me think, but she would see an old blackbird and she'd say there is Johnny Zeke stopping by and then she would laugh. He was a mean one, she said giggling all the while. I didn't think much of that being a youngster but now that she's been gone for more than 20 years, I find her words carry a bit of the wisdom that connects grandchildren to their grandparents. I could hear the sounds of old Ireland in her talking.

   Her eyes would go to a different place when she saw the birds in her backyard. She had names for every bird that frequented her back yard. We used to play cards and go to bingo. I felt a bit of the pang as I realized how long it had been since we talked. Nearly twenty years since I had last heard her talk.

She always told me wisdom was in short supply. Men like to get all full of themselves. The worse ones would start thinking they were God himself. She went to church every Sunday and a few times during the week.

I had thought when they lowered her casket that I had heard the last of my Granny. But I found as I walked that the birds got a way of reminding me that love don't stop at the grave door. For that I am grateful to the spirit amongst us.

She would say that the cardinal sitting on the telephone line was Cousin Gene. Died young and she bowed her head remembering back when. She used to tell me that John Lamey was a soft, kind, quiet man who liked to tell stories and that the oriole captured his spirit. She would look at me and point out the two bluebirds drinking from her fountain. They reminded her of the gay bachelor farmers, Will and Fritz, just down the road. Said they sat next to each other every Sunday in church. Some of the happiest people she ever met lived right down the road. She would look at me and say God and his happiness shines its light through all kinds.

She is alive and well, telling me the other side isn't so bad. There is a happiness in the air and dead people don't have the burdens the living do. I swirled my glass of Jameson and listened to Tom Waits. I smiled, took a deep breath, and heard the whisper of Happy Valentine's Day.

Chapter 81

I miss Dad. Miss that feeling of the hair raising on the back of my neck.

I come from a long line of arguing types. I used to hear the stories about how the kitchen table was where the arguing took place. All the kids and grandma. Republican roots.

My grandparents lived in a run-down old place along Main Street, across from the St. Rose of Lima. That place got tore down. I remember being there once. Grandpa played an Accordion.

The cemetery that runs along the road is where my Grandpa, Grandma and Uncle are buried. Grandma died in 62 from the sweet tooth and Grandpa in 68 when the road veered left and he went straight. My Uncle died on a curved road in Kalamazoo.

Sometimes I could find my folks out in Lewiston. It had been a long time since I had been in the Rustic Bar. I wanted to meet up with the Lewiston Newspaper man. There was an old guy in the corner, broad faced, tired eyes, dusty clothes. Worked for the mill, I'm guessing.

"What are you drinking?" I asked.

"Warm, warm beer."

"Never heard of anybody drinking warm, warm beer." I shook my head.

"Long before refrigeration, man has been drinking to forget. Sadness."

"I'll have a Jameson." Warm beer just didn't sound good.

"What did you say, Honey?" The bar maid started chuckling. "We only serve real whiskey in here. Canadian.

Are you man enough?"

The old guy whispered, "It is best not to argue. Just nod your head, smile, and tell her that her hair looks wonderful."

She brought over a full glass, not a shot glass, but a full glass. I wasn't going to make it to Elgin tonight. Wasn't certain what Altie would say, though he would probably laugh and say he doesn't pay me to write like other people. "You are going to see empty storefronts when you drive through town. Memories, dreams that left town for the highway or faced a divorce or a death. The lights are mostly off. A reminder to the past and days of living but that isn't the story in this town. No, no, it is the kids."

"You can see it, feel it when you walk in their school. There is something going on. The teachers are embracing learning, computers and reading. And the kids are looking to create."

I was enjoying my Canadian, just listening.

"Town dies when there is no singing, dancing, celebrating. Kids need a place for their energies."

He nodded and the bartender with the pretty hair filled his glass. She had a nice way of talking. "Lotta good times were had in Lewiston at the Rustic Bar. Wedding dances and get-togethers. Fights and hardships. Oh, these walls saw and heard it all. Damn shame its dying years being a bit ugly. No, this girl had nice legs in her prime."

"Us old folks, us white hairs grew up when it was mostly quiet. I remember the days before TV, listening to a ball game on the radio. Sounds from a whole world away. And I remember listening to Hank Williams Sr. and Patsy Cline, George Jones and then those Outlaws on the juke box. Used to be over there in the corner."

220

"There was a dancing room in the back and a nice kitchen. Boys would come in from the field, the barn or like me the mill. Enjoy the company of others."

"I was here the night the Stockton boys came to town. Can't even tell you what they were fighting about but the Reps and the Merchelwitz's went at it tooth and nail. I was three sheets to the wind. My legs didn't work too well, when drinking, so as they started to fight, I decided it best just to sit this one out. Beer bottles got cracked over heads and one of them got thrown through the front window. Cops came, and they kept fighting all the way to jail."

"Town is coming to life. People need that feel of a town. That winning football team gave the town pride. The band and choir and arts same thing. Good things going on in Cardinal land."

"I'm covering the Caledonia-Plainview game for Indian Creek Press."

"A newsman? Let me tell yah." He waggled his finger. "Those linebackers play downhill on Plainview. Tough to move the ball. I ran into the Lewiston coaches, now and they tell me in that first game Cal stood up to them. If that good wide receiver, Frank, had made it to the end zone it might have been a different game."

You never know where you'll find a story. Spend so much time getting where you are going you miss what is right in front of you. I made a mental note to call the coaches tomorrow as I put my story into the Fax Machine.

"Say, Pretty Hair. I'll have another Canadian."

Chapter 82

He didn't quite seem right. He was sitting next to me at the Rustic Bar. Downtown Lewiston. His eyes were in a different place.

"Lost my Maggie a year ago. We came nearly every day. A couple beers excepting Sundays. It let us settle from the bustle of work. Never had kids."

I nodded, stared into my drink wondering what demons were coming. I swirled my drink and had more.

"She died and that's when I realized death is just a way of talking. I never felt closer to Maggie than I do now. It's a longing. I feel like half a person now that she's gone. Don't even know myself no more. Lost identity.

"I forgot how to talk, socialize. Maggie used to take care of that. Maggie had a gift for the gab. I used to love the bar because we'd come to the bar and she'd banter with everyone. Gave my ears a chance to breathe. Constant pounding. I got pretty good at tuning her out. Mastered saying huh. But for two hours she pretty much left me alone.

"I'm stuck with my own thoughts. Maggie gave me a grounding, a sense. I didn't tell her I loved her nowhere near enough. Leave thinking and talking to Maggie. I miss her. I feel her everywhere. On my walks, drives and on the coldest of days I feel a void. An empty spot. It's her way of talking from beyond. Maggie lives. I kept her clothes after she passed and some nights the grieving runs wild. I take comfort in the smells of her clothes. Memories, memories are all we got. People say gone is gone and I shake my head. She filled me up. Showed me how to live, to love. She is here." He was pointing at his heart. He paused, took a deep breath.

I asked, "What is the name of this fair lady?'

"Magy Magooley-Norton. I'm Norton."

"She was Irish?"

"Cut from the very cloth. She was a quiet one. A worrier, till she had her second. Then she was all giggles. By the time of her fifth, wasn't a man in the place who would stand up to her. I carried her home more than a few times. We couldn't have children."

I was feeling a bit awkward.

"You see, I was missing a nut. Born that way. My cousins used to call me One nut. One nut Charlie Bastards," he said, as he laughed. "Anyways, I felt bad my whole life. I remember our wedding night. We honeymooned up in St. Charles. Room number 7, White Motel.

"Best move I ever made was marrying Maggie Magoo. That's what I called her when we were happiest. There were happy times in my living. Only thing missing was the joy of children, grandchildren. We did what we could to cover our pain, share our fortune in finding each other. Maggie started buying shoes and pencils and whatever kids needed for the schools."

I nodded at Pretty Hair. Said I wanted a warm beer to honor my two new friends.

"Warm or warm warm. Hurry up."

"Warm-warm." I nodded at Ray.

"City shut off my electricity, can't pay what you don't have, so the beer gets warmer as the week goes on." I was beginning to like this town and I put the next chapter into the fax machine.

Chapter 83

Far too many of us think we know it all. Fact is, we are all a bit ignorant about some things. That's okay, you wouldn't want me handling a gun or driving a semi-truck or fixing anything mechanical. I don't do carpentry or plumbing or most anything very well that requires a different kind of thinking. Some of us just think differently and our blind spots are in different places.

We like to think that the other guy doesn't think right. In our early years we hung with people who had a relaxed way about them. They were our friends. When I think back to high school and look around that cafeteria, I see nothing but people caught up in their own worlds, sharing ideas about their life and where the social gathering was on Friday night.

There are people who think discipline is the answer to our problems. Work harder, make more money, go to church, raise the flag are some of the things we do. Those folks who walk that talk still got problems and sometimes I think they spend too much time imposing their beliefs upon others, causing more problems.

I hear my friend Frankie say organized religion is the root of evil and that before there was religion there was a spirit, an energy. He keeps telling me to look at the stars. He says early man has been staring at that moon forever knowing there was something magical about the nature of it all. Even before written words there was a spirit and he didn't see church or the Bible as a way to attain that spirit. Frank is dead now, but I still hear his words and when I see his children and grandchildren, I know Frank is carrying on.

Myself, I don't go to church more than a couple times a year. I find it noisy and the quiet time my body and mind needs doesn't get satisfied sitting in a church pew with fifty other equally distracted people. I find my needs met in the quiet sanctuary of the woods or even in an empty church on a winter afternoon. God have mercy some say, but the God I hear is just happy I found a way to enjoy the wonderful beauty in the center of us all.

We have become more superficial through the years. We have gotten away from the real meaning of man. "I" is not defined as man at his best. Thy self was third in the eyes of many behind the Lord and Friends. The person who placed the importance of others in front of them was most respected.

Each year as Christmas approaches, I think about the people who have left my life. I feel them, smell them, and even sometimes hear them. My Grandpa has been dead for 50 years but I felt something as I drove by St. Mary's Church in Minnieska, Minnesota last month. I felt a calling to see the world through his eyes. I visited the pews and confessional booth and I stepped where he stepped so many years ago on his wedding day. I saw that river as I looked out the front doors from where he stood facing the pews as a married man. I saw old cousins wanting to get the party started and I saw happiness on most everyone's face. I saw my Grandma in her youth and heard the voices of 100 years of praying.

Chapter 84

"Dying changed my thinking," my daddy said. He was a Marine and this day, Memorial Day was our day for remembering.

I was a bit late when I got to his resting spot. The crowd of the day had gone back to the rat race of living and the cemetery was back being quiet with the drone of the highway, a distant mower, chirping birds and the sound of the American flag as it lightly moved. A gentle reminder.

He told me how he walks after a lifetime of not. Movement gets his mind a thinking.

"No recliners in heaven," I said.

He chuckled, saying being dead isn't quite like what they say. He still was working through the issues. "I was a hard-headed thinker," he said. "Nobody was going to tell me anything. My ideas were set. It took dying to change. Beliefs don't hold water on this side."

He seemsed to be different as he worked through dying. In the old days we struggled talking and we now seem to be standing together. I no longer feel the urge to be in a different place when he is near.

"Dead is a good place. No better or worse and you start to find yourself as you let go of all that you are carrying. You see what matters."

I kept walking and felt the dead images of the past as I made my way through the old dead town. My memory was triggered as I saw the names of earlier times. The old Republican told me that war is horrific and the politicians who sends the young to die, live in a special place on that other side. Fran is raising hell and his scorn is that of his old party. I hear distant drums echoing those thoughts.

226

Enemies don't exist on this side of living. You start to realize where your wrong thinking comes from as you enter that realm of reason. Memorial Day is hard as we look at what might have been for some of us. No kids, wedding, marriages, funerals. No watching your children or grand-children playing ball or acting in a play. Gone, gone.

Go talk to the old folks who lost a child to the war machine and if you are able to hear they can tell you the horrors of that lost child. We honor the dead fallen but we must never forget the broken hearts who were left with the pain of death. They too lost dreams and stand as a testa-ment to man and the ability to overcome a most painful hurt. Early dying and the dealing with the emotions left behind makes living within the shadows of death a war in itself.

I could hear the rumblings coming out of the west-ern part of the old town asking the politicians why they wanted to kill the children.

"Profit, profit," the politicians chant.

The old preacher said, "Greed won't get you through the gate. You sold your soul."

I heard the Hell proclaimers cry, as they listen to the tangled webs of being.

It is not easy walking through these shadows they say. These folks have feelings, emotions and they see the world with the experience of living and dying. We want to know why you don't hear our quiet whispers as you yell from the pulpit, sit in the pew or pretend you have answers. We want peace amongst all people because over here we get along, that's when you start realizing the old beliefs don't hold water but cause problems as man plays the dance of living. Its peaceful amongst us here on this side of living.

The storytellers were up the road a bit. They could weave a lovely tale as they told the tales of living. Listen to them long enough and not a chance in hell would you ever want to see a battle, a war, a fight.

We are here to help. That next life is quiet as we go upon our ways. It is not the land of I in this other place. Your world, that world you are living in has become so much about the self that us dead folks have begun to wonder if you ever heard the words we spoke. Hard-headed are the children of the dead.

"Living you were the same," I said. "Thought you knew all and dissent was frowned upon."

"We made our share of mistakes on your side. You are filled with beliefs, things you believe in. Most of the things you believe in are the myths that run through all our forefathers. We didn't know what death would bring. Over here there are no beliefs. It is of the space. Being in the quiet and your body is filled with a quiet, a peace. It is lighter, less burdened."

Navy Man chimes in saying, "They have lost their way of thinking. Their identity. We took pride in science, tomorrow, and learning. Became a bunch of no thoughts, not able to think. Blinded. There are problems in this world and my Republican Party thought government could help address the problems running through us. It is not the government who has failed, but ourselves as we pound our chest and wave the flag of I as an aspiration. They yell 'I' at the top of their lungs. Trickle down nonsense."

"Feeling okay, Fran?"

"Haven't felt this good since I left. Politics. I miss the arguing, the reasoning and the sense a solution was to be found. Hard to get politics out of your system. But it
228

goes when you step on over here. You get time to think. Can't see a thing in that party of mine today. That party of Goldwater, we were thinkers and now we are caught up in a different way. It is an offense to how I lived."

I hear the Irish voice of Jimmy Boylan. "I fell on a grenade, I did. Blew myself to smithereens. Would do it again to save the lives of my men. My men made it back, and I've gotten to watch their children become parents. They are my family, my brothers in arms. But no children for Jimmy Boylan. They got a life and all the good and bad things that make it up. I got a front row seat and a window into their lives. Good men they were and are who carried the burden of seeing their buddy Jimmy taking his own to save theirs. I never hesitated."

Jimmy, Jimmy Boylan. The common good stood at the center of us and we were willing to die for that. Other countries weren't like us. They were ruled by Powercrats and Kings and pampered Princes, War Mongers and Bullies. America was hope, the World dream that the world could be a better place."

I twirled my Jameson as I thought about the magic of the day. The remembering and the being and the thoughts and the words of some old friends. I gave them a salute and a pause of reflection and thanked them for being part of who I am.

Chapter 85

I like the winter walks. My Daddy never liked walking but today I hear his heart and remember the things we didn't much agree about as I walk down the hill for my afternoon coffee. He was with me and said it felt good to breathe.

Dad has been gone a little over a year now and yet we have better conversations. He seems to have gotten better at hearing and I think my thinking is clear. There is little friction and we no longer dig in our heels and take opposite sides.

He asks me to take a walk through the woods and tells me that he never quite appreciated them. He asked me to sit near a tree and feel it warm my insides. No hands, he flashed and laughed.

He told me again about the wild mustard, and I wished we had stopped and walked through the trails of his youth. Walking when he was living was not done much and eventually his legs stopped working. He tells me that I might have the family disease, and its best to never stop that daily walk.

I tell him the mosquitoes, bugs, gnats, and hot weather make walking miserable. He tells me he hasn't run into any bugs on his side of living. I look at him, seeing the twinkle, and realize we had learned to be different in a lighter way. I feel together with him for the first time and wonder what else?

We get going on our walk and I feel a lightness slip out of me. I hear him whisper that he is going to visit family and I wonder how long before family realizes old Marines never die; they just go fight a different way.

I finish my walk and head in for my coffee. I see familiar faces. I see Mrs. Schwarz and think of Rodney and Cliff. She is smiling and makes me think about long ago days.

I started walking this afternoon, thinking about my

dad and how he enjoyed a piece of pie. I could never figure out if he enjoyed the talking or the pie itself. I was going to have a coffee with the piece of pie and I hoped he would show up so we could tell the same stories.

I saw the Peterbilt Jacket and I straightened up. My Uncle Wayne had never served in the military, one leg being shorter than the other, but I can't recall ever respecting a man more. He looked at me, and I felt the sadness that all great men have. I think he missed family.

Wayne used to drive a Semi from coast to coast. He preferred the open road, and every time he saw the mountains his heart would beat faster. He had been gone nearly 5 years now, and I wondered what he had been up too and where his journey had taken him.

He never had to talk much to get his point across. It was easier to let Lois do the talking and he still thought of her every day. He had a way of saying things and Kurt and Karmen mostly listened as they got through those early years enjoying life.

He said that he tried to make it for most family outings and that he missed the warm bread. He hoped at Thanksgiving there might be some of that good, warm banana bread on the table. Just the smell could get his stomach going. He liked the trucks the boys drive and Matt and Brad have made him proud to be a Grandpa.

He said he had to go and that he would be around a lot over the holiday season. He told me that he thought when he left that everything ended. He had never wanted to leave.

I sipped my Coffee hearing him say something about a garage and a stock car and next season being a lousy winter away.

I felt tired as I walked home. Those two men, Dad and Uncle Wayne, had been part of me for my 50 plus years. Now, at least for one day, they were alive again. I heard my phone ring. I saw the number 452-9288 and I began to wonder what was next.

Chapter 86

After Dad had passed, it was a while before we talked. I had visited, but I suppose we were each going through our grief cycle or that the pain of death was intense enough that not much was said. He did send a letter and I passed it on.

Dad was a Marine and you could feel his heart when a flag waved. He would sit up a bit, and I could almost hear The Halls of Montezuma running through him. That was the way we rolled as I felt him remembering. I drove a car through the fields of his youth as he shared his reflections of all that was gone and missteps along the way on his last road trip.

Dad could never get his words out right. The tone of his voice was too fierce, too intense as I tried to think about what he was saying. Those loud noises ran through me like static, and I would get tense listening to the pain of his words.

There had been a drowning and a lost farm to the dust bowl in his youth. He was a small town boy through and through. He took delight in talking to farm folks. I never took to that kind of quiet, and it took me quite a while to find the space where I felt best.

He was Republican enough that he quit going to

church. All that shaking hands and pretending righteousness was not who he was. He thought churching was more about hard thinking, and he never much liked the songs except for the ones with a little military to them. He might have done better at a different church but the easy chair caught him most every morning as he drifted through retirement. He felt paralyzed by the depression which weighed upon his head.

I could feel things as a youngster that I kept to myself. Through time, I learned to let go of the old way of thinking. I've found talking to the dead brings me back to a pleasant time. Kind of like good friends you've known forever.

Those old folks love to hear your story, and there are even some days where it is nice to tell your story to someone you've not met before. They can have the quiet voice of a farmer or a teacher or a learned friend on his or her own journey. They all got wisdom when you hear that the words are no longer harsh.

They mostly get me feeling good and they remind me of things that mattered. They have had enough of crying and understand this is how life works. They would like more than anything just to touch your hand and feel its warmth. Their life is blind to that and they miss that part of their life.

I never remembered laughing with Dad. We saw different things, and I keep seeing the old marine in places where a laugh was right. He never stood down and in the end he did so gracefully that I shall remember his way when my time comes.

I walked past the stones of the old priests and bishops and that's another story. I heard the tales of the church pew ladies and the bingo workers and the men with grease under their nails and sawdust in their hair. They all got a different way of looking at things. They spoke in quiet words. My heart still twittered when I heard an Irish lilt lifting from a grave and I knew it was good to be alive.

I heard my daddy whisper to listen to their stories and learn from what they have to say. Their story is life itself and I think there is more I don't know. His voice is quiet, soft, and I think what a wonderful day. Grace has fallen upon my daddy's heart, and a day with him is like no other. All it took was dying.

Chapter 87

"Seven years! You've been gone seven years. What have you to say for yourself?" I asked.

He sat smoking his pipe, rocking on the rocking chair outside his new home. St. Mary's Cemetery. He looked all around and said this is the American dream.

"Your guy lost," I said.

He nodded and said, "It don't mean so much on this side. We don't need governing. Anger, drive, all gone when you when you step over. Money has no influence on the ways over here. Those big stones in the cemetery are like weights around your neck. Man and his ego wanting to be remembered."

I told him the grandkids still talk about him and that they smile when they do.

"My golden years," he said, "were the best of times. Seeing grandchildren grow into fine adults and being part of that is what mattered. What's in the backpack?"

234

Once again, Science girl had packed me a backpack with all the fixings. Bloody Mary's, Coffee and some Jameson.

"Drink for us," I said, thinking it might take the whole bottle to get over the demons of tribalism we carried between us. I was feeling good. The hair on the back of my neck wasn't standing. He was an old school republican who defended that way of seeing his entire life. I had left the party of my forefathers and our relationship drifted. Politics and Fox News. Limbaugh and Hannity. We stopped talking and grew more set in our ways.

It was November, a bright sunny day where the sun warmed your face and the wind told you what was coming. A beautiful day for walking about the cemetery.

We finished that bottle, we did, and as we let go of the things that we carried between us I felt a lifting. Time heals all and there are few things better than letting go of the dislike holding us down.

Chapter 88

A Birthing; I was most honored to meet you, to hold you, to feel you and to feel the rhythm of those feelings you got running through you. Seems like you are headed for a fine, fine life.

Now I told your Daddy and your Aunt and Uncle a lot of things when they were just beginning. I told them everything I knew. I talked to them like I'm talking with you. Love pouring out my heart. I kept thinking for thirty years as life told me its story.

I figure you won't remember having this talk being

you left your Mother's womb a day or so ago. I can only imagine the stress in seeing the light as that nine-month life you were living came to an end.

Life anew and the innocence of life is shown on your face. Life hasn't yet thrown you a curve. That's when the chickens come home to roost and you see what you are made of.

He had started grunting. Hanson men sometimes do their best talking with a grunt or nod of the head and I'm thinking the gene got passed on. The first signs of talking. A grandpa he can talk with, how lucky I am. That was when I started hearing the quiet whispers.

"Get a feel for him. Listen to his breathing, his heart. Watch his eyes, pretty soon they'll dance," I heard my grandma say.

"Let the boy enjoy it, Ma. He's got the best job in the world. Nothing like being a Grandpa," Grandpa said

I looked up from my grandson. A room full of fore-bears, happy, smiling and eyes watering. I looked to my left where strangers sat, or stood, mouths ajar and eyes showing the joy only a birthing can bring. In-laws, I'd never met.

I saw dead younguns from the other family eyeball-ing each other from the other side of the room. I thought of Grandma and Grandpa being married up in the Minnieska church looking out over the river and cousins looking for the prettiest girl. I smiled and thought about being young and my grandson's heart. Life had delivered me a blessing.

Chapter 89

Good to be a Grandpa on such a fine sunny, delightful day in late March. The grit of a Winona winter had lifted. Green splotches were showing here and there. Walkers were walking with an extra bounce. Yesterday had passed and I was thinking about being alongside friends.

I was out on a date with my granddaughter. She was all of three and the pandemic had kept us apart for far too long. Mom and Dad used to worry about senile old Grandpa, but they were in the beginning stages of raising a fine, independent daughter. There was no doubt who was in charge and it wasn't me.

JoJo and I started talking ice cream right off the bat. Forever in pursuit of the finest ice cream in all of Winona. I told her I liked mint chocolate chip and she told me she liked gummies in her Gelato. I didn't know the difference and it all tasted good.

She eyeballed me, "How long has your thinking been upside down, Grandpa?"

"Been that way forever," I told her. "I kept it to myself. Kept it hidden, locked up inside, tucked away. Unhealthy you know, keeping things bottled up. Makes my head explode."

"You're goofy, Grandpa. You are not in a comic book or in a cartoon. Just not quite right in your thinking."

I told her that's some good insight for such a little squirt and she told me she had an older brother and a younger one too. "I have to use all my tools to get my way. Mom and Dad aren't easy."

She told me she wanted to go to Nate and Ally's. "They let me put gummies in my ice cream."

I told her that store was once a grocery store. Then a hardware store and office supply store. It has beautiful brick on the insides and if you listen closely you can hear stories echoing throughout.

"Oh Grandpa. You can't hear voices bouncing off the brick walls. Can you?"

"I told you my thinking wasn't right. You want some of the Blueberry and Cherry fruits on your ice cream?"

"Green gummies, sour gummies, silly Grandpa."

We took our ice cream outside and sat staring at the Merchants Bank. I told her that her great grandma used to sit and have her ice cream at the Dairy Bar and that Great Grandpa used to eat at Ruth's Restaurant pointing towards the Merchant Bank Parking Lot.

"How are we supposed to learn if all of yesterday's reminders are now parking lots?" she asked.

"Kind of smart for your age," I said. "Memories are what we carry to our end days. So important. Old time buildings don't have much value to the merchants of money that trample our yesterdays. Easy to forget when reminders are under a parking lot."

Sometimes a scoop of ice cream is all it takes to get a conversation going and we spent the next half hour talking about Grandpa and Grandma and what they were thinking while they sat in the little cafes of yesterday.

Chapter 90

It was turning dusk and the dead folks had seemingly turned in. I heard the last church bell and took the time to remember the dead of my past. It is hard realizing life carried on beyond the ways of my learning as change gets harder by the day.

I thought about my Dad and Grandpa and the things they kept to themselves before leaving. Perhaps Grandpas whispered in our ears the stories of life mostly forgotten and those lay dormant until triggered by the world we live in.

Now that Dad is gone, we talk often. A dutiful son wasn't me so much when living. Death allows us time to sort through old feelings.

I've always liked the light that fills this river valley as the sun rises, those early morning hours as we hustle and bustle to our daily doings. Come evening, time gets slower, the sun shares its warmth with the other side of the globe. I feel myself breathing. Peaceful times are harder as the golden years start creeping into my bones and the world moves faster.

The sedan delivery truck pulled up and Frank said he had a story. I asked where he was playing this evening and he said he was playing Rascals and thought about asking him who he was playing with but remembering all the bands and friends he played with would leave someone out and that isn't right.

I told him Cheryl and the kids were well and he said he knew. Watching is part of dying as he watches the people he was once part of he says.

He told me he was feeling it and that life was different but kind on his side. Never thought death would be like this. Just not part of his thinking. Fran and June were the best kind of parents he said.

That was when he told me he came from another seed. Told me he was adopted at birth and thought nothing of it. He said, "I had four parents but only in dying did I find where my heartbeat came from. When you hook up with kin you feel the myths from your ancient pasts. Bonds to the dead. My Dad, Fran, and my biological father, Guy, shared many traits but in Guy's words I heard the rumblings of my ancient past. Something different, beyond the seeing was what I felt with Guy and Donna. Oh, don't get me wrong Fran and June will always be Mom and Dad."

I wondered what that must be like, being surrounded by people whose heart beat differently, whose ancestral yearnings weren't the same. I looked back and marveled at the smile Frank carried.

"I met my brothers and sisters," he said. "They liked to rub shoulders and bounce and laugh and I felt at home like playing in a band. I felt Guy and the rumblings of his heart as they matched mine."

I felt for Donna. A pregnant college girl, enamored with a football player. She left school and they carried on with their separate lives. The future wasn't very bright for a single mom in the late 50's. She hoped and prayed for a better place, never knowing what had happened until Frank's youngest, Corey, found her. Guy had no idea, though Donna says he knew.

Donna, now the other side of 80 had never told her children about their brother and Guy wishes he had met his oldest son. Frank had a blast as he saw his life come full circle and he got to see what oldest daughter Beth will look like as she grays. Spitting image.

He got to see his mother and father after spending years wondering about the rejection that comes from adopting. I had heard stories about the orphan train stopping at the Red Depot. Names like Koscianski and Bundy and countless others took that route. In Winona, that wasn't so important.

Chapter 91

"What do you mean I can't go to Howie's one hundredth birthday party?"

"No Sir, Doctor's orders."

I eyeballed the Nurse, figuring if I raised a fuss, they'd take away my morning smoke and walking privileges.

"I'll be calling my daughter."

I had kept my Volkswagen Bug stored at Kurt's place. He last told me he started it every Friday. It sounded good as ever. It had been a couple decades since I had driven and I wasn't even quite sure where Howie lived anymore but missing his hundredth was out of the question.

I woke early, telling Harold as I walked outside that it was a day for two smokes on my walk. He nodded, saying, "Don't let the robins get the better of you."

The sun was just making its way up over the horizon. Old or not it was still my favorite part of the day. I was a bit worried about stealing my own car and if Kurt knew what I planned, I'm not certain he would let me drive. He always told me I couldn't drive when I was normal, and I'm guessing senility took away a bit of my edge.

I should have known the old boys would have taken care of everything. Wayne and Kick had the bad boy polished and running as I approached the house. They seemed proud of their work.

"Kurt and Sandy are out suntanning California way. Won't be back for another week. You need someone to ride shotgun?"

"Is that you Kick? A long time."

"Wayne called and said he needed help. Didn't have much going and knew Kurt always kept something cold in the fridge."

Wayne piped in. "It's a bit hesitant going from fourth to fifth. The old lady hasn't been out on the road for a while. All new belts, ready to roll. Have fun."

"Kick, cruising with you would be a blast, but I'm not certain I'd get out of Winona. This is something a man has to do on his own. Say goodbye to an old friend before he joins you."

I was a week late for the birthday as I started down old highway 61. I noticed some strange looks as cars buzzed past. I felt thirsty as I drove by Linehan's and Twin Bluffs. I started thinking about old times, old friends, and that after all the running and crazy stuff we did, we were still friends. I put the pedal to the metal and said what the hell.

Happy Birthday Howie.

Chapter 92

"I hope that your family is impressed," I said. I was combing my hair for the first time since high school just to show them a different side to my being. Forty years not combing my hair.

"What is wrong with you?" she asked.

I smiled. She was part Al. Part Rita. Together they were an amazing bouquet of energy and their last master-piece is like nothing I had ever met. I worked for a long time on a closed psychiatric unit where stories get told but she had curly hair and multi-colored cupboards, Einstein on her walls, and she could light a campfire. I'm a lucky guy having a lady with sizzle.

She had a lot of stuff inside her thinking but that's how love works. If we had met when young there is not a chance our relationship would have survived. Time is a funny thing; it doesn't work at the same speed for everybody but it's constant. Physics. She's still teaching and I'm a slow learner.

2020 has been an unusual year. I stopped going to the barber and so my hair goes every which way imaginable. Some folks just go get a haircut. Hansons have a different way to their thinking. Jerry Jeff sung a song called Pissin' in the Wind that sums me up. Or at least where my best learning comes from.

Science girl retired this past year. Sleep patterns are a reflection of health and before she retired more than a few times I caught her shadow boxing while sleeping. Taking punches at students she left hours ago. Teaching takes something out of you.

Our granddaughter, JoJo, says I'm goofy in my thinking. She is only two but my family is so grateful Cheryl is in my living. Keeping another bum from living under a bridge. Al and Rita show up in her demeanor and actions every day.

Our bodies are pretty good. Each of us have body parts running inefficiently. A lot of half dead body parts we say. We are sure this bug going around would enjoy gnawing on the dead meat inside us.

I put the brush back down and joined Cheryl downstairs watching NCIS. She and Gibbs were chasing some bad guy. She joined me in wishing you a Happy Holiday.

Chapter 93

Larry. My neighbor.

Dead. Larry Gorrell has passed, gone on.

He was a mentor. My lack of social skills was never more evident than when Larry and I talked. He was light witted, friendly and happy. Comfortable with himself.

I struggle a bit talking so I shared my stories and the respect we felt grew. That is what neighboring and friendship is all about.

I think Larry is smiling. He was the last time I saw him, but I think him being a chapter in a book and a recurring character in my stories would make him laugh. He had a way with words and ideas.

His last words were rather remarkable and so when Larry visits and we pour ourselves a scotch we'll have a little talk as he goes about explaining himself. Then we will laugh and talk some more.

Chapter 94

I was talking to Wes, Nora, and Auggie as we were out for our spring walk.

"It must have been 1977 or so when I first started hearing and seeing things most people don't," I told the kids. " I fought it for awhile, but eventually schizophrenia became a way of life for me, a way of thinking. I was a young man when those voices started taking over my thinking. They have been with me, by my side, for nearly 40 years now. Old, dead friends, dear friends, I've come to call them."

They were all a bit young when I planted the seeds for learning. I told them young, because schizophrenia was not something you talked about or shared with others. Buried it, tucked it away, tried suppressing it all the years before the grandchildren started popping out. I figure they have already figured out that Gramps ain't quite right.

Those voices kept talking but I mostly ignored them while doing the child rearing. I met witches under bridges and the shadows of living were always close. In my early years, I shared quarters with the not quite right minds of Thomas Eagleton and Ernest Hemingway.

"Schizophrenic?" Little Nora asked.

"Greek. Early twentieth century. Split mind," Auggie responded.

"Your mind works in two directions, Grandpa?" Wes asked.

"On a good day, Wes. Sometimes it is in two different places, physical spaces and then some time sequencing."

We were sitting in Windom Park, surrounded by all the big houses.

"Do those houses have spirits in them, Grandpa?"

"The whole neighborhood does, Kids. The whole neighborhood."

"Are they nice spirits?"

"Only the best. And they love kids. Whole town is filled with spirits and they all love kids."

"Can we go visit them? Can we, can we?"

"They will find you if you have the gift, but I wouldn't wish for anyone to be given the gift of schizophrenia."

"But you have it Grandpa."

"See that blue house there on the corner? That was

245

the home of Moses Varney. Moses had a voice that would turn heads, a snap to him, like a whip crossing your head. He wasn't meant to live in civilization. He only stayed here a few years then it was off to the woods. He comes back now and then just to see. He told me once that Winona was the best town he ever lived in and when he moved here just after the settling there was no place like it. Then it grew, till it got where it is today. It used to be just muddy, dirty roads, and horses and mules constantly got in the way of traveling.

"He told me one night that the Indian grave openings let loose the spirits of the dead. Winona has given the dead a life he said and then the remembering starts. He gets sad as he recollects how we treated the Indians."

"You can't say dead people are living Grandpa. Science can't measure it."

"Not yet, but science is only starting its learning. You see that big, white house on the corner? That Mr. Garvin, who helped found Bay State Milling, was a thinking man. Had a contraption in his garage, a turner, that turned his car around. Garvin Heights and Farmers Community Park and he donated for the upkeep of the park. Getting outside is good for one's thinking, he said. If you nose around I'm sure there are some who remember Mrs. Garvin. Louisa, she died in 1968. Wingold Flour was what his company was known for when I was growing up. They used to sponsor little league baseball and basketball teams."

Wes was looking at me. "You all right, Grandpa?" he asked.

"He just sees dead things," Nora said.

"How can you see something that doesn't exist?" August asked.

246

"If I see it, doesn't that mean it exists in my sense of reality?"

"Oh."

"Hey, you kids want to go see my grade school? Maybe talk to some people along the way. Maybe later go to Nate and Ally's or the Zesto stand." I love being a Grandpa.

Part 9 The Journey Continues

Chapter 95

I was having my beer at the Athletic Club. 5th and Mankato. Stories were pouring out the woodwork, walls, and stools. Swirling, swirling, dancing. Polka music could be heard coming from upstairs and the sounds of bowling pins were coming from the basement.

Walking inside reminds me of yesterday. I feel myself relaxing as I rub shoulders with a different time, a different people. You can see yesterday alongside today, in the walls where Polish history talks.

"Hey bleeping Hanson," Frankie Red Nose greeted me. Frankie had a gift for swearing.

I just liked the way he talked. I asked him if he was happy that this building, the Athletic Club, the Polish Community building, was being recognized on the National Historic Register of Buildings. "Dancing with the big boys, now," I said.

He said the story of the Polish people was not well known and he thanked the people who made it happen. I told him it was the stories that were of interest and that I didn't know architecture but this building looked secure, like a fortress, a castle without ornament.

He looked at me and said, "It's the Polish soul you're

248

talking of that makes us who we are." He gave his chest a pounding.

It was a matter of pride, Polish pride, being a member of the club. It meant you understood the hardship of coming to this country with hope and a dream and a pair of hands that could work and determine your own tomorrow.

"You got any idea, Hanson, what it's like to leave forever the land you came from?" Frankie went on. "Do you know what it's like to say goodbye to the grandparents and everything you know? Hop on a slow-moving boat that didn't look real sturdy and move to a country where your language was spat upon and you were thought of as dirty and unclean? To hear whispers and see raised noses as those that were here before you crossed the street or didn't say hello in passing? Well, this place gave us a spot to gather, to be with our own.

"I was a member of the club and I bowled and danced. You should have seen some of those parties that were thrown for weddings and baptisms and funerals here at the Athletic Club. We would dance all night and come back in the morning.

"Large gatherings were hard to manage in the small houses inside a neighborhood that was a larger family itself on the East End. We had no place else where we could talk Polish, Kashubian and not be looked at distrustfully. We couldn't swear in the church. We could be ourselves in this rock of a building."

I looked around the place. Guys dressed in the times of their living. Grandpas wearing fishing hats talking to their grandkids about their own Grandfathers. Seeing the child's eyes open wide and grow bright believing every word that came out of Dziadek, Grandfather.

There were men wearing suits and ties rubbing shoulders with the boys at the chain making company and the meat packing plant. Different times, same place.

"This building was a place for the times of your life and the old people were revered and admired," Frankie said. "A place where having a beer with your buddy's grandfather was a sign of respect. Different times, different times when families gathered yesterday at the Club." He turned quickly, swinging wildly over the head of the guy sitting next to him, his grandson. "Potater, you fall on your head again? I thought your days of being crazy were no more. Let the gentle Polish heart breathe, live, grow soft as you age. It's the Polish you are searching for. You have to let go, relax, let go. Carrying on battles that have stopped making any sense. I told you that when living and it's like seeing a rerun on TV as you keep running into brick walls from my dying spot."

I don't think Potater knew his Dziadek was talking. He didn't have the gift of seeing the dead like some do and I heard the boys down at the junk yard saying it ain't all he's missing. Tater's one of the junk boys.

Being a Townie I asked Tater if something was wrong being he was staring deeply and quietly into his beer. His mind seemed to be in a different place.

"Just another brick wall in a life of brick walls," he said. "My genius doesn't go in a straight line." He tapped his noggin. "Lose track of who I am, lose my place. Little heart problem. A life of cigarettes, beer and living hard."

So Dziadek said to me, "This building was a dream come true for my father when it was built. A place we could gather to celebrate life moments. A community believing

250

in a better tomorrow."

Too bad Tater couldn't see that, hear his grandpa's life.

I looked around the place and lifted my glass to yesterday, seeing time wanting to talk. A building on the National Historic Register and I felt the Polish pride that built this building rising.

Chapter 96

I was sitting in the Athletic Club sharing a drink with yesterday. The bar was full of old faces and honest laughter from the times when people found a way to get along. "The Historic Winona Athletic Club captured the Polish soul like no other place except for maybe The Square Deal which once stood in the parking lot next door. It was that kind of bar and everybody knew everybody."

"I grew up on East Third. My Mom was a Kukowski. I had a brother and a sister. The people in the East End did a great job getting me ready for life. I was a priest who felt most at home working with the broken hearts, forgotten people."

"I did a lot of my priesting in state institutions with the people who had life fall on their head. The less fortunate and those unable to live amongst us. I heard their stories, their anger and saw how life fell."

"These were our brothers, sisters and cousins and their stories for far too long have been swept under the rug or put into a closet. Never spoken of once put away. The hidden America."

The stories were filling my senses when the Priest sat

on that bar stool next to me.

"Hanson! Bleep what are you staring at?"

I ducked as Chops tried slapping my head, just missing.

"You gotta stop the early drinking. Drink too much of that whiskey and you'll be seeing the demons. Makes you a bit whacked."

I shrugged my shoulders and smiled as the woodwork spoke of a grand and glorious past that told the story of immigrants and successes their forefathers so long ago could never have imagined. All here at the Winona Athletic Club.

Father Dan whispered, "If the Square Deal were standing, Chops would have a seat at that bar. Greatest guy in the world but his thinking just isn't quite in place. Nothing wrong, he just thinks in a different way. He hears the echoes of his past and tries to keep one step ahead of the devils calling."

I nodded my head and heard Frankie. "I had a cousin like you," he said. "First thing in the morning, he would crack a cold one. He said his Uncle Frank taught him the art of drinking a beer when he first got up. You aren't alone in the East End, I tell you, Hanson. What time do you start drinking?"

"Drinking isn't my problem, Frankie. You don't happen to see Father Dan next to me?"

He looked at me, slurping his beer and calling me a bleeping idiot for seeing what ain't bleeping there. Effin nuts.

I turned to Father Dan.

He started talking about the river and the people of it. "That river gets you. It shakes out your worries and

252

problems of living. Its gentle soul can tame the wild hearts. It's where I found my peace in a world controlled more and more by timekeepers wanting more. The river remembers today, tomorrow, and yesterday as it rolls down south."

I sipped my whiskey feeling the goodness that was Father Dan wondering where the kind souls have all gone as time spoke in a building called The Athletic Club.

Chapter 97

I was having a smoke in the back of the auditorium. I was remembering old teachers, friends, and girlfriends. I was saying goodbye to a grand dame. Her death march had begun long ago, and all that was left to put her out of her misery was the wrecking ball. Cause of death? Demolition by neglect.

After a bit, Petey joined me. "I loved this building," he said. "Me and my friends had fun. The additions like the shop classes and gym and band and choir all taking in the back of the school. It was like classroom recess. We could do something with our hands. Create and make.

"Oh, don't get me wrong some of us knuckleheads got hollered at a few times. We didn't pay attention easily. We kept thinking about doing other things like skipping school or grabbing a smoke out back of Erickson's or heading down to the Hurry Back.

Petey had lost a few pounds from the last time we saw each other but his mannerisms hadn't changed much. "You listen to teachers for a couple hours, Hanson, and you are ready to do something else, learn something else, find a way to spend that built up frustration that comes with the hard learning. Like I said, learning don't come easy to some of us and our natural abilities were best seen in classes which didn't involve as much sitting. I'm talking woodworking, instrument playing, physical education, and cooking."

I guessed Petey was right, and some of those kinds of classes could be right here, in this auditorium. The greatest thing about the auditorium was the feeling that you were part of something bigger and better than your mere self. You got on that big stage and the butterflies would start. You felt good about yourself as you overcame the fears of performance. Fourteen hundred seats if you counted the balcony and more than a few hung over that balcony screaming and yelling as electrified music came to Winona and lifted our souls. It was a huge stage and to a kid, it was larger than life.

Winona in its day stood by kids. This auditorium was built for the community and that opening night in 1929 or 1930, you couldn't get a seat. Opening night was Glee Club and the place roared as Winona expressed themselves. That auditorium was built to be shared by the community and the school. An example of early-stage public-private partnership.

Those Winona State Professors had a great deal to do with the entire setup because education was something Winona believed in. The Board of Education placed the K-6, the 7-9 and the 10-12 school settings in place. 6-3-3. Winona State was highly influential in the introduction of Music, Industrial Arts, and Physical education into the school curriculum. That's why the auditorium got historical status attached to its being. Winona was state of the art and cutting edge. And the acoustics in the falling down building still ring true.

Anyway, I wasn't the best at book learning. No, No but I'm eternally grateful to those two Winona State University Music professors that established the Winona Music Series. In the 30's, 40's and 50's Professors Grimm and French had connections to Columbia Artists Management out of New York, and Winona became a regular stop for tours between Minneapolis and Chicago. Paul Robeson and the Vienna Boys Choir were two of the acts in its earlier years. Music is a language of the soul.

When they built the building they put in big glass windows to capture the natural light. Our Winona forefathers looked at everything trying to save a buck. It has been sad to see it age right before our eyes. She wasn't that pretty but she had good bones and on the inside of the grand old building you could feel the heartbeat of a town.

Chapter 98

You traipse around enough sidewalks and bars and churches and schools and you'll start seeing what matters. Old Winona knew what mattered and our forefathers now weep.

I was standing across from the auditorium, directly in front of the library talking to Old Man Bauer. He lived in the house where the gas station now stands. He was a photographer who captured images of his time. Picture taking was something Winona always took to.

"Why there were people who claimed they could tell what a man was all about just by looking at one of my pictures," Old Man Bauer said.

"How often do they get things right?" I asked.

He said that some do. "A good photographer can capture Man's inner self." He looked at me. "You're nuts aren't you?"

I smiled and said, "It's a special gift. Most of us don't survive. We get locked up, put away. Taken to trial, burned on the cross. How dare you think differently? They cried as my brothers died. Yeah, I'd say nuts." I nodded and added that I remembered the words of Mr. Addington on my journey. He told us to do what it takes, to make yourself better whatever path you follow. A fine, fine teacher. I just took a different path to where I'm standing. Came to dying while still living.

Old Man Bauer gave me the hairy eyeball, saying something about dead people weeping as the trolley car went past. Back and forth down fifth all day the trolley car went. People got aboard to buy their groceries, spend their money, meet and greet, say hello.

"What do you mean people weeping?"

"The auditorium," he said. "It was the heart and soul of this town. That place brought Winona together. The whole town would show up, not just parents and grandparents. They were the kids of Winona and they mattered. Those acts that came through brought light to all of Winona. I sometimes wonder what you people are thinking. You can't take money to the grave. You must all be falling asleep when the preacher man preaches. That auditorium is nicer than the colleges. It was a source of pride for generations of Winona folk.

I took a look at him and said, "I thought photographers were mostly quiet folks."

That must have lit a spark for he started yelling about tearing the hearts out of Winona. "Old dead people weep when their buildings go down and this one, this one was life as it was meant to be. Progress, progress is hard on us old dead folks. I mean we wept when the Opera House came down and the Redman's burned. That little theatre down by Merchants Bank? Parking lots now, I tell you. Our gathering spots gone."

He wasn't done railing at me, just a took a breath and went on. "I ran into old man Kertzman the other day," he said. "He owned a dredging company up Lamoille way. As practical of a man as I've met and he told me that the auditorium reminded me of his daughter. She played the harp on that stage. Nothing made him prouder than the moment when all of Winona watched and applauded. Just a man remembering his daughter while taking care of business. He swung by to remember and rekindle his heart with the best most proud time."

I told him I'd like to take a selfie with him.

He said,"This is beyond the seeing. Find a champion."

I scratched my head and like that he was gone.

Chapter 99

It didn't surprise me none when Bev Porter stopped by. It was the night before her visitation and wake. Word moves fast on that other side. I wasn't going to be able to make it to her wake and visitation. Body has too many things wrong with it to survive the bug and it seems to like spreading in crowds.

I was having a smoke on the stoop of the old high school auditorium when she showed up. It was good to see her.

Even in the darkest of dark days her face and body language said, "Hi. Sit down, let's talk." Her eyes still sparkled. Bright and wide open. "I ran into Jim," she said. "He told me that he was shocked to see Grandpa when he passed. It took him a bit longer than a day and a half." She told me she'd had a good life. Family, work and love. What else matters?

She said she was headed to the Eagles and added, "Jim told me that when an eagle dies, the spirits soar. Then they gather to remember. All the dead Eagles who have left us gather at the club and raise their glasses. Jimmy tells me that Eagle members from when the club was on the Morgan Block show up. He said it's nice seeing old friends you never thought you would see again.

I took another hit.

She told me to keep writing. "Take a deep look inside. Don't you worry about stepping on toes. They need shaking up. Tell the kids hello and stop on down. 7th chair. Eagles Club."

Rest in Peace, Mrs. Porter.

Chapter 100

The night skies over Farnum Farms shine bright. The stars dance, shooting, flying, shooting stars. A crackling fire and good, good friends. Christine, Fred and Science girl. Just up in the Coulees, round the bend. Frieda, the seeing eye dog, kept guard on what we couldn't see.

Christine has bright, dark eyes reflecting a life of reading and reflecting. Those eyes were full of light and dancing when she pointed at me and said, "He is bat shit crazy."

My heart started bubbling as I thought of my granny as she spoke in the folk language.

Science girl was mumbling something about chemicals and metabolism and how these drugs, these steroids, take over the thinking of some. Your mind changes speed and for a few days you ride high before the energy goes. The buzz ends, the adrenaline leaves and the ailment that got you the steroids for in the first place starts settling. Breathing, coughing, become a chore for those that get the bug. Hard sleeping, hard waking, hard. It's not pretty. More steroids, more steroids he'll be wanting.

Fred added that Kings have long gone mad. All countries, all cultures, all beliefs go crazy. Mad Kings, kings gone nuts. They start thinking they are God himself as they lop off heads, stretch arms or coat them in honey and let the ants go to work. Caligula. Madness has a history and the French and English Kings carry some seeds.

I told Fred that from my sitting, I wasn't sure God was a male. We got that god figure in our heads. White throats you know. Life tells me that any God is going to be carrying a great deal of the feminine spirit. Least a great God would.

"I've long thought evil had filled his soul," Christine said. "The devil's fruit blossoming. Deadly sins all around." Frieda started growling and I wondered what was beyond the seeing.

Fred started poking the embers and said, "Frieda, it's fine. We'll be all right. Let them pass; they'll be gone shortly. The dead will be waiting for us when we step over. Relax," he said, showing his love for the dog sitting right close to Christine.

Science girl told us to put some more logs on the fire. "Make it big; make it large. Raise the light. Let the spirits soar, she roared.

A backyard fire with people who felt like kin. Life rumbled as the flames of the fire star took us back to earlier times. Fire and sizzled meat. Smells and telling stories.

"Another log and make it larger," Christine said.

Christine and Science girl started howling as we listened to some Dan Hicks on the outdoor phonograph. I could feel the burdens going. He was singing the songs of relaxing living and the good man soul. Singing the kinfolk music, with a beat that reminded you of fall.

Fred had four peace pipes and we started smoking to ancient gods no longer talked of in this one-size-fits-all world. We raised our glasses to the Moon God, smoked the peace pipe and let go of the thinking, holding us to this place.

"Frieda is able to see the dead," Christine said. "She's always barking at something not there. She start the night with growling. Then every couple of hours she starts yipping. 2 am. 4 am. She's at it all night long." She turned to Fred. "What is wrong, Fred? Is it dog dementia. She is 11."

Fred shook his head, but of course, he had to figure it out. He started looking for disturbances taking place at that certain hour. Thought maybe the city was up to something. He found nothing, and I thought sure as shooting it meant Frieda was headed down that dark path of dementia. Frieda kept on growling.

"The growling bothered me. I like to figure things out," Fred said, "so as I walked around the neighborhood like I do asking everyone I ran into if their dog was exhibiting any behaviors like Frieda and her two-in-the-morning growl. None of my neighbors had seen anything quite like that.

"You have to hear this," Christine said.

"I'd been doing some insulating. It was hot and so I decided to stop in for a beer and let the workday go before I headed home. Strasser's Tavern, a drinking establishment with dates dating back to 1890 or something. The walls in that place talk," Fred said. "While I was there, Tom walked in. We had bought the farm he was selling. So we got talking nice and easy-like. I mentioned Frieda and the problem. He jerked and drew his shoulders back and asked, "What time did you say?"

I told him it was two-in-the-morning like clockwork. "That's my Mama," he said. "The last ten years of her life she got up to go to the bathroom every night. My brother, who was the priest at the Holy Trinity Church right across the street, lived with Mom during her last 10 years. Never moved out. This was his home parish. His whole life happened here within 6 blocks. He said it was uncanny how regular she was. Family. I miss the two of them, Fred."

Fred told me the story and it made my day. Frieda protecting us from things we can't see. Dogs just got different ways of seeing. We clinked our glasses and wondered what Frieda was barking at in the deep fields of Farnum Hills.

Chapter 101

It feels nice to breathe. To be able to watch TV and not hear the messages of hate coming from the commercials or the radio ads preying on the fears we carry inside us.

I like the feeling of getting along, live and let live. Now when we get past this pandemic we can once again gather, dance and hug. Science seeing tomorrow before us blind folks do.

That hate we hear gets inside our thinking. Not healthy, carrying the devil's seed because hate blossoms into thoughts that spread to action. All attached to that inner core of hate. The devil's fruit blossoming from the seeds of hate isn't leaving sometime soon.

Socrates once said an unexamined life is not worth living. That was in ancient Greece, before the times of Jesus, after Buddha and before Muhammed. He was given a choice. Death or Exile. He chose death and so he was given death for corrupting the youth of the time. Getting kids to think.

Making kids think was a death sentence in ancient ways. Challenging the ideas of the status quo was what Socrates and Jesus did and they were given death by those they challenged. Jesus appealed to a vast group of people who were oppressed. Was Buddha's last meal poisoned or was it old age? Muhammed died in the lap of his wife.

We live in very different worlds and our mixtures of beliefs intermingle. It's who we are. America. World citizens.

Chapter 102

I was sitting in the Do Drop In. It was a place where old and young gathered. The old duffers blamed the young duffers and the young folk talked back.

It was there on Second Street only a short while before it moved to Third Street. Not too far from the Bluff Country Coop which was the Mississippi Queen. Open early and late. I go back to the parking lot that now stands in its place and am proud to announce that the spirits of our past are alive and well there.

They tell me that death changes everything and is a good, good place. They are together now laughing at the latest living version of who they once were. I guess that don't change when you step on over.

First time I ran into someone from the other side was when I was having coffee one morning, end stool at the Do Drop. He was more than willing to talk, and he was of quiet tones so I was able to listen and learn.

Frances poured my coffee, looked at me and shook her head. Some folks knew early on I wasn't quite right in the head. Love you Auntie.

This was a fall day. I was working on my winter skin and feeling the call of my roots, my early days of thinking. Visiting the old folks, the gone folks. Revisiting my thinking and where it comes from and wondering if time had changed the now dead and their thinking. Those quiet whispering roots make me who I am.

Chapter 103

The old guy whispered to me. "It's the devil's seed I tell you. Preying on everyday folk and their fears. Coming right out of the TV and Radio. You have to let it go, Hanson. People need people."

I turned to Old Doc Lafky at the Do Drop In. He and his family had been in and near Winona forever.
He said this period of time we are living in now might be the craziest of craziest. He said the first world war was born of ancient hates and this entire town was gripped by the stories of blood and guts strewn on the battlefields. "Decency had left us," he said. "We were fortunate we didn't have that television adding fuel to the fire. The flu epidemic made the whole world sick in one way or another."

I nodded saying this election cycle and pandemic have made for a long, dark and cloudy year. Cabin fever might be tough this spring. People might be shooting people left and right.

"Best way to beat that is to take your shirt off and stand outside in the cold," he said. "Make sure the lock ain't locked and let the cold jar your senses. You'll forget what ails you."

He gave me the hairy eyeball to make sure I was listening, then he went on. "Once a week is usually enough and just a couple minutes. Make you appreciate a warm sweater and a fire. Winter walking of course is the best. Quiet, everything is quiet. Good shoes and a coat but the cold air will clean your soul and keep the demons from setting in your bones."

"I can feel them Doc. Knees, joints, stiffness. I can just feel the dead folk working through me. Everything gets messed up. Body feels funny."

He took a sip of his coffee. "That must be something feeling the dead like you do. I got no pills for you. You must be one of a kind but you're in the right town. There's no other town quite like Winona. Not sure I'd want to be anywhere else with the bluffs and the river and the hiking and biking. Keeps the demons at bay."

Chapter 104

I was talking to Charles Potter down at the Do Drop In. Most people didn't know his real name. He was best known as Mr. Potts. He had an opinion about everything and didn't care what others thought.

When young we mostly egged him on, seeing if we could get him to blow his stack. Laughing the more we got him going.

Charles was a voracious reader. One morning in the late 70's I was having my bacon, eggs and toast and Charles was all wound up talking about how the propagandists were planting images inside the TV set. "You can't see them," he said. "Just a small splice is all that's needed to enter your sub-conscience." He shook his finger angrily. "Russians," he cried. "Stalin still talking and America hearing. A brutal man in a land of harsh weather and no hope. He ruled with an iron fist and planted that seed clear across oceans landing on our kitchen tables. The devil planting that seed of fear in us. We heard him. We built fall-out shelters in our schools and held drills where our children sat under old wooden desks. Joe McCarthy and J Edgar Hoover seeing shadows where none were. Russians, brilliant Russians he said, making our forefathers fear. And Bobby Fischer went nuts in the dark world of the mind."

I asked Charles about the dollar bill knowing full well that his voice would soon fill the restaurant.

"E Pluribus Unum," he cried. "One from many. Our country's motto from the times of Adams and Jefferson and Franklin but now the fear of Russians coming has changed our country's motto. Those days of Eisenhower as the cold war raged in the hearts of Americans trickling down to us students sitting under desks.

I sipped my coffee as Bess filled up Mr. Potts cup.

He said thanks and turned to me. "In Russia people speak the company line. To those that raised their dissent, there wasn't anything Stalin or Khruschev would not do to stop them, silence the noise. On a good day rather than using guns or poisonous mushrooms to kill, Stalin would send his opponents to cold Northern Siberia where death happened slowly and relentlessly. We were unified in fear back then yesterday. Russian bombers weren't loading weaponry on the Interstate like some feared. We survived but fear still echoed inside. Propagandists continue planting those seeds that seem to blossom each election season." Now Mr. Potts he didn't look much like anybody else. His thick bottle glasses and unshaven face spoke. He smelled a bit like yesterday.

He wore a greasy hat where he kept his good ideas tucked away. He read these big thick books cover to cover. One after another. He didn't stop for anything.

We figured he came from money, being he didn't seem to ever work. Same thing for breakfast every morning. Pancakes, over hard eggs, and white toast. Grape jelly, hash browns, two slices of bacon and two patties of sausage. Forty-nine cents.

He had some dental problems so he had just a couple teeth left. Eating sometimes took him longer and between every bite he'd have a drag off his cigarette. He had all day and sometimes he just stayed for lunch.

He sat in the back booth reading those thick Oxford History Books. Some said he was a professor who lost his marbles. He didn't quite see history like most folks. His history was of the people. Not the rich and powerful but from those who toiled in their shadow.

After going off on the changing of the country's motto he started up about the pledge. He said that changing too was from the fear. "It comes in many ways," he said.

Soldiers came back from World War II with stories of the war and Russia standing up to the German invaders. The news spoke of centralized planning in their godless country. Thoughts of them taking over the world were not far away. The Russian bear, the Red Machine was coming. Coming to take over the world, take away our freedoms. And the newspapers, radio stations and TV sets reminded us. Fear sells.

"Fear has always been used as a motivator," he said between bites. "The Pulpits talk of hell and the pain that awaits those who don't follow the rules. Old coaches threatened running till we puked if we didn't perform. Make us tougher. And cruel parents withheld their affections and used belts in this world of living hell." He looked at me to see if it was registering.

I took a sip of my morning coffee not too far from where we once had breakfast. It's hard to hear the sounds of yesterday in the noise of today. Mr. Potts has been gone awhile but it was nice to see him this morning. Remembering some of the folks this holiday season who once made a difference in my living as I sit under the new bridge and stare at a frozen river. Mr. Potts Thank You.

Chapter 105

Time for the Mystic Sage. It was the holiday season where darkness kept getting darker. All the bars and grandma houses were dark. It was a holiday season we'd mostly forget.

Stoner and I were like hell or high water. We always got out to see the Winona Christmas lights. A tradition between brothers of different mothers.

We didn't have any alcohol in us with the bars being closed so we were able to stay between the lines fairly easily, though driving 15 in a thirty kept happening.

Stoner had picked up me and Science girl. We hopped in the 69 VW Microbus he was driving. It was that cold night before Christmas in the year of the darkness. The wind whipped and we began driving through yesterday. Stopping in to see all the old friends who happened to be living in a space we'd eventually find. He passed me the joint and I said what the hell, being I might not get to next Christmas.

We were shivering, getting warm by rubbing shoulders was the only way to roll in those vehicles with bad heaters. He wouldn't have any propane heater on in the van when he drove so the only way you could get warmed up was to fit a dozen people or more inside that VW Microbus.

I started seeing all the natural heat lost from that engine being in back when who do I see but Wild Jim giving me the whack off sign and saying pass me that joint. I eyed him up being sometimes the smoke can distort the seeing.

"I ain't found Lynda yet," he said. His eyes blazed blue from somewhere deep inside himself. "Merry Christmas," he said holding on to the smoke as long as he could. Sucking, sucking the last every little bit of THC out of the end. He was a hardhead of the first order who had a few cracks in his skull. He took off his stocking cap and his hair stood up in all different directions as if he'd been living with that stocking cap covering his head for a month. He carried the odor. He shrugged his shoulders and said. "What's a man to do? I was born tough and then fell on my head when living. Made me who I am. Look at this face," he said. "Life spoke," he roared.

I noticed Science Girl staring. Her eyes were wide, wide open. A brilliant light and she yelled at Stoner to change the music. "Save me from the darkness of these two brothers of different mothers. They ain't normal. Find me some Christmas lights."

Stoner of course didn't hear a word Science Girl said. He was at his core a military man. Everything in order. His dad was a Sergeant. He took no guff.

Like most who grew up in an environment of strictness, he had a bit of rebellion in him. It's the way it flows with Fathers and Sons, Mothers and Daughters.

Routine ran through him and he remembered most everything. We were going to follow the same route we first did 41 years ago and stop at the old houses where the best of our friends had called home. In the old days he would have a hit at every one, then move on to the next. Stoner said that we had to start the tour by visiting Mrs. Beighly just like we did 41 years ago.

Old habits die hard, you see, so Stoner lit one up as we pulled up. I wasn't much interested but the impending date was getting closer and that bug, that damn bug might find me tasty.

I took a hit and passed it on. To my surprise that microbus was now filled with a dozen folks and they filled that VW microbus with the smell of burnt leaves and a foggy vision. Everybody loved Mrs. Beighly and so we decided we would spend time with her just talking.

She was delighted we stopped by and the coffee pot got brewing and being it was Christmas time she had made a big batch of hot chocolate and cookies for all of us. She said that she was worried that all her children's friends might have forgotten.

We all stared at her and Dorothy Bagel started quivering. "That casket ain't never stopped my feeling, Mrs. Beighly. I can sense the dead, feel 'em all around me. Dead people go beyond the curtain."

"That's just the weed talking," Parker Rice said. "Stuff will take you away. Set you in a different place, makes your synapses run at a different speed."

Mrs Beighly smiled, shook her head lightly and said, "Children, let's enjoy the time we got together. I mean if this isn't showing life don't end when you stop breathing. I don't know what does. Been dead a year and a half. What a wonderful place.

And so began the 41st annual Winona Christmas Light Tour.

Chapter 106

Big Jim was sitting on the stool next to me. He was one of my best buddies and I don't see him enough. One of those guys who keeps me grounded. Keeps me in touch with my writer roots. Us writers can go a bit nuts as we tell the stories running through us.

Jim started talking about the game. "Vikings. I been watching since Van Brocklin, Bud Grant, Osborn. Kassaulke. I like the way he hits. That Kassaulke was a hitter." He raised his arms and screamed, "Defense."

All eyes were now staring at Jim. He bowed, his head with a smile on his face and whispered, "Is she coming?"

"Lisa knows you Viking fans need to let go. Hard enough carrying those 4 losses inside your heads all these years. All those years of not winning. You must have some messed up thinking."

"Reason has never had a place inside my head. I fell on my head, feeding the pigeons, right off the barn roof. Coma. 3 months." He showed me his big fist and we fist bumped. He glanced up at me with the light dancing eyes of a man who had changing in his past. He smiled and said, "Linda, St. Peter, hundred 90, St. Paul, St. Paul. Linda."

"Are you always this way?"

"Defense, defense, defense, wins games. Hit the quarterback, knock him down. Defense," he roared as he pounded the bar.

The Bartender, Lisa, walked over and got right in the face of Big Jim. "Those bottles are about an eighth of an inch from the edge of falling off. Before you started yelling it was a quarter inch. They fall, you pay."

"Defense," he roared and the bar glasses shook.

I turned and saw Vikings entering the bar. Wally Hilgenberg and Fred McNeil, Korey Stringer. Even in death these men stood large and the crowd milling around the bar became quiet paying respect to the traditions that helped make them who they are.

I heard my buddy Charlie whispering, "Those boys played the game for the love of the game. Metropolitan Stadium and Bud Grant standing in the cold, facing the elements. That is when football was football."

Chapter 107

The plumbing had started clanking when he walked in. A tall fellow with black and white greasy long hair. Boney features and long, narrow skinny feet, toenails long and uncut. Green, gray, gnarled looking.

He nodded as he took the top bunk. A pointed goatee and some scruff for a beard and beady blue eyes looking in a different direction. Inward.

He said nothing as the room filled with the white smoke. Then he mumbled, "Death comes out different than it's painted."

I asked if he'd seen the dead.

He chuckled in a deep-voiced kind of way. "I thought a great deal like you did when I was living, before the dying. Things just change, your way of thinking just changes. Now Hanson, you hear and see but you are blind to what you can't see. That's what that Jesus fellow did. He lifted the blindness that exists in the mind. He lifted the mind, woke people up. He was enlightened.

"You were raised on a Sunday Morning pew sitting,

right out there on West Broadway. Those priests don't talk much about after the casket closing. They ain't never been dead you see. I been dead for a good long while and I've yet to see a gray-haired man ruling from above. Nothing like that."

The plumbing kept on clanking and I thought about how young men became men at the YMCA that used to stand on the lot of an old mansion where great warriors roamed and danced and told stories of love and honor as I ran to the shower to get ready for a swim.

A shower never felt so good. I had sensed one of my basic human myths had been challenged. I had a good grounding and a kind Catholicism running through my bones. I know some of the boys went places they shouldn't have but the priests of my youth were fine men who carried with them that meaning existed beyond our seeing.

I decided as that warm water hit my back that I needed sleep. The voices and the visions of my seeing were driving me away. Hearing things coming from shadows and whispers was the last part of my living that brought me the faces of the voices. The sounds of schizophrenia finally started making sense about the time I got halfway home. I finished my shower, got dressed, and said goodbye to Daryl and Bethany. Folks doing laps shaking loose the negative energy running through them.

Chapter 108

The old building, auditorium has been there forever. Part of the neighborhood. The sounds of life, kids, can still be heard coming from the hearts of old men and women who performed on that stage. Their voices get a little emotional sometimes cracking as they remember. And the woodwork, oh yes, the woodwork still talks about the place of some of the best times of our lives.

The concept of there is something that is greater than I echoed through that building. I was just a little kid the first time. The Winona Winhawk basketball team were playing basketball against the Red Wing Wingers. Sitting in seats way in the back, my mind overwhelmed with the stimulus of all those noises and sounds of its people working their way through my head.

I have never heard Winona so clearly as I did that evening and I'm not sure who even won that game. Chuck Williams was court side announcing and Gary Evans was scribbling for The Winona Daily News. Winona roared that night and I felt what being a town was about.

My buddy Ted was telling me how all the grade schools would have their school play on the big stage and grandpas and cousins all showed up to see the kids perform. Old barmaids and waitresses would be carrying the baggage of living showed up because a child reaching for the stars is life itself. They might not have attained what they dreamt of but they would never get in any youngsters way. It was a magical place that old theatre with that overhanging balcony.

I was there one night. It must have been '74 or '75 when a band by the name of The Flying Burritos Brothers showed up. My buddy Riff hung over the rail with probably 50 to a hundred more music-crazed people, hanging, just hanging over the edge. Whole place was like that stomping, chomping, dancing and raising our voices to the words and the music that matched our times.

I can't imagine what it felt like to play a violin or a fiddle or a bass on that stage with everybody watching. A single spotlight with just you and your instrument. Heart pounding, stressed. Just a kid playing in a full house on a big stage. Feeling young again. That old building was the heart and soul of this town where the river ran crooked.

Chapter 109

The boys like to share their stories. Talk about what was and what they missed. The consequences of war are harsh. This is Stoner down by the lake talking with the old soldiers.

They come in the morning, old soldiers for a cup of coffee and a talk. They sometimes wish for a bit more privacy and none of them to a man likes the beating down sun. Shade leads itself to better talking, thinking, and the cars and their noises are distracting to their ways of getting by.

Some of the boys died before they came home while others passed as old men with stories untold. Some still live with minutes to go in the scheme of things while others, the younger are looking at years before wisdom creeps into their thinking. All bricks in the pavement.

We chit chat about what they never got. Their mom and dads, grandpas and grandmas, the last goodbye. The children they never had or the love they felt for one girl or guy that he or she thought of. Others came home and kept the memories of war and the dying that happens in the field tucked away. As if not talking will fill that void, that pain, that hurt.

They wish they had talked a bit about the pains and hurt of those wars they fought in. Maybe then, maybe then. They stop, quietly waiting, hoping it don't take dying, for realizing, to get us. It hits us all differently, living and the dead in different ways and at different times. But they say that it takes most of us dying to see living.

They don't seem to have much regret for living their lives as they did, but they say it takes dying to see those patterns of living we get trapped in. I guess slowly the BS gets squeezed out of us, till death removes all.

"Voices, they hit me after Nam, you know. Dark shadows scurrying just outside my seeing."

"Greyness?"

"Shadows, day and night. Not just my seeing but feelings, hearings all moving differently than they used to."

"That's nuts."

"Life. But anybody who knows me understands other than quirks, I'm harmless."

"I think I'll hold back judging. Oh, was Stanley mad this morning."

"I missed that while I walked. What's his problem?"

"No sleep. He could smell the Barbecue, his stomach he said all upside down. Good Barbecue smells wouldn't let him sleep in the first place and then he was up to the toilet at least four times. Smells get his stomach churning he says. He says good food cooking is filling the back alley of the Morgan Block."

"You didn't feed into his bathroom routine did you? Did you? How many helpings did he have?"

"He said he went through the line four times. Twice a day. I didn't know about the other."

"We got any listeners left?"

"To be honest the phones have been ringing off the hook, advertisers hawking their wares. Puetz out there at Sugar Loaf Ford is hawking a hybrid Lincoln that gets 42 miles per gallon."

"It got any juice?"

"You should ask but I heard him growl that's American engineering under that hood and Ford don't sell dogs."

"You asked him about that Pinto?"

"Where it belongs," he said. "American car manufacturers, dropped the ball, went brain dead, got fat, complacent when they made cars like the Pinto. They blamed the workers when it should have been placed on their desk."

"That's how we do things at Sugar Loaf Ford, my desk. The big companies were not prepared for the Japanese way and its business ran us over. We were not prepared for times that were a changing just like Bob Dylan sang, if you want to call that singing."

"Took us awhile, we were set in our ways and that leads to a failed business practice, no matter the business. We should have heeded Mr. Dylan and his words and applied the changes coming to our business. Sign of a good storyteller you know, words echoing and making sense a long time after."

"You are pretty articulate for a kid who grew up working."

"I broke a lot of turkey necks on the way. One hundred hour weeks. Back then things weren't as automated and as long as you weren't working with knives you could think of other, better things. Nothing wrong with my roots; that turkey plant up Altura way was one of my stones, part of my own myth. A place that helped me see."

I had never touched a turkey other than one cooked.

I hit myself in the head. Damn writer channeling another from just a brief meeting. I apologized to Mike who was a nice guy with a strong handshake formed by the hard work of his roots.

"So, you did cut Stanley off before it got worse?"

"Yeah, Grippen came running to the station. I was scared. Have you ever seen him run before? Grippen? I hadn't. Scary sight! He comes screaming down the street. Yelling the FCC is going to shut us down for his talking. Huh, I said? Yes, Stanley talking about his bowel movements right on the air. Turn out the lights the party is over."

"You told him there was no medication to stop Stanley from talking? Just the way he talks. You have to redirect that talking or he will carry on forever. Get him talking in a different direction. I mean I stayed away from Stanley as a youngster. Hair all over like he had. I wish I'd a gotten to know him. Probably a nice guy once you got beyond the seeing. He found a puppy dog in his later years. Loved it like a baby. You get any lawyers calling wanting to represent your first amendment rights?

"Not yet, then again the FCC hasn't shown up.

Chapter 110

Once again, I needed a walk. My teeth and my knees and my back were aching. My head was on backwards so I put on my hat and jacket, grabbed my pipe and radio, hoping that a nice, cool Winona walk would straighten out my thinking.

I left Pleasant Hill and began the long walk down the hill and into the town when I heard the old words of brothers and friends who walked and talked at that school on the hill. Not many teachers left from my time there but when you walk through the marbled halls and hear the echo of the words and faces that never leave one's thinking. Brother Frank, Dr. Dieterman and Father Fabian all gone in the recent past and their voices still echo through my thinking. Tom Etten, Tom Etten where oh where has your spirit flown?

I carried on across the bicycle bridge which used to be a road and headed towards Hyvee and Wellingtons looking for the road and then the path that went in the back of the Holzinger Lodge. I hopped on that path and could feel myself breathing as the sounds of nature entered into my thinking.

I saw shadows of old friends and lovers, holding hands and talking in the quiet way. Immortality, I guess ed, walking on that path behind Holzinger, along the bluff where the echo of life-after rings most true.

I felt the dead spirits as they started talking. Old friends and new acquaintances, asking what I'd been up to. "Did you bring a drink or a joint or a good laugh under that hat you are wearing?"

I heard old neighbor Fran telling me to bring a marti- ni and the kids and grandkids and greats as well. "We'll talk smart and watch Jeopardy,. Have another and laugh some more. Bring me the cheap vodka," he cried. "It charges my soul as it burns my inside, rebirth from the burnt remnants of yesterday's living, like a forest after a fire.

I nodded my head as Fran sucked the olive of life and remembered the best times and loves of his life.

I heard Rip Streeter screeching that it's five o'clock and where's his drink and Wall Street Journal. And I heard friends chuckling like when they were young hearing Rip, rip. Good men out just beyond the seeing.

I waved at Judge Chaleen and noticed the grass was unturned. I wondered what the good judge saw now as the dark side got shown in its brilliant light.

"Step beyond the casket," he said as I walked by.

I went to visit my grandfather of one leg. He spent much of his life drinking to cover the pain of the bullet that grazed him in that Civil War at The Spotsyvania Court House. Doctors wanted to amputate but he'd been at Gettysburg where men died from minor doctoring. It was there he started his whiskey drinking, covering the pain of being in the wrong place at the wrong time.

I carried on and heard church bells ringing from way downtown. I crossed the highway and started listening to the quiet sounds of the town that was.

Chapter 111

"How come you didn't visit?" The voice crept into my being.

"Oh, who are you?"

"John Brown. I was right, you know. I thought there was something to being dead while alive. I saw the shadows while living. That's why I put ventilation ducts in my mausoleum. Everybody thought I was nuts after the horse kicked me in the head. Gets lonely not being able to talk with the living. Ain't no better place to do some learning than out here where the spirits talk. Closed minds, closed minds.

"Mama made a fortune you see in those Winona

early days. She knew them all right up to Henry Huff. A better scoundrel wasn't to be found, she used to say. He was a prick as he pranced in a mean, mean fashion. She could tell the best stories my Mama could. Made her money buying and selling claims and then property. Pa worked at The Empire Lumber Company and Mama had a little bit of that Eastern Money that helped build this town."

"A horse kicked you in the head?"

"She was a beautiful horse. Wild and free, mostly untamed and I let my guard down. I couldn't see the same after that. That was when the shadows kicked in. Mama got a trust written up to protect me during my remaining days. She's been dead a long time. 1876, cold fall day for a burying. She left it all to me. Lawyers spent years slowly siphoning off the assets. Had no children."

"You were a man of privilege?

"I suppose so but then a horse did kick me in the head, destroying my life so I was fortunate I had some money. I wasn't alone, not in this town, full of not so right thinkers."

The radio turned on and I heard live music from St. Cecilia's Theatre. The Bus Boys were singing a song about half a brain and you could feel Winona breathing to the sounds of their times.

I'm not quite sure what the old nuns were thinking right now as the music played. They were a pretty strict lot back in the day. It couldn't have been easy trying to tame the wild spirits that came to that beautiful campus called St. Teresa's in the west end of town but when I look at those buildings those nuns must have done a fine job of shaking down deep pockets and boorish Bishops.

"This is Stoner Thompson. I'm out here front row

281

of the balcony in the beautifully restored St. Cecilia's with my friend Petey Hawaiian and I've never seen such happy nuns. Life brought back to life they proclaim and not a pointer-stick in sight. Winona has always been a place where people weren't set in stone. There is nothing better than being happy and Winona was full of happy people not quite right in the head.

"Me and Petey went out road tripping through the streets of Winona before the concert. He was driving his light blue Olds Delta 88 with the power seats trying to look inconspicuous when we drove by the Madison school. It was quiet and the sadness was compounded by the words on the sign. We could hear the voices of yesterday as we took a walk around the block and we wondered why that sign wasn't thanking Winona for the memories of a great run. You can hear the violins singing when you listen right up close to the Madison School on seventh."

Chapter 112

I was walking downtown, past the Hardee's toward the library when I heard him walking beside me.

"My name is Roger, Roger Garrison," he said, his Billy club dangling on his left hip and the .38 Colt with the six inch nose hung from his right. His walkie talkie stood behind his holster and his hair was no longer gray. He was sporting a new badge and wore it with the humble pride of a good cop.

He looked at me and said, "I hear you been nosing around in the death of Lena Weinberg. Us men in blue were given direction to look the other way." His eyes had a bit of twinkle dancing behind the steely blue and I asked what he meant. He said Lena Weinberg and his voice got louder. I could hear the voices of the book dwellers from the shelves behind me telling me to hear what he was saying. He said he was a cop following orders. He wondered if our paths had once crossed.

Not saying it was blood we had between us; it is just how life works in the Rivertown where everybody knew a bit about everybody. I asked him about his family's arrivals and when he said 1867 I knew our paths had indeed shared a story. More than likely our grandparents or great grandparents, maybe bowled or sat in the same class or got into a fight, played ball for Booby, Max, or Earl during times before.

He liked meeting and talking with people, he said. "I knew everybody on my beat, their kids and where they came from. House to house, business to business. I had the greatest job in the world, and never did have to raise a pistol."

I asked him if he knew Lena. He took a deep breath and said he pledged silence when it came to Lena. He had wanted to investigate, the whole force did, but the suits who ran the politics, said no and threatened those jobs that we depended on.

I offered him a pecan roll from Winona Bread and Bagel as we sat drinking some lukewarm Hardee's coffee on the steps of the library letting the late afternoon sun warm our face.

"She never would have done what they say," he said. Garrison's walkie talkie went off. "Roger, Roger, we got problems. I need a squad car to Johnny's. Snit, Ed Snitkowski is off the wagon and standing on the bar threatening to bash a beer bottle over crazy Cyl's head."

"Eva, Eva. I'm retired."

"Well so am I. You didn't know? It's magical over here."

"It was shocking getting here, Eva, and I miss so much. I yearn for the old feelings that being a cop brought but my guard is over, my duty done. Trying to teach Hanson, but he has a mind of his own. I turned in my badge."

"Roger, Roger we pinned your badge on you, a cop for ever after. Your eyes were closed. I always figured good cops had a special place on this side and to be prepared. We see things no man or women should see. It can wear you out. You should have heard your beagles howling, just howling on your dying night. Started crying I did. But, Roger, hear me out. Snit needs you. Locking him up has never done him any good. I got other guys I could call but they likely would get the beer bottle on top of the head. The only person I ever met who could settle Snit down was you. One more ride for Eva, please."

"I could never say no to my dispatcher. One last cruise for the boys in blue and guys like Snit and the good things in life. This is old car 101 heading down to the East Side. Hanson, yeah Hanson follow the money and you'll find Lena"s killer. This is Roger. Out."

Chapter 113

"We got a mess down here. All cars report to Sixth and Mankato! We got Officer Garrison and his car top down in front of the Watkowski Funeral Home. I repeat car 39 rolled his car in front of the Watkowski Funeral
284

home."

"This is car 104. Officer Garrison is in need of medical care. Cars blocking the streets East, West, North and South. Everybody in town is headed to the East Side and Roger went barreling through the four way at Broadway and Kato, running into the front end of a semi. He must have gotten 15 feet off the ground, coming to rest on his top."

"Worried about Snit he was. I got Praxel on the way. I had to wake him, you know, after the pileup we had coming down Stockton Hill last night. He was not happy. Seeing dead people messes up his sleep."

"This is car 103. We were all having coffee and donuts at the Happy Chef, getting ready for Roger's welcome back party. They had the scanner on, you know. It's how we kept track of things. Old ladies in corner houses and our dispatchers knew them all. When we heard Roger was stuck upside down we put on the sirens, hell bent on saving Roger. That damn railroad. They got the whole town blocked from Goodview to Louisa."

"Now settle down, 103. There is no reason to hurry!"

"No hurry! We got a cop down, Snit and Cyl are going at it. The trains are blocking us from helping. Can't get to the scene. Townies got the roads all jammed up. And you tell me not to worry. What kind of dispatcher are you?"

"Now just a minute, 103; what were you doing drinking coffee and having a donut on your shift? There are criminals out there on the streets and you're having a pastry!"

"It was a hot beef sandwich I'll have you know. A man can't work without something warm filling him. Besides I do my best detecting, sitting over a cup of coffee, listening to the chatter coming from the booth one over. That's when I heard."

"Heard what?"

"The scanner!"

"I called Elmer down at the rail yard and he said an engineer is entitled to a break every four hours and when it's break time, work stops. Why those city planners didn't make overpasses I'll never know. Penny wise, pound foolish and now we got a boy in blue stuck inside his car on the sidewalk of a funeral home and we can't help him."

"I got a call from Mrs. Swenson, switchboard operator at Bell Telephone. Said the party lines were overheating. These townies listen to the police scanner and then they got the Party Lines and then they gotta see for themselves. Keeping a secret ain't easy you know in town."

"Chief Carstenbrock isn't going to be happy."

"This is 104. Is Praxel coming?"

"Broadway is backed up to Hamilton."

"Well put on your lights."

"The boys won't give up their place in line. They are all headed to Garrison's going away party. Dead folks won't miss that."

"It is a shame, I tell you. It was just a gag, just a gag. We had a retirement cake and were ready to party. Ready for a girl to pop out of it. Snit and Cyl got fake blood all over them. It looks like a massacre happened in the East Side and now Roger is upside down. This is not good."

Chapter 114

I was going to bed and Father Vic was getting up. It was freshman year. Strangers in the night. We shared a light.

We were brothers bound to an attachment to the wee morning that I called bedtime and he called morning. He was praying and I meditating. Out there in the church by the apple orchard where the deer come to play.

"The land of the dead is a delightful place, Hanson," he told me once. "Holy, I feel Holy here as I feel my ancestral being. I hear the sounds of my fathers in the Valley of St. Yons."

It was crazy. I was a dumb 18-year-old. I knew most everything, never realizing life was just beginning to talk. My learning journey was just getting started.

The first time we met I was smoking a joint on the church steps. He walked in the quiet way of his forefathers. I just about swallowed that joint that I was inhaling as I saw him. My mind started racing a million miles an hour. Caught.

He looked at me. He must have seen the guilt on my face and said, "Since time man has used smoke and fire to go to a better place and time. Campfires and incense, the perfume of a beautiful girl that smells just right. Smells can transfer your mind to somewhere else. You'll be seeing the dead if you keep smoking that. It's not for everyone and I'm seeing some dark shadows in your coming days."

I chuckled. Still in the invincible state. I was relaxing talking to a teaching priest. Campus was full of questioning, asking about the things we couldn't quite see. Priests of all persuasions. Nuns and Brothers. PHD folks on every name plate. And they could flat out teach. It was the mission of their founder St. John Baptiste De La Salle.

Father Vic said, "My first holy place was inside the Sisters of Guadalupe Church in Taos. On those hot days I would spend it inside the cool. Most of my friends would be outside playing and I'd head to the church, the adobe Church. An escape from the harsh reality of the sun, the harsh reality of the poor. The reality of oppression and the hope that the church brought. Time will show, Hanson, the decay of civility and the break-down of the family."

"That was my first holy place," he said. "It's where my grounding comes from. Where I first felt my dead forefathers. I started seeing the dead folk at a young age. Great spirits lie in the beyond. If you don't hear yesterday talking in your seeing there ain't much hope for you ever being a writer."

I nodded hesitantly. This was a new kind of churching to me. I asked if he heard dead people talking.

"Not like you, but I walk beside them. Their way of seeing. Hearing the tales of time. I like walking amongst the dead, amongst the wreckage of failed ideas, broken promises," he said. "Poorly conceived ideas. It's man and his ego. Trying to capture that god spirit is futile."

"He kept on ranting. "Our church has lost its way. That spirit is of acceptance of those who look different, talk different, think different. We shouldn't be looking to purity as the path of living. The human dimension is not meant to be perfect. We are full of those deadly sins. The human dimension is not pure, wasn't meant to be. The spirit is accepting of that human dimension. Black and white thinkers in an abstract world is what is going on. Getting in the way."

288

I took another hit letting the quiet of the morning fill me. Deep breaths, feeling nature.

"We get in the way. Some of us have even begun to restrict access to the body of Christ. We should ask ourselves why we would want to close the doors to something so wonderful. Food for thought as I feel the errors of my brothers."

"For most of our history those of us who were popes saw little of the outside world. There were even three popes once upon a time and it is rumored there was a woman amongst us once. I would have liked to have met her. She must have been a great pope to get past our rules."

Our church was so much more than following the dogma. Rules and words written long ago by men who were not there at the time of Jesus and his dying. They wrote through the window of historical time creating a myth. Lessons sprinkled throughout the book."

"Think, Hanson, Think. We were given a brain. Unleash it. Stand up for truth. Our basis of truth will crumble as all things do in light of time. The other side, the dead side have lost their voice. Learn their language and hear their truth. We were meant to think. To turn our backs on that freedom of thought, conscience, is to turn away from who we are.

"We should be talking about that spirit that runs through us. We have forgotten that wisdom of the ages as we sit on our throne saying what is right and wrong.

"That spirit loves all of God's children and does not discern color, race or sexual being. It is love that it speaks. The spirit cannot be forced. The spirit lies beyond this human dimension."

"Least that's what God tells me every morning when

I wake. He tells me to plant seeds into the minds of people and watch them bear fruit. It is not obedience that is desired but the warmth and openness of the space we share. Family means many things to many people and for a group of mostly white-haired old men to define its entirety is presumptuous to say the least. God tells that to expand the ring of acceptance and to pray for those who close doors to receiving the spirit of Christ. Hell has long been part of the myth. We would all do well to examine our consciences. I was a child of Hitler's war. I saw my church start to crumble and I moved forward determined to save the world of my own youthful vision. The only peace I ever found was within the walls of that church before Hitler came. I have lived with those horrors all the years of my life.

"Until now, as I have let go of the beliefs that trapped me, I saw only one way, one vision. We must allow the expression of conscience thought and get out of the way as the spirits reveal answers to the old questions that eluded those before us."

Chapter 115

I went walking through campus. Past old faces, old memories and missed lessons. It was the wake of a soul mate and I went walking through his times. Brother Finbar McMullen has left us.

His real name was Donald but when a Christian Brother professes his vow they take on a name of a Saint. Donald became St. Finbar. Myths and magic run through the veins of Old Ireland and in the spirit of the times Finbar McMullen found himself. The ancients said St. Finbar was the King of Fairies and the Patron Saint of Cork. He was all of that. He lived up to his name. An actualized myth.

I sat on the stones of my thinking listening to the sounds of learning as they echoed through the marble hallways of St. Mary's and Heffron Hall. A place in time when Finbar and I first met long ago. I drifted through my thoughts when I noticed Brother Raymond Long, eyeballing me not two feet from the end of my nose.

"I thought you were nuts. You can see the dead?"

"I guess I can. How have you been?

"You heard voices, saw shadows when we last met. And now you see faces. The progression of an insane man?"

"Does it matter? My insanity?

"No, no. Thanks for hearing us dead folk. Seems like nobody listens to the whispers beyond what they see." He paused, taking a deep breath. "It's a big day. Finbar will be here within an hour. He embodies all that is a Christian Brother. We knew his examination wouldn't take long. Justice, young people and education is Brother Finbar. The soul of a brother. How good is your seeing? What do you see on the lawn?"

I took a gaze and said green grass, beautiful trees and a couple sculptures. Am I missing something?

"You don't see the thousands of brothers, nuns, priests, professors milling around. Are you telling me you can't hear the beautiful piano playing of Brother Lawrence?"

"A party on the steps of a dying?"

"A celebration of life, an entrance to the hereafter. Like a baptism for those who left living. An awakening. A St. Marys tradition. Life beyond the curtain. These are hallowed grounds. Let's go meet Finbar and those he never thought he'd see again."

To be continued...

Made in the USA
Monee, IL
03 October 2023